Pat MacEnulty holds a doc University. Her bachelor's d She is the recipient of an I Florida Arts Council and se her writing. Serpent's Tail p stories, *The Language of Sharks.*

Praise for Pat MacEnulty

Sweet Fire

"Her lean, easy prose propels her story beyond the personal, making for more than convincing fiction" *Observer*

"[MacEnulty] writes about her subject with sympathy, wisdom and—an unexpected blessing—humour" *Guardian*

"[A] gripping debut novel . . . terrific" *Uncut*

"An amazing view into the mind of someone driven to recklessness by unknown demons" *Venue*

"It is entirely to MacEnulty's credit that she confronts the demons head-on in a hilarious, unflinching, vital account, devoid of sentiment or platitude" *Herald*

"A searing generational riposte to the consequence of turning on, tuning in and dropping out . . . a formidable indictment of the 'depleted souls' produced by the conditions of capitalism" *Literary Review*

"*Sweet Fire* is a sparkling debut from a dazzling new writer . . . Trish is one of the most likeable junkies in modern literature" *bookmunch.com*

"Throw away any preconceptions you have about first novels: *Sweet Fire* is a beautifully written, eye-opening story that you can neither put down nor forget. Nineteen-year-old Trish is one of the wisest and most likeable junkies in modern literature. I never expected to laugh while reading about a heroin addict, but Pat MacEnulty, like Lorrie Moore and Jane Hamilton, writes with such finesse that humor and pathos go hand in hand. Add in her poetic grace and narrative drive, and you have a superb novel. I loved it" Elisabeth Hyde, author of *Crazy as Chocolate*

"Hold this book. Savor it, like a box of chocolates, or a bag of dope. Fight the urge to devour its bittersweet pleasure, because when it's gone there's no guarantee of more. This is America's *Trainspotting*, where the smooth and terrible allure of heroin binds the heart of a narrator you have to love—and can understand without learning another language" Vicki Hendricks

"A frank, moving depiction of a nightmarish slice of American life" *Kirkus Reviews*

The Language of Sharks

"A spare, disciplined prose that no one will be able to read without thinking of Hemingway. But MacEnulty has made the style her own . . . Every story is a new demonstration that MacEnulty has that rare ability to convince, wholly, in very few words" *Observer*

"The dirty realistic landscape sometimes steps aside for bittersweet coming-of-age flashbacks, but mostly we're in swampy hell. Harry Crews would love it" *Uncut*

"Drug and alcohol addiction, prostitution, abusive relationships and their complicity in it all laid bare in confessional and profound prose make a tale of unflinching honesty about women's right to survival" *Buzz*

Time to Say Goodbye

Pat MacEnulty

A complete catalogue record for this book can
be obtained from the British Library on request

First published in the UK in 2006 by Serpent's Tail,
4 Blackstock Mews, London N4 2BT
website: www.serpentstail.com

Printed by Mackays of Chatham, plc

10 9 8 7 6 5 4 3 2 1

For my family

"And what you see is hell, for fear *is* hell"

A Course in Miracles

Prologue

1978

Vera Lee was a fast learner. She had learned from Lance Underwood how to discern a Merlot from a Pinot Noir, how to drive a Jaguar XKE Roadster at 110 miles per hour down Tamiami Trail, how to appear attentive but jaded when attending the Broadway touring production of *A Chorus Line* at the Jackie Gleason Playhouse in Miami Beach, who the hell Mikhail Baryshnikov was, and how to cheat at blackjack, bribe a judge with sex and shoot to kill. All in just a few summer months.

She had learned a few things from her former boyfriend, Trent Lewis, as well. He schooled her in two subjects: marijuana cultivation and burglary. She didn't think she'd ever really use the knowledge she had gained about growing Sensimilla in a closet—the seed germination process, the perfect height and temperature of the lamps, the fertilizer and pruning required. She had seen where that information landed Trent: five years at the medium security prison outside Ocala, Florida. (Of course, she'd wound up with a much longer sentence, but that was another story.) But burglary would prove to be very useful right now. Trent had shown her how to jimmy open a lock with a screwdriver, how to remove a window pane from a jalousied window to reach a door lock, and what to do if you didn't have a pair of gloves handy (wear socks on your hands). But Trent had also taught her that the most important quality for a successful burglary was boldness. The best burglaries were those where you didn't have to break anything at all, removing a case of coke, for instance, from a parked delivery truck, strolling inside a motel room and taking the camera and the watches while the occupants were at the pool.

That's what Vera Lee set her mind to as she moseyed into the garage of Lance Underwood's Fort Lauderdale mansion off Las Olas Boulevard. Just walk in like you own the place, she told herself. Vera Lee had been waiting in the courtyard behind the stucco arches, surrounded by palmetto plants and giant green elephant ears since about five in the morning. It had been a long walk from where the trucker dropped her off on I-95, but she was too wired to be tired. At around eight that morning, Lance drove out of the garage. The maid, Consuela, arrived around 8:15 and pushed a security pad to open the garage door. It was simple enough to slip inside the garage after the maid entered the house. Vera Lee waited a few minutes as the garage door closed automatically behind her, then she went through the unlocked door into the kitchen. The trick was not to get sidetracked by thoughts about the last time she was in this house, not to think about what happened to Lois Underwood, not to remember the steak Diane that Lance had cooked on his indoor grill and fed to her piece by bloody piece as she sat at the bar with a gin gimlet.

Her heart pounded hard as she slid around the house like a Persian cat. She heard the television click on in the den at the back of the house. If the maid found her, she'd smile and act like she belonged there. She had never met the maid but seemed to remember Lance mentioning that she didn't speak English, something Lance found useful and which could prove useful today as well. But what if Lance came home? She wondered if the police had notified him when she'd first escaped. Was he expecting her to come to him? He had made all those promises, how he would hire another attorney to appeal her case, how he'd help her get free "when the time was right." But she didn't believe him anymore. She hoped she'd let enough time elapse since her escape, hoped that the police had stopped waiting for her to show up at the scene of her abhorrent crime, hoped that this would be the very last crime she'd ever commit. It was a miserable, pathetic life, the life of a criminal, and landed you in a wretched place with crazy treacherous women. Of course there were a couple of exceptions, namely Godfather and sweet Mandy, but most of those women were baby rattlesnakes.

She wanted a cigarette desperately, but she didn't smoke anymore, thanks to the advice she'd received from the esteemed attorney.

"Your beauty is your most important asset," Lance had told her, his pale green eyes steadily assessing her. "Smoking destroys a woman's beauty. You won't always be sixteen, you know."

"Beauty? I happen to be smart, too," she'd retorted. And he had burst out laughing.

"Smart? Maybe, but thoroughly uneducated. What was the last book you read?"

"*Valley of the Dolls* if you must know," she answered.

He shook his head, went to his bookshelf and came back with a slender volume by a man named Carl Jung. It was about dreams.

"Read this. Learn something. Use your mind."

She had obediently tucked the book away, later read it and not understood a whole lot—except one thing that seemed fairly important: we can only hide so much from ourselves. The stuff that we try to block out of our minds, it comes to us in dreams or illness. She'd never been sick, but she had plenty of bad dreams.

Vera Lee stepped lightly up the staircase, staying close to the wall. She could hear the maid in the kitchen loading the dishwasher. The hallway floor upstairs was covered with large red Mexican tile. How much would have changed, she wondered. She peeked into Lance's study. Same big mahogany desk with the throne-like black leather chair behind it, same bright view of the canal through the large window. She'd heard him talking to other lawyers, to judges and to his clients on the phone—the mellow voice that soothed their fears while she sat on his lap and he twirled a lock of her blond hair around his finger.

She continued down the hall to Lois's room. Would he have kept her things? The woman had been dead for almost a year and a half. Vera Lee turned the door knob and went inside quickly, shutting the door behind her. The room was dusty, the air old and stale like bread left in a bread box for too long. Vera Lee caught her breath. She saw herself in a large gilt-framed mirror surrounded by lavender-striped wallpaper. It was a shock—the red hair and the extra pounds of prison weight that she'd put on. But she was still "stunning" as Lance had once called her—maybe more so. There was a comfort in looking at her image, as if she were with a long-lost friend.

Her eyes roved around the room. The mattress was leaned against the wall, the curtains down, hems torn, every drawer was emptied, clothes were piled into boxes. He had obviously searched the room thoroughly, but hadn't thrown anything away. Perhaps he hadn't ever found what he was looking for.

She opened Lois's closet. Shoes and open purses lay scattered over the floor, but the clothes were still on hangers, dresses along one side, slacks and blouses on the other. As she quickly sorted through the clothes, she remembered how she had huddled inside here one late afternoon when Lois came home unexpectedly. She had slipped into the closet and found the notebook, hidden under a stack of shoeboxes. And there was a letter—written by Lois. She had just started reading it by the light through the crack in the closet doorway when she heard voices in the bedroom. She dropped the letter and shrank back against the wall.

"Is she here? Now?" Lois had demanded. "Are you sleeping with her, Lance? Are you fucking her? Isn't that statutory rape?"

"No, no, no," Lance insisted. "I am not sleeping with her. What do you take me for?"

"I don't know. I don't know you anymore. You're involved with these men, these despicable characters, and now this girl. You've been seen with her everywhere, Lance. The theater. Restaurants. I heard you took her to the ballet, for God's sake."

"I'm trying to help her, sweetheart. That's all. You have your charities, and I have mine."

"Charity? Lance, I know what you're up to. I've kept records from our bank accounts, and I even know about your little secret account in the Caymans. I have it all documented. I know about the Panamanian deals, everything. I could sink you like that."

She snapped her fingers, but then Lance had moved in on her, grabbing her arms, holding them down, kissing her neck. She pushed him away, but it didn't stop him. He slowly pulled off her clothes, his hands caressing her shoulders, her back, kneading her ass. He put his mouth on her naked breast and wedged his hand between her legs. Vera Lee watched, mesmerized, from her hiding spot in the closet as Lance eased his wife onto the bed. He didn't bother to undress himself, just deftly unzipped his black trousers and pushed between her helpless bony legs, thrusting hard. Vera Lee thought that Lois would stop him, scream at him, fight back, something. But instead she turned passive and cooed like a pigeon. Waves of jealousy ran through Vera Lee. Lance had never kissed her like that, never. He had never made love to her in spite of all the attention he gave her. He was like some glorified pimp, sending her off to give blow jobs to some old cigar-smelling judge in order to get some foreign thug off the hook.

When Lance was done with Lois, he had tenderly kissed her pale stomach as she ran her fingers through his silvery hair. Then he lifted her up and carried her into the bathroom. Vera Lee listened as the bathwater ran. She shoved the letter and notebook back under the shoeboxes. A few minutes later, Lance opened the closet door, and with a quick jerk of his head, he signaled her to leave. She had run downstairs and out to the backyard, then down to his yacht where she hid uneasily. It was the only time she ever went on that boat. She didn't like boats, didn't like the ocean. It wasn't always like that. Her father had owned a charter fishing boat, but Vera Lee's childhood was best left forgotten.

That day was Vera Lee's only acquaintance with Lois Underwood until Vera Lee shot her a month later. But that encounter had been erased from her memory just as the blood had been scrubbed clean from the hallway downstairs. She didn't remember doing it. But, surely, she had done it. The police said she did. They found her with Lois's car and Lance's Walther P38 from his beloved gun collection. The Broward County prosecutor said she did it. He said jealousy was her motive. And the jury said she did it. After all, she had killed two other people. What further evidence was needed? So it didn't matter that she couldn't remember anything about September 26, 1976.

Now she needed to steal a few clothes and a little money and move on quickly. But that wasn't why she came here. She could steal clothes from a store and turn tricks for money. No, what she needed was a little insurance—something to make sure Lance Underwood would not want her to be caught. She looked again at Lois's clothes. How she had envied Lois's life. Lois was a patron of the arts and had been involved in an exhibit at the North Miami Beach Museum called "Art to Wear." Lance was proud of his wife and showed Vera Lee a picture of her from the paper, modeling some extravagant outfit. Vera Lee looked through the clothes—there they were, the famed Art to Wear pieces, a caftan with feathers and little voodoo dolls adorning it. A sweater made of Mardi Gras beads. A jacket made of patches of dark brown suede with some kind of plastic strips between the patches. Maybe Vera Lee just wasn't very sophisticated, but she thought the jacket was hideous. She took it off the rack and held it up to the light of the doorway. Yep, it was ugly all right. She looked closer at the strips of plastic. What was on them? Damn, she thought. Lois was not only beautiful. She was clever, too.

Chapter 1

2004

Rodney Ellis never liked funerals, but now Willie was looking at him expectantly, wanting an answer.

"Yeah, man, sure," Rodney answered. "I'll give your eulogy. Just let me check my calendar and make sure I'm available. What day will it be, by the way?"

Willie leaned back against the headboard of the hospice bed and tried to laugh. Instead he coughed, his eyes watered and his emaciated frame, which had once been a hefty 230, shook. Rodney glanced out the window. He saw a concrete birdbath surrounded by pink rose bushes and a mimosa tree: a pretty scene, like someone's idea of heaven.

"Oh God," Willie said when he finally got his body under control.

"Sorry," Rodney said. And he was—sorry to see his friend of almost thirty years looking like a crumpled beer can on the side of the road, sorry that sweet Debbie Price was losing her husband, sorry that the Gainesville Police Department would be deprived of one of the gutsiest detectives on the force. Rodney shook his head and rubbed his brow. Then a deep involuntary sigh escaped his chest. Cops weren't supposed to die of cancer. They died of gunshot wounds or heart attacks or boredom after they retired—not this, not prostate cancer. Willie seemed to read his mind.

"I always thought I'd be killed by an asshole," he said. "I just didn't think it would be my own."

Rodney put his hand on Willie's bony shoulder.

"I'll be sure to mention that in your eulogy," Rodney said.

"You know, Rodney," Willie said, leaning back, "there's things I won't miss."

This was the first time they had talked about his dying. Rodney's inclination was to tell Willie not to talk about it, to lie and pretend that he wasn't dying. But that wasn't what Willie was looking for. He needed someone to be strong enough to accept it. Rodney was pretty sure that Debbie wasn't that person, so Rodney asked, "What's that?"

"I won't miss the kitty houses," he said. Rodney laughed. The kitty houses were those places inhabited by someone with a bizarre need to house cats they couldn't afford to take care of. The smell of cat piss and rotting cat food was overwhelming in those places. Then there was the haunted feeling as the cats perched on sofas and old TV sets and window sills, watching as you walked through to find whoever it was you were looking for. A few times it had been a decomposing body—someone whose only friends were stray animals.

"It is amazing how some people live," Rodney observed. "The things you see when you're privy to the interiors of their lives."

They had discussed this topic before—how you never know what's going on behind the façades, and how most of the time you don't want to know.

"Rodney," Willie said.

"Yeah?"

"There's something I want you to have."

Rodney's stomach lurched. He didn't want Willie to give him anything. To gain anything, anything at all, from the death of a friend is a terrible feeling. But Willie had his red-rimmed eyes pegged on Rodney and something about his expression slid inside Rodney. It was an expression that said, I didn't ask to be this imperfect person, I know I'm ridiculous, the whole human enterprise is a joke, but love me anyway as I love you.

"I want you to have my Luger," Willie said. "It's an American Eagle, fairly rare. A sweet piece. I want you to have it."

"I don't know, Willie," Rodney said. "That's something that ought to go to your son."

"David's getting plenty, the whole Willie Price estate. You, I want you to have the gun. I had Debbie bring it over. Open the drawer."

Rodney pulled the drawer open. There was Willie's prize gun—a Stoeger Luger, 9 millimeter with a 3⅝-inch barrel. Rodney pulled it out and examined it. The long barrel gleamed and looked almost blue. It was a sleek weapon with a beautiful wood grip that fit the hand perfectly.

"It's a beauty, huh?" Willie smirked, showing his teeth, which looked long and white in his gaunt face.

"Yeah," Rodney nodded. Rodney had never been as fascinated with handguns—he'd been a sharpshooter in the military and preferred a rifle and 300 win-mag bullet—but there was no denying the craftsmanship. For his own sidearm, he was still using a Smith & Wesson .38 police special though most of the guys on the force were into the 9 millimeters these days. They'd get a nice surprise when he pulled this out at the range.

"Take it," Willie said.

Rodney shook his head and put it back in the drawer.

"Later, man. I'll take it later. It's still your gun, okay?" He tried to hide the quaver in his voice. Willie didn't say anything for a moment.

"Okay. I understand," Willie said.

An hour later Rodney walked through the hallways of the department headquarters to the office he shared with Detective Lanelle Thomas. Twyla from records met him in the hallway and blinked up at him. She wore her usual black outfit that made her look as if she'd stepped out of a 1950s beatnik bar, and her purple hair hung in frizzy strands around her thin face.

"How's Willie?" she asked.

Rodney shrugged. "Dying. He's got maybe a week at the most."

"It's so sad," Twyla said.

Rodney nodded his head and continued toward his office.

"Oh, Rodney?" Twyla said. "They've got someone interesting in the back holding cell. Brought him in late last night."

"Who would that be, Twyla?"

"A guy named Trent Lewis. He's here for drunk and disorderly behavior, flying without a license if you know what I mean, but I did a little research on him and he's got an interesting history."

"How interesting?" Rodney asked. He wished Twyla would just say whatever she wanted to say, but that was not the way she worked. If you pushed her, she got flustered and you'd never find out what was on her mind. Most people didn't have the patience, but Rodney had discovered during the past few years while she'd been in the records department that she was one hell of a researcher, even if she was an odd duck.

"Remember the sixteen-year-old girl who got arrested for those three murders back in 1976? According to the records, you and Willie were the ones who busted her for some minor traffic violation—turned out she was wanted for three murders in Fort Lauderdale."

There were some cases that Rodney would always remember. He would always remember Danny Rollins, the sicko who terrorized their little college town by murdering a slew of college girls. He would always remember the brilliant gay professor who had been killed and mutilated by two teenage boys, and he would always remember the day he and Willie arrested Vera Lee Gifford. She was a blonde in a bikini, stoned out of her everlovin' gourd as she idled in the middle of traffic in a stolen convertible with a vintage Walther P38 in the trunk. "Lordy, look at this baby," Willie had said, admiring the gun. "It's a near-mint condition P38 with the 480 code on the slide. This is a very rare bird indeed. German military, Hot Rod. Made sometime around 1940."

Rodney didn't know the relevance of the gun at the time, but he would never forget the way the girl fell against him and muttered something, called him Daddy. He'd been on the force about a month, and here was this girl, leaning into him, her small hand clutching his shirt, saying she was sorry, saying she wouldn't tell. He was not a man who was easily moved, but he'd felt sorry for her and uncomfortably attracted to her at the same time. When they brought her in and found out she was wanted for three murders, it had all seemed unreal to him.

During her trial, he'd traveled down to Fort Lauderdale to testify. He remembered looking over at her as she sat next to the public defender in her jail outfit. She didn't have anyone to bring her street clothes, but even so she was a beauty with startling blue eyes and full lips. She had a fragile, vulnerable quality about her, and yet somehow she was a stone-cold killer.

"You do remember," Twyla said, interrupting his reverie.

"Oh yeah, I remember her."

"Well, this guy, this vagrant, Trent Lewis, he was her boyfriend once upon a time. I read up on her case, and it seems that one of her victims was the wife of the attorney she hired to represent Trent. Weird, huh?"

"Nothing people do is weird to me anymore, Twyla," Rodney said. He turned to go into his office and pushed the image of Vera Lee Gifford from his mind. He didn't want her to infect him the way she once had. He didn't want to think about her or her old boyfriend. Willie's impending death suddenly made it all seem irrelevant. Then in spite of himself, he thought of something and turned back to Twyla.

"Twyla, didn't Vera Lee Gifford escape from FCI about a year after she went down?"

Twyla shrugged. "I don't know anything about that," she said. "In fact, I was only two years old when you arrested her."

"Thanks for the reminder, Twyla. Why don't you do a little checking up on that? I don't seem to recall them ever finding her."

Lanelle was on the phone when Rodney walked in. She glanced at him like a mother hen. She was a big-breasted, dark-skinned woman who had never in the entire time he had known her displayed any anger either to a suspect or to a fellow officer—not when they spit on her or threatened her or talked dirty to her in the case of certain suspects or the subtle discrimination he knew she had felt over the years from her peers. When something upset her, she closed her eyes and seemed to vacate her body momentarily only to return a few seconds later and get down to business. She reminded him of a statue of Buddha he had seen in Cambodia once—utterly at peace in the midst of chaos.

When Lanelle hung up the phone, she looked at him as if waiting to see what he had to report. He shook his head, so she didn't ask about Willie. What was there to ask anyway? They all knew he was dying.

"We've got work to do," she said, holding up a piece of paper with a scribbled address.

"What?"

"A fresh one. Motel maid, fifty-three years old, bludgeoned to death in the Days Inn on 13th Street. Uniforms are at the scene now."

"Let's go," Rodney said.

The coroner met them at the motel room and handed them some latex gloves and some booties. Rodney and Lanelle ducked under the yellow tape.

The motel room was clean, beds made, the floor looked vacuumed. Interestingly, her cart was inside the room next to the door. A technician was checking it for prints. Rodney followed the coroner to the bathroom. The body was wedged between the toilet and the bathtub, blood splattered across the floor. He could see a deep gash on the side of her head. He slipped on the gloves and pushed the hair away. She'd been hit with something hard and sharp. Her eyes were wide open.

"Why the hell would you kill a motel maid?" Lanelle wondered.

"Maybe she didn't use hospital corners when she made the bed," Rodney said.

"I hate it when they forget to do that," Lanelle said.

The coroner, a short man with round glasses magnifying his round eyes, used his laser pen to point out the blood drops.

"See how the blood is shaped like a tear drop. That's a high velocity spray there. The blood impact came pretty fast."

No shit, Sherlock, Rodney thought. Every coroner in the country probably watched way too much CSI and somehow thought that no crime could possibly be solved without their gruesome insight.

"Well, a blow to the head is likely to do that," Rodney said.

"Have we got the murder weapon?" Lanelle asked.

"Nada," said one of the uniformed officers. "I've got somebody checking the dumpster right now."

"What's her name?" Rodney asked.

"Thelma Jackson," he said. "She was on duty yesterday afternoon. The manager says this was her floor. They got busy and didn't notice till this morning that she hadn't punched out. One of the other maids found her."

"When was she killed?"

"Late yesterday afternoon, maybe early evening?" the coroner said, leaning over to measure the size of the blood drops.

"Sexual assault?" Lanelle asked.

Sherlock the coroner shook his head. "I doubt it. If someone raped her, they took the time to put her clothes back on nice and neat. But we'll check further."

"I'm sure you will," Rodney said, standing up. Except for the blood, the place looked clean. Little wrapped bars of soap and miniature shampoo bottles by the sink, fresh towels. Apparently she had just finished with the room when someone snuck up on her. It didn't look like she'd had any time to put up a fight, which was lousy for them. No fight, no physical evidence—or at least not much.

The motel manager stood outside the room, looking as if she might faint. Rodney approached her to learn what he could about Thelma Jackson. The air was humid enough to swim in.

"Thelma lives, uh, lived, with her mother over on Sixth Avenue. She's always been a good worker, never gave anyone a bit of trouble. She started out here when she was on work release from prison about six years ago. They're the best workers we get. They'd always rather be at work than stuck at the work release home or whatever it is," the woman said. She wore eye make-up so thick, Rodney wondered how she kept her eyes open. "Are y'all gonna be done soon? I hate for any of our guests to see this yellow tape. It doesn't look good."

Rodney and Lanelle glanced at each other.

"It's the only color we've got," Lanelle said. "Sorry."

Rodney made a call to the Gainesville Parole and Probation Department while Lanelle went to the next room and spoke to the maid who found the body.

"So what's Thelma's story?" Lanelle asked as they drove to Thelma's mother's house.

"Convicted murderer. 1970. She killed her abusive husband. Six years ago, some do-gooder lawyer can't get her clemency so gets her paroled instead. She goes to Gainesville work release, gets a job as a motel maid. When she gets out of the work release center, she keeps her job, stays out of trouble and winds up dead in a motel bathroom. You could say, what goes around comes around or you could figure that somewhere along the way Thelma Jackson got a raw deal and that life basically sucks."

"It's better than the alternative," Lanelle said. They were both thinking about Willie. They drove through town to Thelma's house. Most students wisely deserted the sweltering town as soon as finals were over, so traffic was light. Even the homeless migrated to some cooler clime.

They found the small wooden railroad house in need of a new coat of paint. Gainesville didn't have a particularly dangerous ghetto. Some gang activity, property crimes and a few assaults, but even that usually stopped short of homicide. The fact that Lanelle was a motherly black woman made their work in this part of town a little easier. People respected her. Rodney did, too. She was a good detective and a good person. Next to Willie, she was the closest friend he had—maybe the only real friend, besides his daughter, Amy, and Buddy.

Thelma's mother opened the door, took one look at them, and crumpled.

"Don't tell me something happened to my baby," she said.

"Ms. Jackson, can we come in?" Lanelle asked in a gentle voice.

The old woman unlatched the screen door and opened it wide.

"It's Thelma, isn't it?" she asked.

"I'm sorry, Ms. Jackson. She's been killed," Rodney said.

"I knew something was wrong when she didn't come home last night," she said, turning her back on them. They followed her inside. She collapsed in an old flower-patterned chair. Now this was a woman who'd had a hard life, Rodney thought. Slumped in the faded wingback chair by a rotating fan, she was small, and the expression on her face was of utter desolation.

"Thelma was a good girl. Why anybody would want to kill her . . ." the woman moaned.

"Ma'am," Rodney said, sitting on the sofa. "Thelma went to prison for murdering her husband, didn't she?"

"That was a long time ago. Back in 1970 when we lived in Perry. She was only twenty years old, and he beat her and starved her, made her live in the woods. He took a hot iron to her one time. An iron! She still has the scar on her back. Yeah, she killed him. And if she hadn't he would have killed her. We moved here when she got out of prison and ain't had no troubles with nobody."

Rodney glanced at Lanelle.

"Well, I know she did her time, Ms. Jackson, but I'm just wondering if there was anyone who might have hard feelings about the murder. Some relative of his who might have wanted revenge?"

"After all this time?" The woman lifted her gray head and looked at him like he was crazy.

Rodney shrugged. "I'm sorry. It's just that this doesn't look like some kind of random killing. And apparently it wasn't a robbery."

The old woman began to sob; Lanelle put an arm around her.

"I'm sorry you lost your daughter, Ms. Jackson," Rodney said, rising. Grieving parents always tore at his heart. He thought of his own daughter and how he would feel if someone told him she had been killed.

Rodney studied the room and noticed an old desk in one corner. He rose and slowly walked over while Lanelle comforted the distraught mother. A pile of papers sat on the desk—bills, junk mail, a calendar. He noticed a card with a picture of a large bird, a heron, flying across the sky. He reached down and thumbed it open. Three crisp one hundred dollar bills. No signature. No message. Was Thelma turning tricks? Nah, she was fifty-three years old and, besides, what kind of John would put the payment in a pretty card like this?

"Probably shouldn't leave money laying around like this, Ms. Jackson," Rodney said.

The woman looked at him in consternation, her brow furrowed, eyes gleaming with tears.

"What are you talking about?"

"These hundred dollar bills. Better put this in the bank."

The sun was momentarily covered by clouds, and the light

streaming through the window was blocked, causing the woman's face to fall into shadow.

"That's a birthday present for my niece," the woman said.

Rodney nodded. Nice present for a niece, he thought.

Rodney and Lanelle spent the afternoon asking neighbors, co-workers and friends about the habits of Thelma Jackson. She didn't get out a lot except on Friday nights when she went out to a bar called The Presidential Lounge and drank Beefeaters and tonic till around midnight. No one knew of anyone steady in her life, and her momma said she always came home.

"I've known her since she got out of prison," one of the maids at the Days Inn said. "She stays clean as the board of health. She don't want to go back there, and I don't blame her."

"Maybe there was someone she knew in prison," Rodney said to Lanelle on the way back to the office. "Maybe an old lover got out and came to see her. You can't stay locked up as long as she did and not get into something."

"I'll check with the work release center, see if any long timers have been recently released," Lanelle said.

He pulled the Chevy into a parking space behind the building and turned off the car.

"What is it?" Lanelle asked.

Rodney sighed and stared out the window.

"You gonna talk to me or I do have to take you to the interrogation room?" she asked.

"I don't want to do this," Rodney said.

"Don't want to do what?"

"Don't want to try to find Thelma Jackson's murderer. Don't want to talk to one more broken-hearted mother. Don't want to file one more goddamn report." He paused, then admitted. "Don't want to go to Willie's funeral. I told him I'd give the eulogy."

Lanelle didn't answer for a few minutes. Then she said, "This day in and day out mayhem can get to you. Maybe you need to take some time off." She paused and then said, "Can I ask you something personal?"

"Damn, girl, you can ask me anything," Rodney said with a dry laugh. He always enjoyed flirting with Lanelle. She grinned momentarily, then grew serious.

"Do you ever have flashbacks? Of Vietnam, I mean? I know you saw some ugly stuff while you were there."

"No, partner. I don't ever think I'm back in the jungle, but I do remember it very, very well," he said. "Why do you ask?"

"I don't know. I guess all this stuff on the TV all the time about the war in Iraq made me wonder. I still remember seeing the body bags on TV from Vietnam. I was just a kid, but they left an impression."

"Don't worry. You won't see any this time. They learned that lesson."

"That's what I'm afraid of," Lanelle admitted.

Someone momentarily blocked the relentless sun from the window. Rodney looked up and saw Twyla. He and Lanelle got out of the car. Lanelle headed inside, but Rodney could see that Twyla had something to say.

"I did some checking on that girl, the murderer who escaped from FCI. They never did find her," Twyla said. "Did you talk to Trent Lewis?"

Rodney shook his head. "Lewis is just a vagrant. And Vera Lee Gifford is probably dead somewhere. Girls like her don't usually live long on the streets." He was feeling especially cynical today. The smell of death festered in his nostrils from that motel room bathroom. Funny the way things stayed with you. Like after-images on a TV screen. He kept seeing Willie's gaunt face, blotched from the chemo, and then Thelma Jackson's wide open dead eyes on top of Willie's. He'd seen a lot of death in his day, but maybe there came a point when it saturated your consciousness and you couldn't take any more.

"Well, it's too late now anyway. He was bailed out a couple hours ago."

Twyla headed toward her car—a Volvo about twenty years old. He knew the only reason Twyla worked for the police department was that she couldn't bear to leave the college town atmosphere. There weren't many jobs for people with a master's degree in English in a place like this unless you wanted to teach, and one look at Twyla told you that kids would eat her for lunch.

"Hey," he called to her. "Who the hell bails out a drunk and disorderly vagrant?"

Twyla turned slowly to look at him. The late afternoon sun fell across her, and her purple hair sparkled.

"I don't know," she said.

Something told him he ought to check it out. But something else told him to forget it. Let it go. He wiped the sweat from the back of his neck and decided to listen to the second impulse.

"See ya later, Twyla," he said and walked inside.

Chapter 2

"Do I look like a billy goat when I pull my hair back like this?" Chelsea asked.

Patsy Palmer looked at her ten-year-old daughter in her black velvet skating outfit, thought for a moment and then said, "Dang. You know, you're right. You do resemble a billy goat." Then she started laughing one of those hard-to-stop laughs. The idea of her beautiful little girl looking like a billy goat was just too ludicrous to bear. Chelsea began to laugh with her.

"Don't do this to me while I'm driving," Patsy said, wiping away tears. Then she shook her head and said in a perplexed voice, "Gee. I wonder why I never noticed how much you look like a . . ." She couldn't finish.

"Now, you're doing it to yourself, Mom," Chelsea said, giggling helplessly.

"Oh, Lord, I can't drive," Patsy said. "You always do this to me." She wiped more tears away from her eyes and chuckled.

"Let's not tell Kyle what's so funny, okay," Chelsea said.

"I think it's one of those you-had-to-be-there kind of things," Patsy said as she pulled into the high school parking lot. It was summer time, and heat waves rose off the black parking lot in front of the driver's ed trailers. The door to the trailer opened. A handsome blond boy came out, followed by a bunch of teenagers, girls in their ragged-bottomed skirts that were all the rage and boys in baggy jeans and whatever ghetto shirts were hip this season.

Patsy waited for Kyle to come to the car. He stopped, waved

at one of the girls and came over. He hadn't had a girlfriend yet, at least as far as Patsy knew, but it wouldn't be long. He slid into the back seat.

"Hey, Mom," he said.

"Hey, Babe. How was driver's ed?"

"Did they show the gross movies?" Chelsea asked. "Like Dad always talks about?"

"No, not yet. We just learned all the boring rules," Kyle answered.

Patsy pulled out of the parking lot and headed home. As they drove home Patsy made mental notes of the various houses for sale. She knew a young couple who were moving to Charlotte, and they wanted to get in a good school area. The houses around here were fairly pricey, but people would pay big bucks when it came to getting their kids in a good school.

After dinner, Patsy put the dishes in the dishwasher. Tom had cut up and barbecued a turkey on the grill. It wasn't great, but as Tom said, at least they had some room in the freezer now. Now Tom was holed up in the bedroom watching television. The politics of the day enthralled him. She tried to ignore it all. She hated politics. Patsy had two interests in life—her children and her work. Actually, they were more like obsessions.

After making a couple of calls to some clients, she went upstairs and peeked in Kyle's room. He sat on the floor of his room with computer parts scattered across the floor.

"I hope this isn't my computer you've disassembled," she said, coming inside the room and stepping over green boards with squiggly silver lines over them.

"No, this is an old one," he said.

She sat down on his bed and studied him. A jet rumbled past in the sky outside. Patsy rubbed her foot. One wall of his room was covered with a mural that he and Tom had painted of the solar system. She'd never known that Tom had any artistic talent until he painted that wall. He never displayed any since then.

"So what's going on in your world?" she asked.

"I was thinking about time," he said.

"Oh." Whatever he was about to say would be strange, she was sure of that.

"Yeah. I was wondering. What is on the other side of now?"

"The other side of now? What?" Patsy laughed. Sometimes talking to her son was like talking to an alien.

"I mean, imagine that time is like space. Think of it as a wave floating along. If you look behind it, there's only void. In front of the wave is also just void. The only thing that exists is this constantly evolving wave, but as soon as it exists it disappears into the void—it becomes the past."

Patsy leaned back and gazed at him. "Honey, you think about some mighty deep stuff. Don't you ever think about things that other boys think about—like girls?"

Kyle was silent for a moment. He took a soldering iron from its holder and placed a piece of solder on one of the circuit boards.

"Did I tell you about Alessandra?" Kyle asked, concentrating on his work instead of looking at her.

"That sweet girl who's on the math team with you?"

"Yeah."

"Tell me what about her?"

"Well, I emailed her a poem I wrote."

"A poem?" Kyle had never written a poem in his life.

"Not exactly a poem. A mathematical equation. But kind of like a poem. See, if you know how to read equations, you'll know what this one means."

"An equation that means something. Tell me," Patsy asked. She slid off the bed to be closer to him. He smelled of boy sweat—a tangy scent. A thick shank of hair hung over his forehead.

"It means that everything was nice and orderly, but then it got all messed up, but in a good way."

"Oh," Patsy said.

"She probably thinks I'm an idiot," he said. His long lashes brushed against his cheek.

Patsy brought her face close to his.

"She probably thinks you're a genius. Which you are," she whispered. Then she kissed his cheek and stood. "Don't worry about it, babe. If she's got any sense at all, she'll hang on to that equation for the rest of her life."

He glanced up at her. "Think so?"

Patsy nodded. She left the room with those odd feelings that parents get as they realize their children are growing up, and she wondered exactly who she'd be without them. Chelsea was her best friend, her giggling companion, but Kyle, Kyle was the one person in the world she trusted. Even more than Tom. Maybe it's because he looked so much like the way she used to look, a younger but so much wiser version of herself. Of course, no one knew she was originally a blond. She'd been a redhead for such a long time even she wasn't sure what her natural color looked like.

She stepped into Chelsea's room. Chelsea sat on top of the fluffy white comforter of her bed, wearing her kitty-cat pajamas. Her room was still decorated with Pooh Bear pictures from when she was little. But Chelsea was already in the double digits and Patsy would have to redecorate the room this summer.

"Already had your bath?" Patsy asked.

"Yep. Will you tell me a story?"

"What story do you want to hear?"

"The one about the two princesses," Chelsea said.

"Okay," Patsy lay down on the bed beside her daughter. A small lamp in the shape of a half moon glowed on the bedside table.

Once upon a time, there were two princesses. They lived in a magic tower of light by the sea. The princesses wore pretty dresses of silver and gold. They sang and played games every day. During the day, birds flew around them calling their names, and dolphins leaped from the sea when they were near. At night the ocean waves whispered words of love to the two girls.

The elder princess was as beautiful as the stars in the sky. She took good care of the younger princess. She brought her mangoes and pomegranates and good things to eat.

"What's a pomegranate?"

"I don't know, but they must be good. Hush, now. Let me finish."

Whenever the younger princess skinned her knee, the elder princess kissed it and magically it was healed. They laughed together and were quite content never to leave their magic tower.

But there was a monster who lived down below the surface of the sea. Whenever the moon was dark, this monster would raise its green head and breathe flames at their tower.

"I will eat you both," the monster bellowed. "The elder girl will be my dinner and the younger one my dessert."

Whenever the monster said these words, the two princesses would cower in their bed and hold each other in fear.

"Please stay with me. Don't ever leave me," the younger princess begged the older one. And the older one promised she would not leave.

One day the sea monster rose from the sea and the dark waters churned as he came stomping toward the tower. The older princess climbed to the window, and as the sea monster shot flames from its claws at the princesses she laughed and turned into a giant bird. With a soft flap of her wings, she flew up into the sky. The younger princess had no idea how her sister had turned into a bird. She closed her eyes and begged the gods to turn her into a bird, too. But to no avail. She was stuck in the tower.

When the sea monster came to get her, the younger princess didn't know what to do. She called out for her sister. "Help, sister, help!" The sea monster came closer and closer. Fire shot up from his throat through his mouth and over his long, long tongue and burned the top of the tower. Just when he was about to devour the little princess a huge bird swooped down and with both of its talons it took away the monster's eyes. The monster turned around and around and around—so fast that he caused a hurricane and twenty-four tornados. Then he fell with a loud boom into the sea and he was never seen again.

"Did the bird turn back into a princess?" Chelsea asked.

"Yes, I'm sure that's what happened. And they lived happily . . ."

"Ever . . ."

"Before."

"That's not right."

"After."

"Okay."

Patsy hugged her daughter and kissed her on the forehead and both eyelids. Holding her daughter, she felt a pang of guilt. She wasn't sure what it stemmed from and her mind started to search for the source. Then she stopped. She didn't want to know. She was a good mother. That was all that mattered. That erased everything else.

"I love you so much," she said.

"Bunches and tonkles?" Chelsea asked, her voice fading into sleep.

"Bunches and tonkles," Patsy said, rising from the bed.

Patsy didn't know why Chelsea liked that story so much. She'd first made it up a long time ago, and for a moment, she remembered telling it to another little girl—there was the guilt—she quickly shut the door on that memory.

Tom lay in bed in his plaid boxer shorts, reading a book. Patsy undressed quietly.

"Did you already say goodnight to the kids?" she asked, slipping into a nightgown.

"Yep," he answered. He shut the book and looked at her. "How are you doing?"

"Fine," she said. She crawled into bed next to him.

"Listen, there's something I want to talk to you about," he said. "It's about next weekend."

"Yes?" she asked. Why was he being so serious, she wondered.

"My friend Jay from work said we could rent his beach house for the weekend. He's going to let me have it for the cost of the realty company and the maid. That is a really good deal."

"A beach house?" she said. "But, honey, we always go to the mountains."

"That's right. We always go to the mountains. Always. The kids are tired of it, and I am, too. Sweetie, I know you don't like the ocean, but we're going to Hawaii for my conference in August, maybe this will help you get used to it." He paused. Patsy looked away from him, shaking her head. He continued, "I promised Chelsea I'd teach her how to surf. Patsy, it's not fair to the kids to deny them this just because you have some weird and unreasonable, I might add, phobia of water. Jesus, you take baths, don't you? You swim in the pool at the Y."

Patsy sighed and turned to face him.

"You're right. I have a ton of work to do anyway. Why don't I stay here and you and the kids go to the beach?" she suggested.

Tom shook his head. "No. Then the kids won't want to go at all. We're all going, Patsy. How the hell are you going to handle a trip to Maui if you can't take a trip to the Outer Banks?"

"Well, Maui has mountains," she said. "Or volcanoes or something."

"It's also got a lot of water. This is something you need to get over. You don't have to go in the water, but at least come with us and relax for a couple days."

Patsy felt as if a brick had been shoved down her throat. But she nodded.

"Okay, okay. I'll go. But I'm not going near the water. Nowhere near it, do you hear me?"

"Whatever," he said.

"Whatever," she replied. Maybe he was right, but there were things he didn't understand. Things he could never understand.

Silence.

"Are you going to give me a squeeze or what?" he asked.

She snuggled down and hugged him. His warm familiar body felt good in her arms. It always did. She couldn't stay mad at him for long. His hands traveled along the length of her body. She shivered and felt a deep thirst, a longing, a need. She pulled closer to him and drew his mouth to hers.

Chapter 3

Rodney opened his closet and thumbed along his tie rack. He found a blue silk tie that Amy had given him for Christmas last year and pulled it out. Amy gave him a tie every year, and he always joked about it, groaning when he opened the package. But she had great taste, and he had to admit that sometimes an attractive paralegal complimented him on his choice in ties. He shoved the tie in his jacket pocket and stopped in the kitchen to grab a cup of green tea—Amy had made him switch over for health reasons—and threw Buddy a hotdog from the refrigerator before heading outside to his pick-up truck.

Court appearances were a major annoyance in the life of any working detective, but this one in particular stuck in his craw. It was a conspiracy charge from about four years earlier when the twenty-six-year-old suspect skipped out on his bond. They finally caught him when he made the mistake of going to his eight-year-old son's birthday party a few months ago. He remembered the case well. The suspect, Jeffrey Brown, had been willing to talk, and he seemed to be in the position of giving up some serious names in the dope import business, but oddly Rodney hadn't been allowed to cut a deal with the guy. In fact, he'd been stifled from pursuing the leads at all.

Working narcotics was the most depressing period of his life. He was fine as long as he busted black kids selling minuscule amounts of crack or college students with a couple ounces of weed, but if you started to dig, if you asked questions about how this shit got in the country in the first place, you ran into all sorts of stonewalling. Most of the other narcotics detectives didn't worry about it. They made their busts, took home their paychecks and were glad not to get shot. But Rodney knew that while these punks were getting sentences ranging from thirty years to life on bogus conspiracy charges—often with no more evidence than some other loser's testimony—the financiers and smugglers were living like Roman emperors. His outspokenness had eventually gotten him yanked off narcotics.

He walked through the crowded hallways of the courthouse—the land of the unlucky. A woman nursed a baby on a bench and a couple of teenage boys leered at her. Another woman in flip-flops with enormous circles under her eyes stood nervously against the wall. Rodney was amazed at the people who didn't think to put on a decent pair of shoes when going to face a judge. Then again maybe she didn't have anything better.

He found the courtroom and sat toward the front of the room. Who knew when his case would be called, and he could spend the time thinking about Thelma Jackson.

The case of the state v. Jeffrey Brown was first up on the docket. How about that? And, of course, there was no need for Detective Ellis to testify because Mr. Brown had accepted a deal from the state attorney's office: twenty-five years for conspiracy. Rodney felt sick to his stomach. Some deal. He'd gotten to know Jeffrey Brown while interrogating him about his Miami connection. The guy was smart, and a helluva an artist and while Jeffrey didn't seem to think too highly of his kid's mother, he loved that kid. Now, what would happen? His kid would grow up to be just like him or worse.

As he got up to leave, he heard the bailiff announce the next case, an arraignment actually. The state of Florida versus Trent Allen Lewis. Rodney stopped and glanced around the courtroom. The bailiff announced it again, and people on the benches looked around. A couple of good old boys snickered. At that moment, the doors to the courtroom opened and a balding middle-aged man sporting jailhouse tattoos entered, followed by a spruce young lawyer.

"Are you Trent Allen Lewis?" the judge asked, and the balding man smiled and nodded. Rodney noticed that one of his incisors was missing. The guy was probably in his mid- to late-forties but he had a muscular look as if he'd done his time in the weight room. Rodney lowered himself back into his seat to see what would happen as Trent Lewis and his lawyer walked to the front of the courtroom.

Rodney strained to hear the charges against Lewis and the lawyer's response. Was there something about possession of a firearm? He didn't remember Twyla mentioning that.

"Your honor," the lawyer said, "the gun in question, a Walther P88, is a collectable. Not for shooting. Mr. Lewis was in the employ of a collector and was in the process of delivering the gun. I have some papers verifying this information, as well as permissions granted through the department of law enforcement for Mr. Lewis to be in possession of a non-working gun."

Then the attorney showed some papers to the judge. The judge read the papers with a bored expression on his face and then glanced at Trent Lewis and looked back at the papers. Rodney tried to read the judge's face. It was not a particularly expressive face, heavy on the jowls, but it did seem to say that this wasn't exactly standard procedure. On the other hand, the papers must have been legitimate enough because the judge dismissed the firearms possession charge and thumped Lewis with a two hundred and fifty dollar fine for the drunk and disorderly charge and added a hundred dollars for court costs. The attorney wrote a check, and the two men exited the court room without any more delay.

Rodney followed them outside. The courthouse was in the center of town, and the big Spanish moss-cloaked oaks in front drooped in the breezeless summer day. The two men said their goodbyes. Rodney noticed that the young lawyer ignored Trent's outstretched hand, got into a Mercedes and drove away. Trent stood on the sidewalk and shoved his hands in his pockets.

Rodney approached him.

"Hey there, Trent?"

Trent turned around and sucked in his left cheek as if sizing up Rodney. Then Trent grinned.

"I thought one of you guys might be in there, checking up to make sure I didn't say nothing wrong," Trent said.

Rodney didn't know who Trent thought he was, but he plastered a friendly open look on his face, patted Trent on the shoulder and said, "You did good. Yep."

"Shit. What do you guys think? I'm stupid?"

"Sure hope not, Trent. Say, what ever happened to that old girlfriend of yours, Vera Lee was her name, right?"

Trent's eyebrows furrowed, and he seemed confused.

"I ain't seen her in near 'bout twenty-seven, twenty-eight years," he said. "She doesn't exactly send me Christmas cards. Wait a minute, who are you?"

Rodney stuck out his hand and said, "Rodney Ellis, Gainesville Police Department. I'm a detective."

Trent slowly took Rodney's hand, and his eyes widened just slightly. He was obviously realizing Rodney wasn't who he thought he was.

"Who were you expecting, Trent?" Rodney asked.

"No one," Trent said and smiled. "Can I help you in some way, Detective Ellis?"

"No, just wondering who you were up here buying collectable guns for?"

"Uh, Mr. Samsonite. Yeah. That's his name."

"Samsonite? Like luggage? You couldn't think of anything better than that?"

Trent shook his head and his expression turned sour.

"What are you buggin' me for? Don't you got enough to do? I hear you got a serial motel-maid killer out there. Shouldn't you be tracking that guy down?"

"What do you know about it?" Rodney asked.

"Just what I saw in the paper. Somebody whacked that broad in the head. Whoo, that musta hurt."

A breeze finally mustered up from somewhere, stirred the Spanish moss and kissed Rodney's neck. A 1996 Ford Explorer pulled alongside them, and Rodney looked inside. A heavyset woman with dark hair sat behind the wheel. She had small eyes that glared at Rodney suspiciously. That woman had never been Vera Lee Gifford, that much Rodney could tell in a glance.

"Speaking of jealous wives, I better get going," Trent said. "Nice talking to you, Detective. Have a real nice day, okay?" Trent turned his back on Rodney and slid into the passenger side of the Explorer. Rodney watched as it drove off, and made a mental note of the tag number.

"Man, you do the crime you got to do the time," Willie said and noisily sucked the straw of the chocolate milk shake that Rodney had brought him. Rodney munched his Rally's burger and nodded. "Thanks for the shake, man."

"Sure," Rodney said. "I know that, Willie. I'm not excusing the guy. He was definitely doing the wrong thing, but that's a whomping amount of time. It's not like he killed anybody. And the thing that gets me is that I know there are bigger fish. It's like being satisfied with a little guppy when there's a grouper swimming past."

"You know when I became a cop I really thought I was helping people," Willie said. "And we did. We helped a lot of people."

Rodney nodded.

"But I don't know if I'd do it again," Willie said.

Rodney leaned back in the armless wooden chair by Willie's bed.

"What else would you do? We were born for this work," he said. "And we've done some good. We locked up some killers, maybe saved some lives."

"But we're little cogs in a big machine, Rod. Remember Gavin Worthy?" Willie tilted his head back and stared up at the ceiling. Gavin Worthy was a name that neither of them had spoken aloud in many years. Gavin Worthy was their albatross, especially Rodney's. Convicted of raping and killing a twenty-year-old pregnant woman, Worthy spent thirteen years on death row only to be proven innocent through DNA evidence. Rodney and Willie had been in on the original bust, and Rodney hadn't slept for weeks when they found out the truth. They had helped convict an innocent man.

He didn't realize that Willie still thought about Gavin Worthy. When Willie was well, they had never really talked about their work in any terms other than normal shop talk. The most philosophical they ever got was when discussing whether Steve Spurrier's assholishness enhanced his abilities as a coach, and they both felt that somehow it did. Too bad he had put on airs and gone to the NFL, a defection that both men took somewhat personally.

"Hey, you know what Twyla told me yesterday. Remember Vera Lee Gifford?"

"The bikini killer?" Willie said with a laugh. "I will never forget her, man. Some tits, huh?"

Rodney chuckled. Willie was such a straight arrow that when he got a little off-color, the incongruity always caught Rodney by surprise.

"Yeah, she was hot," Rodney agreed. "Anyway, Twyla said the boyfriend—not the attorney she was doing but the boyfriend she was doing the attorney for . . ."

"Yeah, yeah. I know who you mean. The marijuana entrepreneur. She 'hired' some attorney to defend her man and then winds up blowing away the attorney's wife along with a couple other inconvenient people."

"Right. Dude's named Trent Lewis. Anyway he gets busted for drunk and disorderly here in Hogtown the other day. That business with Vera Lee Gifford was almost thirty years ago and now he shows up out of nowhere. He had a court appearance this morning right after they sent up Jeffrey Brown."

"It was in 1976 when we busted her," Willie corrected. "Something about that whole thing didn't smell right to me."

"Like what?" Rodney asked.

"Well, when we caught her, she had the sweetest little Walther pistol on her. It was a truly rare bird. One of those that the SS used in World War II. Now, I know the attorney that she supposedly stole the gun from was a collector. Remember that? Soon as I saw that gun though, I knew something wasn't right. No way someone would let some sixteen-year-old chick get a hold of a gun like that. A collector would never shoot the gun. It decreases the value. And he sure wouldn't leave it lying around."

"But ballistics showed it was the same gun used in all three shootings."

"Yeah, I know. But something wasn't right."

Willie paused. Rodney thought for a moment.

"You want to know something weird? One of Trent's charges, which got dismissed by the way, was possession of a firearm. Turns out it was a Walther P80 or something like that. His lawyer said he was delivering it to a collector. Isn't that a coincidence?"

Willie set down the chocolate shake and then scrunched his face up in thought. "The chemo has scrambled my brain cells, but I don't recall there being a Walther P80. It was probably a P88, one of the most accurate double-action service handguns ever made. But it was too wide, about an inch and half across the frame. And way too expensive. They stopped making them in 1994."

"So that would make them more valuable, right?" Rodney asked.

"Oh yeah. Not in the tens of thousands of dollars or anything, but anyone who collected Walthers would have to have one of those babies," Willie said.

Just then Debbie came in. She was a short, plump blonde with a sweet smile. She was Willie's high-school sweetheart and proof that some people were made to marry young.

"Are you guys solving the world's problems again?" she asked.

"Nah, just Rodney's. This case he's digging into is not just cold, it's got icicles dangling from it," Willie said with a laugh that turned into a cough that made his eyes tear up.

"Hey, push that button there, pal. I need another jolt," Willie said, when the coughing finally ceased. Rodney reached over to the IV bag and squeezed the trigger that released the morphine.

Chapter 4

Fancy Lee Gifford pushed the cart down the quiet carpeted hallway, a red notebook on top of the cart with the word "Narcotics" scrawled in black magic marker across the front. The assisted living facility was a good place to collect drugs. Fancy still had an ample stash from her private work, but with Trent around, that would dwindle quickly. The old people could nag you to death, but no one cared. Fancy liked some of them, the tiny old lady in the walker who dyed her hair orange and played Debussy on the piano and the fifty-nine-year-old man with cancer who rode his bike to the shopping center every day. He was a pistol.

The cancer patient had a variety of pain pills from Percocet and Tylenol #3 to the occasional Oxycontin for bad days. Generally, she gave him a Vicodin and marked down one of the more potent pills. She also kept a baggie of dummy pills that she could switch up when necessary. There was another old lady who needed shots of Demerol for chronic back pain. Half went to the old lady and half in the spare vials that Fancy kept with her. She loved the way doctors overprescribed to them. She wasn't hard-hearted. If they were in pain, she made sure to take care of it. They never missed what she took.

Usually, she was especially careful about how much she took, but she'd asked for a leave for the next couple of weeks, and cancelled her private work as well, so she took a few risks. Trent was right. They'd have to be able to move at a moment's notice. Were they finally on the right trail or would it end up just another dead end?

She finished giving out the last dose. Marilyn, the orange-haired lady, had about six different pills to take. She stood wavering behind her walker, swallowing them down one at a time.

"I like it here," Marilyn said. "Except some of these people are so stupid. And their grammar is abominable. Have you noticed that?"

"Well, a lot of them didn't get a real good education back then, you know," Fancy said.

After the meds had been delivered, Fancy strode down the empty hallway to the nurse's station to figure out what she had collected for the night. She knew Trent would be waiting back at the boat with his mouth open like a baby bird. She remembered the day he had reappeared in her life. She had been wiping down the instruments in the pilothouse on *Daddy's Baby* when she heard his voice call out, "Fancy Lee, Fancy Lee, won't you marry me?"

She came out onto the cockpit and looked up at him.

"What sewer did you crawl out of?" she asked. It had been a couple years since he'd been around. Trent was like that. Coming and going.

"Would have come by sooner but I had a job. Took me to the Caribbean where I met some high rollers." He dropped down onto the boat. "Can't believe you still have this thing. Don't see too many wooden boats anymore. Can't you sell it?"

"You know good and well, I'll never sell this boat, Trent Lewis. It's all I've got. This and a crummy one-bedroom apartment."

"You've got me," he said and edged closer to her. She stepped back. Trent was the only man in her life, and that was a thought that made her sad: that she couldn't do any better than this.

"Nice tattoo. Did you get that in jail?"

"I was drunk in Port au Prince when that one happened," he said with a laugh, looking down at the cockroach tattooed on the back of his hand. Then he pulled a rolled-up newspaper from his back pocket. "Got something to show you."

He handed the newspaper to her. She went into the pilothouse and sat down in the captain's chair. He followed her.

"What am I looking at?" she asked.

"See this story here about the woman who runs this theater group in Gainesville for 'at-risk' kids—that's code for juvenile delinquents. Read the whole story. You'll find it kind of interesting."

Fancy settled back and started reading. She didn't tell Trent to go away when he began rubbing her thigh with his cockroach hand. It had been a long time since anyone had touched her like that. But after a few minutes she didn't even notice him. She was much too engrossed in the story. When she finished it, she turned to him.

"So this woman was in prison at the same time as Vera Lee. That doesn't mean nothing," she said.

Trent leaned close to her.

"Remember the letters Vera Lee wrote you, baby? Doesn't this name sound familiar to you?"

Fancy folded up the paper. She knew who would know if this woman meant anything to Vera Lee. She hadn't worked in the prison infirmary all those years for nothing. She knew exactly who helped Vera Lee get out of prison. Only up till now, it hadn't done any good. And who's to say this wasn't just another dead end.

"Look," Trent said. "Remember you said that Thelma Jackson said somebody sent money to her mother on the regular, and she was pretty sure it was Vera Lee. Honey, I didn't spend all those months trolling through the titty bars and strip joints of South Carolina and North Carolina for nothing now, did I?"

"But you never found her," Fancy Lee said.

"I know I didn't. But that doesn't mean she can't be found. And I'm just real curious to see what kind of game she's got going, aren't you? Might be worth a lot of money for both of us."

"I don't care about the money," Fancy said.

"You don't? Shit. I know this boat drinks up every dime you got, girl."

That had been weeks ago. Now, things had gotten dicey. Stupid, stupid Thelma. She shouldn't have threatened them. Fancy bent over and locked up the medicine cabinet, wouldn't want thieves to get in. She straightened up and ran a hand through her light brown hair. Trent didn't understand anything. He didn't know what had happened to her when she was young—what Vera Lee had let happen to her. She looked down at the vial in her hand—a shot of this could knock out a horse. She closed her fist around it.

Fancy locked the door to her bedroom in case Trent came back early. He had wandered off to a bar, said he had some business with someone he'd met down in Haiti. She figured he was just going to look at naked girls. That's what men liked. She knew that. She didn't love Trent, didn't really like him all that much, but he had bulldozed his way into her life a long time ago when he first got out of prison. He'd been looking for Vera Lee and found her instead. And even she needed someone once in a while.

She opened the cover of the old turntable and flicked the switch. The album cover lay on the floor. It looked like a picture frame. On the cover, the word, "Untitled." She picked up the arm of the turntable and dropped it into a groove in the black plastic. The familiar guitar began.

That haunting voice began to sing about a lady who thought everything that glittered was gold. Trent made fun of her for listening to this song as much as she did, for even owning a record player. But she wanted to remember what she had once had—someone who cared for her. Mama left when she was just six, and she could hardly even remember her. It seemed like it had always been Vera Lee, holding her at night, cleaning her up if she wet the bed, singing these songs to her like lullabies. Everyone loved Vera Lee. She was so pretty and so wild. Vera Lee thought that Daddy hated her, but she was wrong. He loved her, too. That's why he almost killed her. He never would have bothered to hurt Fancy Lee. He didn't even know she existed. Maybe he thought he was looking in a mirror when he looked at her round face and hurt little eyes, her dark overgrown eyebrows. Just like his.

Fancy sat down on the floor by her closet and opened the box she kept in there—a box of memories. Here were Vera Lee's platform Candys, a pair of white plastic hoop earrings, a bottle of sandalwood oil with no scent left. And at the very bottom, the envelope.

Fancy pulled up the envelope and opened it. Inside were the pictures. The evidence of what she had done to try to help Vera Lee. Daddy had taken some rich guys to Bimini to go marlin fishing when the man in the white Cadillac pulled up to their little house. She was only thirteen when it happened. The man said if she didn't do it, then Vera Lee would get hurt.

"You want to see your sister again?" he asked her. He seemed nice. He bought her clothes and told her she was even prettier than Vera Lee. She knew now he was lying, but some men didn't care what you looked like—as long as you were young. It was Trent who got those pictures back for her. He wouldn't say how he'd gotten them, but someone wanted her to remember exactly what she'd done, what a bad girl she'd been.

The door to the apartment opened. Fancy shoved the pictures back into the envelope. She shoved the envelope in her medicine bag and unlocked the bedroom door.

"Hey, baby," Trent slurred. He was slobbering on pills. She had given him just a few earlier, but she could tell he had snuck into her stash and taken more.

"You never know when to quit, do you?" she asked. "You won't be happy till you're dead."

Trent mumbled something unintelligible and fell into the bed. Well, he was a warm body, and somehow he eased Fancy's loneliness. Fancy crawled into the bed with him. Soon he was snoring into her ear. She fell into a rough sleep.

Chapter 5

Buddy's whining woke him up—whining that at first melded into someone crying in Rodney's dream. Rodney was soaked in sweat as he leaned over to turn on the light. He was home in his own bed in the house he'd lived in since before Amy was born. Buddy reached his furry muzzle over the edge of the bed and licked Rodney's hand.

"It's okay, Buddy," Rodney said. "Just having a nightmare. It was Dennis Chapman again. Thought he was lost to history, and now here he is, begging me to blow his brains out. And once again, I did it." He got out of the bed and went to the bathroom to wash his face. Maybe he needed to see a shrink. But he knew what they'd do. They'd give him some drugs and tell him there was nothing they could do. He shouldn't have been halfway across the world, killing people when he was twenty years old. But that wasn't the worst of it. The worst of it was when he went back overseas for the CIA, thinking he was gonna be some kind of Rambo-style hero, saving POWs, and wound up putting his childhood friend out of his misery instead, and then leaving God knows how many of the poor suckers behind because the Washington blowhards didn't feel POWs were worth the time or the trouble.

Maybe Amy was right. Maybe he was having some kind of mid-life crisis. And maybe it was because she was gone. Amy had only moved a couple hours away down near Mickey Mouse World, but he had gotten used to her living with him through college and then law school. Now she was off starting her career and getting married. He was really alone. Maybe he should start dating. But not many women wanted damaged goods like him.

Then an image slid into his mental chatter, those blue eyes belonging to Vera Lee Gifford, staring at him across the courtroom so long ago. When he had looked at her, he felt like he was looking into a mirror. He was seeing someone who had been turned into a killer. He wasn't sure who had done it to her, who had turned her bravery into something cruel, but he knew exactly how she felt.

The trial had been down in Fort Lauderdale where the murders had taken place. The bar where she'd worked as an exotic dancer was already back in operation even though she'd killed the owner of the bar and his bodyguard. Those were her first two victims. That night Rodney had gone to the bar and paid a girl ten dollars to swivel her breasts in front of him. He had asked the girl about Vera Lee.

"Vera Lee wasn't really bad," the girl said. "Most of us tried to look out for her. She's just a kid you know. Chuck could have done a lot of time if the cops had known her real age. Anyway, no one misses Chuck or that shit-for-brains Lorenzo either—except for that psycho bitch wife of his. She's the one who ought to be doing time. I know for a fact she's a stone-cold killer."

"What's the wife's name?"

"Sylvia Black. She had always had a hard on for Vera Lee," the girl said.

"A hard on?"

"She hated her. Of course, she hated all of us, but she hated Vera Lee most of all."

He'd bought the girl a Jack Black and Coke. She talked some more. The picture he got of Vera Lee was of a silly little sixteen-year-old girl who liked to have fun, drink a little, snort a little cocaine once in a while, not all that different from the high school girls he sometimes arrested for DUI except that they had parents who made sure they got an education, and she apparently only had a petty-thieving, pot-dealing boyfriend who was providing her with a different kind of education. But now she had gone out and killed people—a couple of bad guys and a woman who had never done anything to her except marry the wrong guy.

"You know anything about this attorney, Lance Underwood, the one whose wife she killed?"

The dancer had giggled. "Lance? All the girls knew Lance. Mistah Monee-Bags. He used to just come in once in a while, but once she started working here, he turned into a regular. Sure, Vera Lee went to him soon as her old man got busted. Not that she had enough money to pay a lawyer like Lance, but I'm sure they worked something out if you know what I mean?" By this time, the girl was no longer dancing. She had sat down at his table, and he was starting to get used to carrying on a conversation with a nearly naked girl.

"Why would Vera Lee shoot his wife, do you think?"

"Who knows? I heard she was so stoned on PCP she didn't know her own name. That stuff will mess you up. I only did it once. Never again, honey. Can I have another drink?"

When he got back to Gainesville after the trial, Vera Lee stuck in his memory, especially her ultramarine eyes. He wondered if she saw into him the way he saw into her. Two reluctant killers looking at each other across a chasm.

"Let's go to Perry," Lanelle said as they walked into Chief Carmichael's office.

"Okay. I got nothing better to do," Rodney said. They explained what they knew about the Jackson homicide. Carmichael wanted to know if either of them had seen Willie.

"I stopped by last night," Rodney said. "He was sleeping."

Carmichael nodded. "Okay. Do both of you need to go to Perry?"

"No," Rodney admitted.

"You two are like Siamese twins. Tweedledum, you go to Perry," Carmichael said, pointing to Rodney. "Tweedledee, you go down to the prison and see what you can find out about her past life."

Rodney took a deep breath.

"Chief, I been working for this department for nearly thirty years. Don't call me Tweedledum, okay?"

"What the hell has gotten into you?" Carmichael asked.

Rodney heard Lanelle say, "He's just on edge about Willie. Don't worry about it." But Rodney was already walking out of the office.

The drive alone to Perry would do him good. North Florida in the summertime was a sultry place. He found the oldies station and let the Young Rascals take him back to his youth—to some sunny day before he went to Vietnam. He remembered the old Palatka cemetery where he and Dennis Chapman played among the tombstones of Confederate war heroes. One of them was his great-great grandpa, who died in 1894. There was a magnolia tree in that cemetery that he had climbed as a little kid and where he had taken Cheryl on Halloween in the twelfth grade to try to scare her. But Cheryl had other things on her mind that night. *I brought your Halloween costume,* she whispered in his ear and pulled out a package of Trojans from her purse. A few minutes later, they were in the back seat of his Impala, and there with her arms and legs wrapped around him, he thought he had finally found home. Was it just a factor of youth, he wondered, or was he only capable of loving one woman and once she left he would never find that kind of passion again? It had been fifteen years since she walked out of their marriage. Since then he'd had a few dates here and there along the way, a couple of short-term girlfriends, but mostly his life had revolved around his daughter and his work. Now his daughter was gone, and somehow between the paperwork and the politics the work had lost its allure.

He knew he was in Perry when he saw the giant billboard for Swain's lemon meringue pie. He pulled into the truck stop restaurant, ordered a hamburger and declined the pie, which looked as rubbery and artificial in the glass case as it did on the billboard. He asked the waitress for directions to the address he had for Thelma's mother's previous home, but the waitress, who was white, said she didn't know "that part of town." She called out the cook, a big fellow with a wide grin, who actually remembered the Jackson family quite well and gave explicit directions to the house.

"Did Thelma have any enemies around here?" Rodney asked the man.

The cook shook his head. "Nah, that man she killed was hated far and wide. Most people were proud of her for sticking up for herself. You can't let someone dog you the way he dogged her."

Rodney thought that hacking her husband to death with a machete might have been taking it a little too far, but it did give her lawyer ammunition all those years later to show she was out of her mind at the time. He paid his bill and left a generous tip, then went outside where truck exhaust lay over the road like a dirty mist.

The little turquoise house where Thelma's mother used to live had a flower garden planted in front. Something about that riot of color put Rodney at ease—a bad thing. He wondered if he was losing his edge. A young woman sat on the porch holding a baby.

"This your house?" Rodney asked.

"No, I'm just visiting my daddy. He lives here," she said. Then she called inside, "Daddy! The police is here."

A middle-aged man opened the screen door and came out on the porch. He glared at Rodney suspiciously. Rodney wished Lanelle had come along. Nothing like a white face in a black neighborhood to grant you instant unpopularity.

"Excuse me, sir. I'm from the Gainesville Police Department, and I'm wondering if you might be willing to answer a couple questions for me."

"Like what kind of questions?" the man asked with a frown.

"I'm just wondering if you knew the lady who lived here before you did—or her daughter Thelma."

"Sure, I know them. Thelma comes here every few weeks to pick up their mail. Why do you ask?" The man crossed his arms, watching Rodney intently.

"Somebody killed Thelma a couple days ago. I wondered if she had any old enemies from over here."

"Thelma's dead? That's a damn shame." The hostile attitude was replaced with genuine surprise mixed with a certain amount of sorrow. The man smacked his lips and dropped his arms to his side. "I can't believe anyone would want to hurt her. She didn't socialize much when she came over. I mean, she'd stop and have a glass of iced tea and tell me about how her momma was doing or sometimes she'd bring her momma. They drove an old Buick and I might do a few repairs while they were here. I'm a mechanic, you know. Damn good mechanic. But Thelma, no, Thelma didn't spend a lot of time getting in other people's business."

Rodney leaned his hip against the porch railing.

"Why didn't she just have her mail forwarded?"

"Well, she did, but there was some mail she got—a letter every few weeks and it never had no return address on it. And I guess they were important letters 'cause she always came to get them. Mmmph. I sure liked Thelma. She had a kind of dignity all those years in the penitentiary never could take away from her."

Rodney had only been standing outside a short while but already the heat was fogging up his brain. He took off his sunglasses and wiped the sweat from his nose.

"When was the last time you got one of those letters?" Rodney asked.

"Just yesterday. I was gonna call over there today and tell her to come get it."

Rodney sighed and looked down at the concrete steps to the porch. He didn't think anyone from Perry had gone over there to kill Thelma. She just wasn't that big of a troublemaker, apparently.

"Well, she won't be coming over to get that letter. Who is it addressed to?"

"It's addressed to her momma. They always are."

Rodney nodded. "Tell you what. I'll take it back with me. I have to see Ms. Jackson again tomorrow and I'll give it to her."

The man shrugged. He didn't want any trouble. He went in the house and came back with a square envelope. No return address. The postmark was Rock Hill, South Carolina.

Lanelle was typing on the computer when Rodney came into the office.

"What'd you find?" she asked.

"I asked around. Went by the Perry police department. Nothing. No one had an ax to grind with Thelma Jackson. Her deceased husband didn't have any relatives that anyone knows of. What'd you find?"

"Nothing much. I went down to the women's correctional institution where she did her time. Her classification officer isn't there any longer but the assistant superintendent remembered her. Said she was a model prisoner. She started off in the laundry but after a couple of years she got assigned to work doing housekeeping up in the front offices, kind of unusual for a convicted murderer but I guess she had earned their trust. Things were more lax back then."

Rodney didn't say anything but he was thinking that Lanelle should have found an inmate to interview. The people in charge rarely knew much about what went on inside. Maybe he'd take a trip down there himself later.

Rodney picked up the phone and buzzed Al to see what he had found out.

"No murder weapon. Coroner says it definitely wasn't rape though she had sex sometime in the past few days. They've got a minuscule amount of semen, enough for a DNA screen, but having sex does not equal murder as we all know."

"Thanks, Al," Rodney said and relayed the information to Lanelle.

"Well, we know it wasn't robbery 'cause she didn't have anything to steal. The people who had been in that room were just some college kid's parents and they'd checked out about three hours earlier. So it looks like she went in, cleaned up the room, someone came in and conked her on the head, hard enough to kill her, for no damn reason at all," she said.

"Well, I got one possible reason," Rodney said, dropping the envelope addressed to Thelma's mother on Lanelle's desk. "The man in Perry says these cards come every six weeks or so to Thelma's mother and Thelma always came over to get them. Remember the card with the money in it at Thelma's house?"

"Yeah. A birthday present for a niece."

"Three hundred dollars for a niece? And it wasn't even a birthday card. It was blank inside."

Lanelle picked up the envelope and held it on her palm.

"There's definitely something in here," she said. "You think Thelma was blackmailing someone?"

Rodney leaned against his desk and shook his head. "I don't know. I mean, if I was being blackmailed all these years by Thelma Jackson, why would I suddenly decide to kill her? And if I did kill her, why would I have sent more money to her?"

Lanelle stood up. "We need to make a delivery, Mr. Postman."

The phone on Rodney's desk rang just as they were walking out the door. He thought about ignoring it, but then something like a hand on his shoulder made him turn around and pick up the receiver.

"Ellis here," he said.

"Rodney, it's Debbie. You better get over here. Willie's asking for you. I think this will be your last chance to see him."

Rodney dropped the phone and ran out of his office, down the hallway and out of the door into the late afternoon light.

Chapter 6

Patsy lay awake next to Tom and stared out the window. Seagulls flew across a pale sky which was slowly becoming lighter and bluer. The breeze with its salt scent wafted through the open window. They'd gotten there the evening before. She had stayed in the house and unpacked the bags of groceries while Tom and the kids took the Frisbee and went down to the beach. She felt guilty for not going with them. Instead she made some spaghetti and tried to keep her mind locked into the present.

A deep sadness moved into her heart. Tom rustled next to her in the bed. She pushed aside the cover and stood on the linoleum. It had been so many years but last night the dream returned. She was about eight years old, leaning over the bow of a boat. She could feel the spray on her face. Everything about it was so real, especially her mother's face just below the surface of the water, sinking, sinking until it disappeared. The wrenching loneliness that she felt in the dream returned full force.

She tugged at the bedroom door, swollen from the humidity of the beach, and jerked it open. Tom still slept. She went outside and sat down on the chair on the screened-in porch. She couldn't see the water from the porch, and she was glad. But she could smell it. A boogie board leaned against the wall. An elderly man walked by with his dog. Tom was right. If they were going to Hawaii, she would have to suck up her fear. Was it fear really? No, it was something more like dread.

She heard the door open and sensed her son standing behind her.

"You want some pancakes for breakfast, Kyle?" she asked.

"How do you do that?" he wondered. "How did you know I wasn't Chelsea?"

"I'm your momma. I know everything," she said.

"Can we go to the lighthouse?" Chelsea begged. "They moved it you know. Can you imagine? I wish I saw that. I wish I saw them move a whole lighthouse."

"Ask your mom," Tom said as he put the last dish in the drainer. "Does she want to go?"

Patsy shrugged. "It's okay with me." It would be better than the beach at any rate though they'd probably want to do that this afternoon. They got ready and all piled into Tom's minivan.

But the lighthouse wasn't better than the beach. It was worse. Much worse.

Patsy stood by the car and looked up at the white and black cone reaching toward the clouds. Her heart began pounding. What was that sound in her ears?

"Why are lighthouses always painted black and white like that?" Chelsea asked.

"They aren't," Patsy answered. "Some of them are red."

"The light inside is made of fresnel lenses," Kyle said.

"It's pronounced freh-nel, honey," Patsy said. "They were designed by a Frenchman. The lights used to be lit with lard."

Tom glanced at her.

"I didn't know you knew anything about lighthouses," he said.

"They were a hobby of my mother's," she answered.

"Nan was into lighthouses?"

Patsy shook her head. "My real mother. The dead one," she said, meaning the one she never talked about.

"Let's go in," Chelsea said, tugging at her mother's hand.

"I'll wait," Patsy said. "You go on ahead."

"Come on, Mom," Kyle said, but Tom interrupted him.

"She doesn't have to go." He leaned over and kissed Patsy's cheek. "We'll be back."

As they walked away, Patsy felt them fading from her life. They didn't know her. They were her family, but they had no idea who she was.

A memory from her childhood came rushing back to her. Her mother, leading her and Fancy Lee up the wrought iron steps of the lighthouse over Jupiter inlet. Her mother had the keys to the place in exchange for cleaning the handrails and sweeping the floor and dusting the cobwebs away from the deep windows. Her mom might have been a floozy who never cleaned her own house, but she loved the lighthouse. There was still a lighthouse keeper, but he was often in his house and the girls could play up in the lamphouse if he wasn't around.

"Once during a hurricane, the lighthouse keeper's son had to come and move the mantle by hand so the light would keep shining. The tower swayed seventeen inches during that storm, girls. Can you imagine how scary that was?"

"Is the tower haunted?" she had asked her mother.

"Yes, it is. You know the Germans used to torpedo ships off the coast right out there during the war. I know for sure I've heard a ghost moaning in here. Probably one of those poor drowned sailors. When a ghost is nearby you feel a chill."

Patsy shivered as the wind plucked strands of hair from her ponytail. She had known her mother was just trying to thrill them with her ghost stories, but now her mother herself had become a ghost.

Patsy got back into the car. She knew they must wonder what was wrong with her, but Tom had learned long ago not to intrude into her fears. He understood that there were things she would not, could not, tell him, but he knew she loved him and more than that, she needed him. The sunlight slanted in through the windshield across her hands.

Outside, birds flew in a strange ballet. They looked like starlings. For twenty-four years she had done nothing wrong. She was as clean-living a person as could be found. The neighborhood women teased her because she didn't drink. She even went to church once in a while and not one of those weird churches that Nan and Jim went to, a regular Presbyterian church that Tom liked.

The diamond on her finger sent tiny dots of light swirling over the interior of the car when she moved her hand. Then she remembered the diamonds of light, tinged with pink, green and blue, that sparkled in a long row on the white interior wall of the lighthouse. The sun hit the lens during the afternoon and created that beautiful shower of light. When she was young, she had watched those bright reflections and imagined they were fairies watching over her. Later she learned that no one watched out for you. She felt a tightening in her throat and closed her eyes. She could see her father coming at her with his belt, tapping his leg. She could remember the hunger gnawing when there wasn't food in the house. She could hear her little sister crying, crying. She opened her eyes quickly. So much of her life before Tom, before these children, was darkness, and she didn't want to shine a light in there.

White clouds floated like barges in the sky behind the lighthouse. The memories churned inside her. It wasn't good to remember, to have those thoughts in her head. She saw Tom and the kids walking back toward her, the wind pressing their clothes against their skin. They looked happy, and she knew she had to erase these memories again and again.

Patsy Palmer didn't have a mother who had disappeared. She didn't have a drunk father who had tried to kill her with the claw of a hammer and she never ran away with a boy named Trent in a red GTO. She had never gotten involved with Lance Underwood. That was someone else's life. She was Patsy Palmer. She had two wonderful parents named Nan and Jim, a great husband and two perfect kids. Hers was an excellent life, and no one, not even a ghost, was going to take it away from her. She got out of the car to greet her family.

Chelsea came running up to her and hugged her.

"Mom, are you afraid of the ocean because of the sea monster?"

Patsy laughed and asked, "What sea monster?"

"The one in the story?"

"There are no sea monsters, babe. Not in real life," Patsy said, running her hand over her daughter's hair.

"Then will you come down to the beach with us this afternoon, please?" she asked.

Patsy looked down into Chelsea's brown eyes. She hadn't known how to raise children. But Nan had helped, and Tom was a great dad. Mostly, though, the kids had taught her with their ready affection and amazing capacity for forgiveness, and she'd always been a quick learner.

"Yes," she said. "I will."

Chapter 7

Rodney pulled his truck into the Presidential Lounge parking lot. Debbie's call had been a false alarm. Willie had rallied and looked to have a little more time. Rodney was glad he had other things to think about right now.

The Presidential looked pure ghetto from the outside—white cinder block with black bars on the windows and the door. Not too many white people frequented the Presidential, but Rodney had been to the juke joint more than once and not just officially. On weekends live blues music started around ten p.m. and went on way past the last call for alcohol. Rodney loved blues and had been known to drink a bit of Jim Beam. The "big eye" had caught him a few times, stumbling out of the place at the crack of dawn. But he was older now, and drinking all night in a smoky bar didn't have the appeal it once had.

"My man, Hot Rod Ellis," Woodrow Wilson said as Rodney crossed the wood plank floor to the worn wooden bar. Rodney's eyes were still adjusting to the darkness but he recognized Woodrow's slim silhouette and his voice.

"Hey there, Woodrow, how you been?"

"Same ol' same ol'. You know."

Rodney sat down on a stool.

"What'll it be?" Woodrow asked.

"A Pepsi cola if you got 'em," Rodney said.

"Shit," Woodrow laughed. "We got some ol' generic cola on tap, man. You on the wagon?"

"Just slowing down in my old age," Rodney admitted. "And I won't lie to you. I'm here officially."

"Thelma Jackson, huh?"

"You heard?"

"Niggas will talk."

"You said that. I didn't."

"You better not, Cracker."

Rodney laughed. "Don't you know better than to disrespect a man of the law?"

"Is that what you are, the man?" Woodrow slid him a tall glass of iced cola. It tasted good, bubbly and sharp on his tongue. Woodrow limped down to the end of the bar and took five dollars from a customer. Then he limped back.

"That old wound bother you?"

Woodrow shook his head.

"I'm glad I made it back it alive."

"Amen, brother, amen. How's Tap?"

"He's good. Real good. His girl Annie just had a baby." Woodrow nodded. There was gratitude in his expression. About ten years earlier, Tap had been in the wrong place at a particularly unfortunate time—a crack house in the middle of a drug bust. Rodney had known the kid from various law enforcement programs where they worked with kids. He knew Tap was a good kid, and though it wasn't exactly legitimate—okay, it was a downright fireable offense—Rodney didn't take the kid to jail. Instead he took him home to Wilson, and the next day, Rodney personally took Tap out to the community college and got him registered for courses. Tap took a few business classes and then opened up an air conditioning repair shop. Rodney had vouched for his loan. He knew the kid deserved a break, and Tap had proven him right.

Rodney sipped his cola and waited while Woodrow poured a beer from the tap for an old-timer a few stools down.

"So who killed her, Hot Rod?" Woodrow asked when he returned.

Rodney shrugged. He didn't like to admit that they didn't have a clue but it was early in the investigation.

"I thought you might have some ideas. One of her girlfriends said she liked to come here on Friday nights. And I know nothing gets past you," Rodney said, and gazed at Woodrow with a questioning tilt of his head.

Woodrow shook his head.

"She was a quiet one. Nice lady," he said. "Comes in, drinks a little. You know, used to be she might go home with a fella, but last couple years, I ain't seen her go with nobody."

"You ever take her home?"

"Once. Little bit after she started coming in here. We had fun, but wasn't neither of us looking for anything else. You understand me?"

Rodney nodded. When you get to a certain age, the need was still there but not the passion. He couldn't remember the last time he wanted to get too tangled up with a woman.

Woodrow served another drink and joked with a young gun who was trying to act tough. Then Woodrow sidled back down and leaned over the bar.

"But I do believe that somebody was popping her, man."

"What makes you say that?"

"Aw, you can just tell when a woman's got something going on. They dress a little nicer, start taking care of themselves, and don't have time to be talking wit' you, homey."

"But you never saw her with this dude?"

"Probably married."

Rodney nodded once again. Well, that was something to go on. Maybe she was killed by a jealous wife or a bored lover. He thanked Woodrow and tried to pay him for the soft drink.

"Hell naw. Your money's no good here, Rod."

"Come on, man. I gotta pay for everything—even a stinking coke. I gotta play by the rules."

Woodrow glanced around the room with wide eyes and then stared at Rodney.

"No snitches in here. Go on, get outta here."

Rodney pocketed his cash and left. It was one thing to go by the book and quite another to insult a fellow vet.

The next day, Rodney drove to the Days Inn and asked for a list of all the guests who had checked into the motel for as far back as they could go. The manager rolled her eyes at the inconvenience, but Rodney gave her "the look" and she got cooperative.

About twenty minutes later, Rodney put on his reading glasses and sat down at the manager's desk to go over the computer print-out. The kid from the front brought out five more feet of the stuff.

"Detective work sure looks exciting," the kid said sarcastically.

"Yeah, this is the part you don't see on TV," Rodney acknowledged.

"Have you ever shot anyone?"

"Hell, I shot a whole slew of people in Vietnam. You want to shoot people? The U.S. army has a gun with your name on it, son," Rodney said.

The kid shook his head.

"I mean as a police officer."

"A couple, but I try to avoid using my gun. I did kill a boom box once though. That was pretty satisfying."

"What?" the kid asked.

"Never mind," Rodney chuckled, remembering the look on the guy's face right after Rodney obliterated the boom box from his fifth floor hotel room during a conference that they had gone to. Well, it was about five-thirty in the morning and that was one incredibly loud boom box. That was Rodney's only post-Vietnam assassination.

Beside him Rodney had a copy of Thelma's work schedule. She worked Sunday through Thursday, didn't take much overtime, and she made minimum wage. It wasn't much of a life,

Rodney thought. She hadn't even made head housekeeper and she'd been here five years. It was no wonder so many people turned to crime.

He pored over the names and the dates for two and a half hours before calling up Lanelle.

"Got something?" she asked.

"Maybe. Somebody by the name of T. Moore has checked in every few weeks around one p.m., well before standard check-in time. Looks like he or she has been coming here for about two years—paying cash and not leaving a tag number. One notation says T. Moore came in a cab."

"Was he checked in the day of the murder?"

"The day before."

"Did any of the clerks remember the name?"

"No, the turnover is ridiculous here. This place is like a toaster. Soon as they get warmed up, they're outta here. The kid who made the print-outs for me started last Monday."

"Maybe T. Moore was making deliveries from South Florida and Thelma stumbled onto his game."

"Maybe. How are you doing on Thelma's personal life?"

"I don't know about the married lover theory, Rod. She lived a pretty tame life as far as I can find out. She even went to church regularly."

Rodney sighed.

"What did her momma have to say about the envelope?"

"Well, she admitted that there was no niece. She said these cards come every so often, said Thelma did a favor for someone in the joint but that she didn't know who it was or what the favor was. Thelma didn't talk about it. She opened the card in front of me. It had two hundred dollar bills in it this time. She kept the money but she gave me the card and I had it checked for prints. Nothing."

"Isn't Thelma's funeral tomorrow afternoon? I think we should pay our respects. A little religion won't hurt either of us."

"Speak for yourself. I'm on a first name basis with Jesus," Lanelle said.

Rodney had just gotten off the phone with Debbie when he heard Lanelle's car horn outside. Debbie said Willie was still sleeping but maybe Rodney could come over that evening. He tossed Buddy a breakfast wiener and Buddy leapt for it like a dolphin at Marineland but didn't land quite so gracefully.

The day was steamy and sweat beaded on his neck in the time it took to get to Lanelle's air-conditioned BMW.

"So tell me how you afford this baby?" Rodney asked.

"I got it used. There's a BMW club on the internet, and, honey, you can get a good used Beemer that these people have checked out for less than some ugly-ass new SUV. And besides this car gives me a little street cred. Ya know, you can't have an ugly ride these days in the 'hood."

Rodney laughed, imagining Lanelle's nice middle class neighborhood as the 'hood, but he knew what she meant. She was able to relate to the pimps, the playas and their women in a way that helped ease them through troublesome encounters. And he could always pull his good ol' boy routine when they were dealing with rednecks. Together they covered a lot of bases.

They drove through the quiet streets. Some bicyclers darted past them. Rodney wondered how they survived the heat.

The church was a brick building with white doors and a white cross on top etched into the blue sky. Fat white clouds hovered overhead. Rodney had been a church-goer in his younger days. He was an only child but had several cousins and they all went together with their mothers. Occasionally their fathers would come, too, especially if there was going to be food afterwards. Nobody could cook like those church women. He wasn't sure why he'd gotten away from the church. It wasn't like he'd stopped believing in God. It's just that after what he saw in Vietnam and Cambodia, he figured God was disgusted with the whole human race.

Lanelle parked the car, and the two of them got out and joined the crowd heading inside. Rodney stopped to glance at the message on the white sign outside. He read, "What will you do when He comes?" Then below it he saw the times of the services and then something else.

Rodney nudged Lanelle and pointed to the sign. "Rev. Terrence C. Moore presiding."

"Terrence Moore?" Lanelle asked, her eyebrows arched.

"T. Moore," Rodney said.

"Holy shit."

"An appropriate sentiment, Detective," Rodney said, and placed his hand on her elbow as he guided her toward the steps.

Rodney sat next to Lanelle and politely listened to the service. He felt conspicuously white in the congregation and he saw the reverend's eyes register his presence.

Reverend Moore was a robust man about fifty years old. His skin was chocolate brown, his face smooth and his eyes large and clear. He was a distinctly handsome man. Rodney glanced at Lanelle, and Lanelle smirked. They were thinking the same thing. The good reverend had strayed. But there was something else. Underneath the warm exterior of the man, Rodney saw a raw wound. Well, one of his congregation had been brutally murdered, so it would be in bad form to look happy. But what bothered Rodney was how the reverend's grief flashed like a neon sign, no matter how hard the man tried to disguise it. Rodney had been in the truth and lies business for a long time. And the only murderers who were good at pretending were the ones who had no feelings, the very young and the very psychotic. This sure didn't look like pretense.

The preacher's voice was deep and melodic as he spoke. "It does no good to interrogate God when something terrible happens. Our minds are too small, our hearts too empty. Do not blame God, but look to the hills whence cometh your help. We cannot understand the great mysteries of the Lord, but we can allow ourselves to be embraced by His Everlasting Love." He paused. His voice had a rhythmic cadence that elicited a shout of "Amen!"

"Thelma, our beloved sister, is with God right now. She is standing next to Jesus, knowing that she has been forgiven for every sin she ever committed, knowing that because she loved the Lord she will spend her days in everlasting life. Let us thank God for blessing us with Thelma's presence while she was here. Let us ask God to forgive whoever has done this to her. Let us ask God to help the police find this killer so that he cannot hurt again. So that he cannot hurt another the way he has hurt us." At this point, Terrence's voice cracked. Rodney watched as the man pulled himself together. Rodney glanced around the room and saw tears falling from faces. Thelma's mother silently rocked from side to side in the front pew.

A choir began to sing an old gospel. "If anybody asks you, where I'm going, where I'm going real soon . . ."

The music wound itself through Rodney's head and turned his thoughts to Willie back at the hospice, his spirit gazing over the horizon. Lanelle reached over and grasped his hand. He gratefully squeezed back. If Terrence Moore had murdered Thelma Jackson, he sure could put on a show. Of course, a lot of the preachers were just that—showmen, but Rodney had never seen a performance like this. The man's sorrow was palpable, it was raw, and a little unnerving. It was as if he were confessing but not to the crime of killing Thelma. His was a confession of love.

"What do you think?" Rodney whispered to Lanelle.

"I'm not thinking anything until we get a search warrant," she said. He could tell she didn't like this. This man was a pillar of the black community. To bring him down on something this sordid would be a terrible stain.

He hadn't been aware of the racial implications of so much of their work until he'd had Lanelle for a partner, but the things she said when they were together made sense. "Look at these homeless guys," she said. "See how many of them are black? But you talk to them, Rodney, and you find out they're not stupid. They're not even uneducated. They just can't find work. They can't support their families. We call them deadbeat dads and throw them in jail and then what happens to their kids? Look at our prisons. More than two-thirds of the inmates are black. Do you think they're just born with a criminal gene? Black men need respect just like white men but the only way most of them are gonna get it is if they have a gun in their hands. Respect is more important to them than their own lives."

Lanelle wasn't a bleeding heart, but she didn't like what she saw happening around her. And she opened up Rodney's eyes to things he'd somehow been blind to most of his life.

After the service, Reverend Terrence Moore stood at the entrance of the church, shaking hands and hugging the mourners. Rodney noticed that Thelma's boss hadn't come, but the other maids were there. Woodrow Wilson was there with his son Tap, Annie and the new baby.

Lanelle and Rodney waited at the end of the line. A woman wearing a black tailored dress stood next to the reverend. Her face was set like plaster, and Rodney watched her curiously.

"That Mrs. Moore?" he whispered to Lanelle.

"Got to be," she said. "Look at the painted-on grimace."

Hers was a grief of a different kind, Rodney realized, as he caught her shooting a hard hurt glance at her husband.

"I think she figured something out today," Rodney said softly.

As the line thinned out, Rodney and Lanelle made their way to the exit.

Terrence Moore held out his hand. He glanced at them with both sorrow and a trace of fear. Rodney took his hand. You could tell a lot by a man's handshake. This was firm and honest. Hell, maybe the reverend would just confess, and they'd be able to call it a day.

"Are you the detectives in charge of Thelma's case?" he asked.

"We are," Lanelle answered. "And, if you don't mind, we'd like to speak to you in private."

"I have to go to the graveside for the burial," he said. "Will you be coming?"

"We hadn't planned on it," Rodney said.

"Terrence," his wife interjected. "Why don't you let the detectives come over to the house with me? I'm not feeling up to going to Thelma's burial. They can wait at the house for you. You can get someone to bring you home, can't you?"

"All right, dear. I'll be home as soon as I can." He kissed his wife on her forehead but his eyes were on Rodney.

Chapter 8

Rodney and Lanelle followed Mrs. Moore's Mercury Sable to a white brick ranch house with green shutters in a neighborhood not far from the cemetery. If their luck was good, they might not even need a search warrant. Innocent wives were much less likely to say no to a police search than guilty husbands were. Mrs. Moore let them inside.

"Can I get you something to drink?" she asked.

"Water would be fine," Rodney said. Lanelle shook her head and said, "No thanks."

Mrs. Moore went into the kitchen. The house was furnished with antiques. A picture of Jesus hung over the dining table. It was not a particularly comfortable house, and Rodney imagined that Terrence Moore had found it stultifying.

"Mrs. Moore, would you mind if we looked around?" Rodney called to her.

She was silent for a moment. He could only see her back as she faced the sink.

"I don't give a damn what you do," she said with a sudden sob. "I don't care."

Lanelle went into the kitchen.

"I know this has been hard for you, Mrs. Moore," she said.

"You don't know anything," the woman said bitterly.

Rodney stole into the bedroom to get a look at the Reverend's closet. He bent down and examined the shoes on the shoe tree. They'd need to take all of them to get a closer look but maybe he could see something that would give them a head start. No doubt about it, Reverend Moore's life was going to get turned inside out. Rodney rifled through drawers, through the closet. Nothing too interesting here. He went back to the living room and found Lanelle leaning close toward Mrs. Moore.

Lanelle looked up at him.

"She was getting her hair done last Wednesday. She thought her husband was at the church preparing his Sunday sermon. Her car is in the shop getting a new transmission, so she had her sister bring her home."

"Where do you get your hair done, Mrs. Moore?" Rodney asked.

"Shirley's. It's downtown. You can call her if you like. I was there most of the afternoon. Then my sister took me to the store. I probably still have the receipt. I didn't get home till about seven. Terrence was here by then."

"Is there anyone who could verify that your husband was at the church?" he asked.

"I don't know. The secretary's on vacation, but maybe somebody else came by," she said weakly. Rodney could see that the seed of doubt had been planted in her mind. If her husband was capable of cheating on her, he could be capable of anything.

"Do you mind if we look in the car?" Lanelle asked.

"I don't know," the woman answered, confused. "He couldn't have hurt her. I know he couldn't."

"Mrs. Moore, I'm not going to deny that your husband is a suspect. We know he was going to the motel where Thelma worked and getting a room there regularly. But if your husband is innocent of her murder, then we need to move on and find the real killer. The only way we can do that is if you'll help us."

Mrs. Moore nodded. She rose from the settee and took the keys from her purse.

"Here," she said.

Rodney and Lanelle went outside. While Lanelle looked under the front seat and in the back, Rodney opened the trunk. He found a set of golf clubs in an old leather golf bag. Carefully taking the clubs out of the bag, he felt something thudding around in the bottom.

He lifted the bag, and out tumbled a hammer. The blood hadn't even been cleaned off. Why use a hammer, he wondered. He stared at the stained claw for a moment. Then he called, "Lanelle, come check out the good reverend's putter."

Chapter 9

Lanelle was fuming as they stood outside the interrogation room, watching Terrence Moore through the glass. The man sat at the table with his head bowed; his shoulders shook slightly.

"It's bad enough that these crackheads and gangbangers are killing people, but a preacher! He's supposed to be a role model," Lanelle said in disgust. Rodney watched her curiously. He'd never seen her so disturbed before. In fact, he had never seen her get riled."Why don't you stay out here while I go in and get a statement from him, Lanelle?" Rodney suggested, taking a sip of his Sprite.

Lanelle tapped her pencil on her thumb and said, "Go ahead. I don't think I can even look at him."

Rodney set his Sprite down on a table and entered the small interrogation room. Terrence Moore had gotten out of the chair and was now kneeling on the hard floor with his eyes shut, his lips moving. Rodney leaned close to him.

"Yea, though I walk through the valley of the shadow of death, I shall fear no evil, for thy rod and thy staff they comfort me," the preacher whispered. He mumbled some more and then finished, "Surely, goodness and mercy shall follow me all the days of my life and I shall dwell in the house of the Lord forever."

Rodney straightened up and asked, "Are you done, Reverend Moore?"

Terrence opened his eyes and looked into Rodney's face. Rodney stepped back. There was a light in the man's eyes that startled him. Maybe he was a psycho and about to have an episode. Terrence stood up. There was a quiet moment, and Rodney felt reality shift ever so slightly.

"I did not kill Thelma, Detective Ellis," he said. "I loved her like my life."

"Well, what did your wife have to say about it?" Rodney asked.

"She didn't know. Not until Thelma's funeral. I couldn't hide it any longer."

"Had Thelma threatened to tell her?" Rodney asked.

"She wouldn't do that. I offered to get a divorce, but Thelma couldn't stand to see another person hurt." Terrence leaned his arms against the chair as he spoke as if the weight were too great to bear.

"What are you talking about? She once killed a man, her husband, when life with him was no longer fun. Maybe you were afraid for your own life?" Rodney suggested. It was good to try different angles, keep throwing in the line and see what makes the man bite.

"She wasn't like that," the reverend said. "She had changed."

Rodney shook his head. He wished Lanelle had come in to do her "understanding routine." He wasn't particularly good at softening people up.

"Please sit down, Reverend Moore. We found the murder weapon in the trunk of your car. Want to venture a guess on how it got there?"

Terrence Moore sat down in the metal folding chair.

"I have no idea," he said, shaking his head as if he were mystified. Moore had been read his Miranda rights, but didn't have a clue how to protect himself.

"Look, are you sure you don't want a lawyer?" Rodney asked.

"God is by my side, Detective Ellis. Jesus forgive me, I am an adulterer," he paused and then continued, "but I am not a murderer. I promise you that."

Rodney stared at the preacher, his large open face, his deep eyes. The man exuded a sense of calm serenity that Rodney found even more baffling than Lanelle's anger.

"Let's start at the beginning then," Rodney began, but Terrence Moore interrupted him.

"Detective Ellis, while I was praying the Lord gave me a message for you," he said.

"And what was that? Is God gonna give you an alibi? 'Cause no one else can," Rodney said, leaning against the wall with his arms crossed.

"God told me that you need to go see your friend. He's in his final hour, and you should say goodbye," the reverend said in a gentle voice. Rodney felt a chill run along his spine.

"This is bullshit," he said. "We'll talk again tomorrow, Reverend Moore."

With that he walked out.

"That was quick," Lanelle said.

"He's not talking. I'm going to see Willie," Rodney said. "See you tomorrow."

"But what about the arrest report? It's not done," Lanelle said, following him down the hall. Rodney wheeled around.

"Tomorrow, Lanelle. I'm not doing it tonight. Do you understand?"

Lanelle stared at him. Then she said, "Sure, Hot Rod. Do what you got to do."

A small lamp cast a yellow glow in Willie's room. Debbie was curled up in a chair asleep. Rodney had seen their son David asleep on a couch in the lobby. Willie's head was leaned up against the headboard with his eyes shut. He inhaled and exhaled in short gasps like punches. All the blood had drained from his face leaving it as white as if he were already a corpse. Willie's eyes opened and stared directly into Rodney's. His mouth moved, but no words came out. Then his eyes traveled over to Debbie. Rodney went to the chair and shook her.

"Debbie, wake up," Rodney said. Debbie looked up at him, startled and pale.

"Rodney?" she questioned.

Rodney nodded. Then she looked over at Willie and saw that his eyes were open. She jumped out of the chair and went over to him.

"Do you want me to wake David?" she asked Willie. Willie shook his head and tried to breathe, but it was obvious that his lungs were barely working. Rodney felt as if he were suddenly made of stone. His mind turned sluggish like a television screen on the blink. Debbie took Rodney's hand and pulled him to the bed beside her. Willie grimaced and twitched his hand. Rodney reached down and took Willie's fingers in his own.

"It's all right, baby," Debbie whispered. "You can go. You don't need to suffer anymore. We'll be okay."

Willie's eyes closed, and his fingers squeezed Rodney's.

"I love you, Willie," Rodney said. Debbie was crying, wrapping her arms around her husband's chest. Willie struggled for one last breath, and then Rodney felt something brush past him. He released Willie's fingers and placed his hand on Debbie's trembling back.

After Willie's funeral Rodney walked with Debbie and her son, David, to the reception in the hall next to the church. He was glad that the eulogy was over. Standing up behind a pulpit had felt especially strange, and he thought Willie was probably getting a kick out of that.

Rodney's daughter, Amy, hadn't been able to come. She was in California, meeting her future husband's far-flung family. He missed her. Rodney, who always avoided funerals, had been to two in two days, and he could have used her company right about now.

"You really got to me with that eulogy," Lanelle said, coming alongside him with a plate of ham and deviled eggs. She looked down at the food. "You know, I don't know why people always want to eat when someone dies. It's like we have to prove we're still alive or something." She looked away, stifling her tears. She wasn't the only one choked up. Rodney heard sniffles all around. Without the class clown, there didn't seem to be much to smile about.

But it hadn't hit Rodney yet. He knew that.

Debbie came up to him. She was holding up well.

"Thank you for what you did, Rod," she said. "That was beautiful. Rodney, you know that Willie wanted you to have this." She pulled a case from her purse and handed it to him. The Luger, of course. He didn't open the case, but instead tucked it under his arm and thanked her.

After kissing Debbie on the cheek, promising to check up on her, and giving his condolences to the rest of the family, Rodney walked out of the reception hall to the garden outside. Twyla stood there, holding onto a large purple gift bag. Lanelle and Al, one of the other detectives, were engaged in a conversation with Chief Carmichael.

"Have any of you seen Rodney?" she asked. "I want to give him something."

Al smirked and pointed to Rodney with his chin.

"He's right there," he said. "You got a birthday present there or are you a bag lady now?"

Twyla was the butt of more than a few department jokes. She'd come to the department to work in records, straight out of college where she'd been an English major. "My thesis is on Adrienne Rich," she told anyone who cared to ask. But, of course, no one knew who the hell Adrienne Rich was. And none of them cared. Rodney, however, had come to admire her quirky intelligence, and for some reason she latched onto him as her surrogate father-figure.

"Rodney," she said. "I made something for you to remember Willie by."

"Thank you, Twyla," he said and looked inside. He pulled out a large scrapbook.

"It's all the cases that the two of you worked on," Twyla explained in her soft voice. "See, it starts off with your latest case and then moves backward."

Rodney was stunned. He had not been one to save newspaper clippings or much of anything else, but here was an incredibly detailed document of his life in law enforcement. He flipped through the pages. She had incorporated clippings, pieces of reports, mug shots and even a narrative of the things she knew about.

"This is amazing," he said.

Lanelle looked over his shoulder. She flipped the book to the last page. There was a newspaper article with a mug shot of a pretty blond teenager. She read the lead aloud: "On Friday night, Officers Rodney Ellis and Willie Price arrested a sixteen-year-old girl on disorderly conduct and reckless driving charges. The girl, Vera Lee Gifford, was wanted in Broward County on three counts of first-degree murder."

"By the way, it was a woman who bailed out Trent Lewis," Twyla blurted out. "She paid cash. Maybe it was her."

"Nah, it wasn't her," Rodney said. Rodney thought back and remembered the disgust and pity he had felt for Vera Lee Gifford. But more than that, at a deeper level, he remembered the way she smelled of coconut suntan oil and the way her head felt leaning against his chest, the blond hair falling over her face.

"She's probably been dead for years," Lanelle said. "That type—they either get caught or get killed."

"True enough," Rodney said, closing the book. He looked at Twyla. "Thank you, Twyla. This is really nice." Twyla looked like she would pass out from the compliment.

Chapter 10

The pregnant young woman stood in front of the white two-story with tears brimming in her eyes.

"This is it," she said, leaning into her husband. "This is the house where I want to raise my babies."

Patsy smiled at the couple and waited a moment before putting her hand on the wife's arm and saying, "You will be really happy here."

The husband seemed willing to go along with anything his wife wanted, and Patsy felt the satisfaction of an easy sale.

"I'll have the paperwork ready for you this afternoon," she said.

Later, after everything had been signed, Patsy left the office and drove to Jim and Nan's condo. Traffic was heavy, and some jerk in a Yukon decided to squeeze in the one car length she'd left between her car and the one in front. They always did that, these people in their tanks, and it annoyed her no end. But she decided not to let it spoil her good day. She wanted to pick up Chelsea and get home in a hurry and try to come up with something for dinner before Tom got home with Kyle. But, of course, Nan had other ideas.

"Patsy, honey, I want you to come in the bedroom and look at a box of old stuff of yours that I found. Do you want me to give it to the Goodwill? I'm sure you can't want it anymore," she said. Chelsea was gathering up her school things.

"I finished my homework, Mom," she said.

"Good, why don't you go wait in the car for me?" Patsy suggested, as she followed Nan into the bedroom. She couldn't imagine what things Nan was talking about. But then in a cardboard box next to the king-size bed, she saw what it was. She pulled a leather jacket out of the box and stared at it. She hadn't seen it in probably twenty-five years.

"I can't believe you still have this thing," she said.

"Well, you seemed to value it a lot and told me never to throw it away, so I didn't, but surely after all this time . . ."

Holding the jacket that once belonged to Lois Underwood, Patsy felt her breath go shallow. Yes, surely after all this time, she could let it go. For years she had checked the Florida papers at the library for news of Lance. His legal exploits popped up regularly and then one Saturday, there was his name in an obituary. No grieving widow left behind. Nothing but rumors and bad will, she had figured. She hadn't even known how she felt about it—just numb. The jacket with its microfiche seams had been her insurance policy just in case Lance ever tried to send her back to prison. That day when she'd broken into his house and found the jacket, she had left him a note and a tiny piece of the microfiche as proof. Maybe it worked because he never tried to find her as far as she could tell. And now he was dead. She was safe from him at least.

"This is the strangest looking thing," Nan said. "Did you ever actually wear it? It looks like it's put together with old photograph negatives."

"I never wore it," Patsy said. "It's not really clothing. It's supposed to be art."

"What do you want me to do with it, honey?" Nan asked, gazing at Patsy.

Patsy sighed. She ought to burn it. The last piece of evidence linking her to the darkness. Or take it out to the dump.

"I'll do something with it," she said. "Maybe I'll cut it up and give the leather to Chelsea for one of her projects."

She folded the jacket over her arm and left the bedroom.

"Where's Dad?" she asked.

"He went to the cleaners," Nan said. "He should be home any minute."

"Well, I've got to go home. It's been a busy day," Patsy said and kissed Nan on her soft cheek. Nan was a picture-perfect grandmother. Patsy remembered how in prison her friend Mandy had talked about Nan and Jim, how they'd forgiven her for killing their daughter, their wonderful Patsy Wofford, in a drunk-driving accident. Mandy and Patsy had been best friends, and it had been easy to pry information out of Mandy about the family. Sweet Mandy. Prison was no place for the likes of her. Sometimes Patsy wondered what had happened to her, where she had gone after prison? Was she married now? They had been almost as close as lovers for those few months they'd been locked up together. Patsy hadn't had a friendship like that since.

She stepped out of the condo into the waning day and looked through the car window for Chelsea. The car was empty.

"Now, where is she?" she asked. She walked past the driveway down to the street. Nan stood in the doorway watching.

"Chelsea!" Patsy called. There was no answer. Then she saw a black Lexus in the street just a few houses down and saw Chelsea beside it. What was she doing? She was talking to the driver of that car. Who was he? Patsy felt her heart rate shoot up. Who was that man? She clutched the jacket tighter.

"Chelsea," she called out sharply. The girl turned to her and waved.

"I'm right here, Mom," Chelsea yelled.

"Get over here *now!*" Patsy screamed. She rushed over to where her daughter stood by the car. "Who are you talking to?"

She yanked Chelsea away from the car and stared at the gray-haired man who looked at her in surprise.

"What do you want with my daughter?" Patsy demanded. A cloud of anger smothered her. The man stammered something, but Patsy wheeled around and ordered Chelsea back to the house. Nan came out with a worried look on her face.

"What is it? What's wrong?"

"Get Chelsea inside, Mother," Patsy said. The rage she felt was like fire burning inside her skin. If she had a gun, she'd kill that man. What was he doing, talking to her little girl? What did he want with her? Damn him. If she had a gun . . .

Jim's car pulled up in the driveway as Nan ushered a frightened Chelsea inside.

"What's going on?" Jim asked as he got out of the car.

"Some stranger was trying to get Chelsea into his car," Patsy cried.

"No, he wasn't," Chelsea yelled, pulling free from Nan. "He was just asking me about my skating competition. He's a friend of Grampa's."

Jim looked at Patsy, perplexed.

"That's Phil Green, Patsy," he said. "I play golf with him sometimes. I'm sure he didn't mean any harm to Chelsea."

Patsy's heart continued to pound. Her knees felt weak, and she leaned against the hood of her own car. This anger, this rage, where did it come from?

"Patsy, come inside and calm down," Nan said, taking her by the shoulders and leading her in the house.

"Mom?" Chelsea said. "Are you okay?"

Patsy staggered into the living room and sank down on the couch. She was still clutching the jacket.

"I don't know," she tried to explain. "I just saw Chelsea talking to someone I didn't know, and I panicked."

"Well, it's understandable," Nan said. "All the horrible stuff you hear on the news every day."

Patsy leaned her head back and stared at the white plaster ceiling. She couldn't fathom the way this rage had blind-sided her. Nothing ever happened like that when it concerned Kyle. But Kyle was a boy, and Chelsea was a little girl. A little girl, Patsy thought. And men could do such awful things to little girls. She felt herself shaking. She had been angry enough to kill that man.

She never should have had children. What if she failed to protect them?

Jim sat down next to her.

"You can't bury the past," he said.

"What?" She looked at him with her eyes wide. "What do you mean?"

"I mean that I know you've got things buried inside you," he said. His voice was soft and warm. He rarely spoke to her about her past; he had never questioned her in all these years.

"Jim's right," Nan said. "I think you should talk to someone. Something's bothering you, sweetheart."

Chelsea sat at the table and watched quietly. Patsy wanted to hug her and say she was sorry. Instead she stood up and walked over to the sliding glass doors that led to Jim's small garden.

"Who could I trust?" she asked quietly.

Nan came beside her.

"There's a woman, a therapist, who speaks at our church sometimes. I think you'd like her, Patsy."

Patsy rubbed her arms and wondered what secrets she had buried in the darkness. She hadn't forgotten the girl she had once been, but she didn't know what had made her that way and she didn't understand why the past kept resurfacing. Why now? Why couldn't she let go?

Chelsea came on the other side of her and slid an arm around her waist.

"Don't be mad, Momma," she said. "He wasn't a bad man."

"I know," Patsy said. Maybe Nan was right. If she didn't get help soon, what kind of mother would she be? And what if she lost complete control? What if she fell back into the darkness? What then? All these years she'd felt so removed from the past. But it was never gone, was it? It was always lurking in the shadows.

Chapter 11

Rodney drove to the house and parked under the carport. Buddy stood up against the fence gate and wagged his tail. He barked a quick, happy hello.

Rodney scratched Buddy's ears and then opened the gate.

"Want to go for a ride?" he asked him, which was a stupid question since Buddy lived for rides. He let the dog in the house. "Go get my shoes."

Rodney changed into some running shorts and a t-shirt while Buddy frantically dug up his old running shoes from the closet, bringing them one at a time in a sideways dance that indicated his enthusiasm for the adventure.

A few minutes later, they pulled up outside "the Swamp," the famous Florida field where he and Willie had spent many Saturday afternoons each fall. Today he went in through the gates with Buddy following him. A tennis ball bulged from his pocket, something to give Buddy a little work-out. Buddy wasn't that interested in running up and down stadium steps. It was sweltering hot, and a posse of clouds had gathered to the east. The usual summer afternoon deluge was preparing for attack. Rodney didn't mind. The rain would feel good. The harder the better, as far as he was concerned.

He tossed the ball for Buddy five or six times, but the heat quickly took its toll on the dog. Then Rodney made a few laps around the field before turning to run up and down the steps. Ever since he had stood over the urn holding Willie's ashes, it felt as if something had solidified inside him. He hoped the running would break it up. But it didn't. Instead the grief burrowed deeper inside. A drop of rain fell and then another. Buddy sat under a shelter and watched Rodney pummel the steps with his feet. The rain began to pour. It poured, and Rodney ran.

Finally, out of breath, he sat down on the bleachers and let the rain wash over him. He could almost hear Willie: "Get outta the rain, you crazy mo-fo." The stalwart Christian, that was the closest Willie ever came to cussing. Debbie used to chide him for this lapse, but Willie liked to think he could step a little out of line and that Jesus would still love him. That and a couple of beers on game day. Willie's big vices.

No one thought Willie a particularly smart guy. He'd had to take the detective test a couple times before barely squeaking past. But Willie had a different kind of smarts. He had intuition, and it was sharp as a laser.

"You always trusted your gut, didn't you?" Rodney said out loud to the rain. The rain answered by petering out into a drizzle, nearly as quickly as it had started. The quintessential summer storm.

Buddy came out from under the shelter and trotted up to Rodney in his most deferential manner.

"Don't worry, Buddy. I'm not going crazy."

Buddy beat his tail against the seat in front of them. The sunlight sparkled on the green grass like someone had dropped a cache of diamond chips across it. Rodney had always been philosophical about death. It seemed you got your allotted time and tried to do the best you could with it. He wondered what Willie would have thought about the arrest they made yesterday of Reverend Terrence Moore. Something about the whole incident hadn't felt right. In most murder cases you didn't have to look too far from home. And usually the most obvious suspect was the killer. Not only did Terrence Moore have a possible motive for killing Thelma, he had the murder weapon. Then a memory flashed in his head. He saw Willie lying in that bed at the hospice center, and heard his voice asking, "Remember Gavin Worthy?"

At that moment Buddy whined impatiently and then barked. Rodney sat up.

"What the hell is wrong with you, dog?" Buddy thumped his tail and grinned sheepishly.

Rodney looked around. The stadium was empty, but Rodney felt strange as if someone was watching him. He thought about the scrapbook Twyla had given him. They had arrested Vera Lee in 1976, same year Jimmy Carter won the presidency. Thelma and she must have served time together. It seemed like a bit of a stretch that the two incidents could be related, but there was another piece of information floating around in his head that didn't quite fit.

Chapter 12

Rodney wended his way across the deep green lawn through granite angels, headstones and marble slabs. It wasn't hard to find Thelma's mother. She wore a pretty blue shirtwaist dress and her gray hair settled on her head in thins curls under a small pillbox-style hat. She stood by a fresh mound of dirt covering her daughter's casket. Rodney observed her from a distance and thought he had never seen such a forlorn figure. Perhaps she was ready to tell the truth.

"Ms. Jackson?" he asked as he approached her.

She turned and looked blankly at him for a moment before recognition caught in her eyes.

"She was all I had," the woman said.

Rodney nodded. "I know. I'm sorry you lost her."

"I just can't believe that it was Reverend Terrence," the woman said. "He's a man of God, Detective Ellis. How could he take away my child?"

Rodney glanced at the thick brown dirt and the fresh headstone.

"The ways of the human heart are mysterious," he said and realized instantly how lame that sounded. There were never good words for a grieving parent.

"Are you sure he did it?" she asked, a sudden onslaught of fierceness energizing her small frame.

"No, ma'am. I'm not sure. That's why I need to ask you something and I need for you to be straight with me." He looked her in the eyes.

"What is it?"

"How long have you been getting that money in the mail?"

The old woman shrugged. "A long, long time. Since way before Thelma got out of prison."

"How long? I need to know this."

The woman chewed on her lip and said, "Maybe twenty-five years."

"Has it always been hundred dollar bills?"

"No. Sometimes more like fifty or even twenty in the beginning."

"Ms. Jackson, did Thelma ever mention a girl named Vera Lee Gifford?" he asked.

Thelma's mother shook her head.

"Why? Who is she? You think she killed Thelma?"

"I don't know. Thelma was in prison at the same time as Vera Lee. Vera Lee was doing three life sentences, but she escaped, and I'm just wondering if there was a connection between the two."

"What did this Vera Lee look like?"

"She was a white girl. Pretty. Blond. Couldn't have been more than eighteen when she escaped."

"So young?"

"They tried her as an adult so she went to prison with the big girls."

The woman's eyes grew big and her mouth formed a silent "oh." Then she looked down at the ground guiltily.

"What?" Rodney asked. A crow flew above them, cawing loudly.

"I helped her," Ms. Jackson said. "She came to my house late one night and she had a note from my Thelma. Thelma's note said to help her out, said someone wanted to kill the girl.

"So I did. I fed her, gave her some clothes, bought her some red hair dye. She was a sweet young lady. So polite. Said her name was Susie or something like that. I was just being a good Christian, Detective Ellis. Whosoever helps the least of these is helping me, Jesus said. That's what I've always done. Is that so wrong?"

Rodney stuck his hands in his pockets.

"I don't know, Ms. Jackson. I don't know much about being a good Christian," he said. Rodney wondered why Vera Lee would send money to Thelma all these years and then come kill her? Did Thelma know Vera Lee's new identity?

"That girl didn't seem like a killer to me," Ms. Jackson said.

"Yeah, but a jury found her guilty of three homicides," Rodney said. Then he reached over to touch the old woman's arm. "We're gonna get to the bottom of this."

She looked up at him. Fresh tears had formed in her eyes. She nodded her head and opened her purse.

"I've got her obituary in here," she said. "I told them what to write."

Her hand shook as she pulled the neatly folded piece of newsprint from her purse. He opened it and another one fluttered to the ground.

"Thelma Jackson has gone home to be with the Lord," the obituary said.

"What's this other one?" Rodney asked, bending down to pick up the clipping from the ground.

"Oh, that's the first article. About the murder," she said. "It's not much." Rodney took the article from her and read it. With everything that happened with Willie he hadn't read a paper in weeks, and he hadn't read anything about Thelma's murder. He looked at the article. It was short. A motel maid didn't rate many inches.

"Was this the only article about Thelma's murder?" Rodney asked, looking at it curiously. Then he realized they almost never release the details of a murder to the press, not before a suspect has been apprehended. So how did Trent Lewis know her head had been "bashed in"?

*

Rodney and Buddy drove along the road past pink and purple crepe myrtles. He'd gotten Twyla to check out both Trent's address—non-existent, according to mapquest—and his girlfriend or wife's automobile tag, also non-existent according to the DMV. He had also tracked down the lawyer who had paid off Trent's fine, but the lawyer swore up and down that he was hired by phone and the money was wire transferred to his account and it was all quite anonymous.

Now, he was heading out past the small town of Alachua to see an old friend. Actually, Douglas Framingham was not exactly an old friend of his. Amy had met him in college. He was an older student, late twenties, but Amy said he was probably some sort of genius. "You should see his papers, Dad. They're brilliant, and they're funny." Douglas was a criminal justice major and Amy had brought him to the house to talk about law enforcement with Rodney. He would never forget the first time he saw Douglas. A big guy, maybe six foot two and two-hundred twenty pounds, Douglas had a big bushy mustache, a shaved head except for a couple of sprouts he had let grow, a tattoo on the side of his head, rings in eyebrows and a silver bar pierced between them. He wore motorcycle clothes and had a mouthful of broken teeth from sundry motorcycle accidents. And he was gentle as a lamb. Bikers sure were different these days from when Rodney was coming up.

Rodney pulled into a long dirt driveway to a double-wide at the back of the lot. A gleaming Triumph motorcycle sat in front. Good, Douglas was home. After graduation Douglas had achieved his dream of working in law enforcement with the DEA, but he'd been disillusioned quickly and he spent the greater part of his time hiding out in his trailer, doing "research." Rodney shut off the truck and let Buddy out to run around the woods behind the trailer.

Rodney knocked on the door. It took a couple more knocks, but eventually Douglas opened the door, looking as if he'd just woken up.

"Mr. Ellis, how are you, sir?" Douglas asked, stepping aside to let him in.

The place was dark and cold as a cave. Computers hummed on long tables set up across what should have been a living room.

"Douglas, when are you going to start calling me Rodney?" Rodney asked.

Douglas smiled, showing his broken picket of teeth, and said, "Sorry . . . Rodney. What brings you out here?"

"I wanted to run something by you. Thought maybe with all your computer wizardry you might be able to help me out," Rodney said.

"I'll try," Douglas said, cooperative as ever, and indicated a long, low, leather couch against one wall. Rodney sat down on the couch and Douglas sat in a swiveling office chair by the bank of computers. "What's up?"

"Well, I'm wondering about a guy named Lance Underwood, a gun collector. Lived in South Florida back about twenty-five years ago. He was an attorney. I tried looking him up, but he wasn't down there anymore. Anyway, he was connected to a murder, actually three murders and a girl named Vera Lee Gifford. The girl escaped from prison in 1978. She's never been seen since. I'm just wondering where this guy might be these days. He's not in DMV's records anymore."

Douglas raised his eyebrows, nodded his head and swiveled around to his keyboard.

"Let's see what's in the DEA database," he said.

Rodney glanced around the place while Douglas punched keys. It was clean but definitely hadn't been inhabited by a woman. The only pictures on the wall were pictures of motorcycles. A metal shelving unit lined with dozens of plastic drawers stood by the computers. Above the computers were odd-looking scopes of some sort. Headsets dangled off hooks. Coils of wire were stacked under the tables.

"Lance Underwood is officially dead," Douglas noted. "As of 1994. Ten years. Seems he died at a convenient time. The IRS was after him. And he was facing a lawsuit by one of his former partners."

"Why does the DEA have a file on him?" Rodney asked him.

"Well, looks like in the 1970s he was aiding and abetting a fellow by the name of Noriega. Oh, yeah, he was probably in cahoots with the Cocaine Import Agency."

"The what?"

"The CIA. You remember when they were financing their wars in Central America and the Mideast. They were deep in the drug trade, man. Pissed the DEA off, but our guys couldn't do anything."

"How do you know? You were in diapers at the time."

"Well, our guys have never trusted them ever since. Remember the crack cocaine epidemic on the west coast. That was courtesy of the CIA, too. So I've heard some talk. Some busts you know you could make, but they'll never go down because the jackals are somehow involved. You can war on drugs all you want as long as you don't step on the wrong toes."

"Yeah," Rodney said. "I found that out, too, when I was working narcotics. It sucks." He paused. "So Lance Underwood was involved with CIA and Noriega back in the 1970s. Does it have anything about Vera Lee Gifford in there? Anything about the two guys she murdered?"

"Do you know their names?"

Rodney thought for a moment. He'd just read that article in Twyla's scrapbook and their names were listed in that. "Yeah, Chuck Staples and Lorenzo Black."

Douglas spent a little longer digging up information but he finally found something. Rodney wondered, if Trent hadn't been collecting that gun for Lance Underwood, who was he working for? That was no cheap lawyer in those Kenneth Cole shoes who came and rescued him.

"Aha," Douglas said, interrupting his thoughts. "They were definitely involved in some big time trafficking, but it was long ago. Looks like they were targeted for a bust, but the girl got to them first."

"Another coincidence," Rodney said. Then he stood up. "Well, thanks for your help, Douglas."

"Anytime," Douglas said. Douglas had an oddly formal manner in spite of his outlaw appearance. Rodney looked at Douglas sitting there with his back straight and his hands clasped.

"You like poetry, Douglas?" Rodney asked.

Douglas nodded sharply and said, "Why, yes, as a matter of fact, I do. I'm especially fond of Japanese poetry."

Rodney laughed. "Then I got someone I want you to meet. I'll catch up with you later, young man."

"Wait a minute, Mr. . . . uh, Rodney. I want to show you something." Douglas had a wide, disarming smile in spite of the broken teeth. Douglas handed him a small headset with a little wire dangling from one of the ear pieces.

"Cell phone technology for bugging purposes," Douglas said with a grin. Rodney put on the headset. Douglas was holding a small button-sized bug and walked to the back of the trailer, saying, "A worm tells summer better than the clock, the slug's a living calendar of days. What shall it tell me if a timeless insect says the world wears away?"

When he came back in, he asked Rodney how he liked it.

"Great. But I don't think that was haiku you were reciting," Rodney said, taking off the headset.

"No, that was Dylan Thomas. I like him, too. Here, you can keep this. Think of it as a token of my appreciation. The button has a Velcro underside. You can hear up to at least a mile away."

Rodney held the small device. Maybe it would come in handy some day. He dropped the headset and the bug in his pocket and thanked Douglas. Then Rodney walked out the door and whistled for Buddy.

Chapter 13

Patsy drove down Highway 16 to the Charlotte satellite of Weddington. The area was undergoing a radical transformation. It was good for business—these houses cropping up in old cow fields. This ongoing facelift was what she loved about living in Charlotte. Nothing ever stayed the same. The city constantly tore itself down and remade itself in a shiny new image. She loved the fact that every week the city scape changed. Old buildings were obliterated to make way for the new. In the fifteen years they had lived in the area, it had evolved beyond recognition. Patsy had no fondness for the past.

She followed the directions through town, what there was of a town at least, past brand new shopping centers with brand new sub shops and video stores.

When she finally found the address, she was surprised to find it on a huge lot in the midst of still-undeveloped acreage. She peered down the dirt driveway and saw a small white wooden house with a ramshackle porch. How different from the cookie-cutter mini-mansions clustered together in the surrounding enclaves. She pulled in and parked in the shade of an oak tree.

Rebecca answered the door wearing a long skirt and a sleeveless white peasant blouse. She looked to be around fifty, and everything about her seemed loose and soft and comfortable. Her dark hair hung to her shoulders. She smiled broadly and her eyes positively sparkled.

"You must be Patsy," she said in a lilting voice. Patsy suddenly felt like a brittle bunch of bones next to this woman, who wasn't exactly "ample" but who exuded a sense of largeness about her.

Patsy entered a hallway at the front of the house. It was dark and cluttered but fairly clean. She looked at the floorboards—the house was probably fifty years old. She smelled incense in the air.

"This place is charming," Patsy said, not adding that it would be impossible to sell except for the lot.

"This is the house I grew up in," Rebecca said. "All this land around here belonged to my dad."

"Belonged?" Patsy asked.

"My brother and I sold it a few months ago." The bright smile on Rebecca's face and her own knowledge of property values in the area let Patsy know that Rebecca had made a pile of money. The whole area would be a brand-new development of half-million dollar or more homes in the blink of an eye.

"Good for you," Patsy said.

"It was. Very good. I'm planning on starting a spiritual center near Asheville, not that they need another spiritual center, but that's where I'd like to be," she said. "But you didn't come here to talk about any of that. Nan said you needed some spiritual counseling. Come into the living room and have a seat."

The room felt cool and comfortable after the warm summer air outside. Bookcases lined the walls. An old oriental carpet covered the floor. Patsy had to become herself again. She had to let go of the anxiety that ate at her.

Rebecca studied her and then said, "You are worried about something."

"Is it that obvious?" Patsy asked, looking for a place to sit. There was a couch, but it had magazines on it.

"Pretty much. Your aura is a mess. Have some water."

Patsy took a tall glass of water from the woman and sat in an overstuffed armchair next to a round antique table by the window. Outside a golden retriever slept in the shade. Rebecca sat in a chair on the other side of the table.

"So you read auras? Are you going to do my tarot cards or something?"

"I'm not a psychic, Patsy. I'm just a spiritual seeker like anyone else. The thing about psychics is that they can only read probabilities. You have free will and the ability to change your destiny any time. Most people don't know that. They just march along to whatever tune the world plays in their ear. What tune has the world been playing in your ears?"

Patsy shook her head. "I don't know. I'm here because, well, I'm having some problems."

"Let's see. You're a successful businesswoman. I know that much about you. I've seen your name on several 'For Sale' signs. You have two children. Nan brags about them all the time. And I see by that pretty diamond ring that you're married. Happily?"

"Yes. I love my husband," Patsy said. Suddenly, being here felt terribly wrong. What was she doing? Risking everything by talking to this woman. She stood up and paced across the room. "Listen, you have to keep everything I say in confidence, don't you? I mean, isn't that what counselors have to do?"

"Patsy, whatever you say here stays here, I can assure you that."

Patsy's heart began to thud in her chest. She felt a blinding sense of panic as if she might die at any moment.

"I think I better go. I don't feel right. There's really nothing wrong with me," she said, realizing that she wasn't making any sense.

Rebecca stayed calmly seated as Patsy headed toward the door.

"It's okay if you don't want to stay, Patsy," Rebecca said. "But will you answer a question for me?"

Patsy turned and looked at her. The light from the window fell over Rebecca's shoulders.

"Whose voice is that whispering in your ear? The voice that's telling you to run."

Patsy covered her face with her hands and began to sob. Soon Rebecca's arms were around her.

"It's my mother's voice. I hadn't heard it in years," Patsy said. "Not since April, April 1978. Then about a month ago, I woke up and heard it. Run, it said. That's all she ever says. Run. But I can't run this time. I can't leave my children. I can't leave Tom."

Rebecca led her back to the chair.

"I thought Nan was your mother," Rebecca said, a confused look crossing her face. "But she's not, is she?"

"No, she and Jim are my adoptive parents. Their daughter died when she was seventeen. I came along and needed someone. They needed someone. It sort of worked out."

"Tell me about your birth mother. Is she dead?" Rebecca asked.

Patsy nodded. "I think so. All I know is that when I was nine, she disappeared. Daddy said that she ran off with another man. That was plausible, but I don't know for sure. Something happened. I dream about her sometimes. She's always in trouble. She's in the water and it's covering her face. She's drowning."

Patsy took a deep breath. She was telling too much, she realized, telling things she hadn't told anyone. Rebecca leaned over and put a hand on Patsy's arm. The palm of her hand felt warm and gentle.

"Patsy, I would like to do some regression work with you."

"What does that mean?"

"It means going into the past."

"Oh, no. That could be a problem."

"Patsy," Rebecca said in a quiet voice. "We need to find out why your mother wanted you to run. We can clear up your past, heal it, forgive it and then let it go. But you need to trust me."

Patsy shook her head. She had lived with this silence for so long. But now she opened her mouth, almost involuntarily, and spoke, "Rebecca, I don't trust anyone. I did some things in my past, things I'm not proud of. Things that could destroy my life and my family's lives if anyone knew."

Rebecca smiled. "Dear One, I am here to tell you that you are not guilty. No matter what you believe. No matter what you did.

In the eyes of God you are perfect." Rebecca gazed at her intently. "Here's what the great masters teach: this life we're living is a dream. Sometimes it's a good dream. Sometimes it's an awful dream. But it is not real. Are you willing to consider that's a possibility?"

Patsy had never heard anything so strange. She glanced out the window and studied the pattern of light on the bushes. The sleeping golden retriever twitched his tail. A tiny sparrow hopped in the grass nearby.

"I don't know. It sounds weird. Crazy."

"Could anything possibly be crazier than this world?"

Patsy thought of the recent news events. She thought of those two planes crashing into the Twin Towers in New York and then those awful photos of those Iraqi prisoners. She didn't understand world events at all. Tom got so upset by it all, but she was just baffled.

"No."

"Good. I'm not asking you to believe anything, Patsy. But I do want you to know this. That I believe we are all guiltless. From Hitler to Saddam."

"That *is* crazy."

"Maybe so. But suffice to say, if I can hold them blameless, I can hold you blameless. Now, I don't want you to go into anything you aren't comfortable sharing with me. But I think we should look back into your childhood. Because somewhere along the line, someone convinced you that you weren't worthy. Someone made you feel guilty and bad. And you incorporated those feelings into your identity."

"Isn't this like psychoanalysis or something?" Patsy felt a strange compulsion to trust this woman.

"Well, it's a little different. I want to take you back to your childhood and I want you to look at some particular event and experience the emotions you felt and then we're going to give those feelings to God and ask that they be healed. Can you try this with me?"

Patsy considered. It was so comfortable in this small room. There were family pictures on the wall, and a set of pretty blue figurines on top of a bookcase, which was filled with books. For some reason she felt calm, as if she were floating on a lake.

"All right. I'll try it. But it has to be when I'm young. Nothing after the age of fifteen." She didn't trust that much.

"Patsy, you will choose where you want to go. Not I. Now, close your eyes and get relaxed. I'm going to count down from twenty to one as you slowly descend a staircase in your mind to the place that needs healing."

Patsy relaxed in the chair. Rebecca's voice pulled her slowly down into a deep place. The room where they sat seemed to quietly drop away. Patsy felt her arms go limp, her face soften and her entire body seem to melt.

The first thing she noticed was the smell—baby powder and Charlie perfume.

"Where are you?"

"I'm standing in front of my mother's dresser."

"Tell me what you see."

"Eleven different tubes of lipstick scattered on the top. And a tray of different colors of eye shadow—gray, brown, blue, green, lavender. Here's some Maybelline mascara. It's sable brown."

"How old are you?"

"I'm about six or seven. My little sister is on the bed behind me, taking a nap. Mama lets me put on lipstick. She smiles at me in the mirror. She has on a short black skirt and a white blouse and you can sort of see through it. She smushes her lips together."

"How do you feel?"

"Happy because I'm with my mama. And . . . and scared, too." Patsy's voice changed into a soft, raspy twang. "I'm going out for just a bit, sugar pie. You watch your sister. And remember, this is our secret."

"What is the secret?" Rebecca asked.

"She's going to see somebody. A man. I pretend like I don't

know. But I do know. And I'm scared for her. Now she bends over and kisses me. And her perfume is all around me, and she hugs me. Then she is walking out the door. I crawl up in the bed with Fancy and watch TV."

"Does your mother ever get caught?"

"Not then. And I never told. I know how to keep a secret. I'm the best secret keeper in the world."

"Okay, I think it's time for you to come back to the present, Patsy. I'm going to count to twenty and as I do so, I want you to climb back up those steps and I'll be right here waiting for you."

Patsy's eyes blinked open and she looked at Rebecca, who had a wide, reassuring smile.

"You okay?"

Patsy nodded.

"Now, I want you to forgive your mama. She shouldn't have put you in that position, you know. Children shouldn't have to keep secrets for their parents."

Patsy nodded, and yet the statement sounded strange to her. All her life she kept secrets. And she hoped that her children would do the same for her. Not that they knew her secrets, but if they did, would they protect her the way she had protected her mother?

Tom came in after work with two bags of food from Boston's Market. Kyle heard his father and barreled down the stairs. Chelsea turned off the television, and Patsy put out some plates.

"I hope you didn't get anything for me," Patsy said. "You know I'm going to bunko tonight, don't you?"

"You didn't tell me that," Tom said. He straightened up and looked at her in that way that always reminded her of an extremely intelligent parakeet. He had a thick head of prematurely gray hair, wide eyes and a soft mouth that always seemed about to smile. He was no beauty, her husband, but his gentle eyes could melt just about anyone, including her.

Patsy put her hands on her hips and glanced over at the kids for confirmation.

"She said so last night, Daddy," Chelsea said.

"I'm starving. I'll eat hers," Kyle said, taking one of the bags from Tom.

"Bunko," Tom scoffed. "Do you all study strategy in between sessions?"

Kyle laughed. "You could challenge Big Blue to a game of bunko. You could be Kasparov, Mom."

"Very funny. No one claims you have to think to play bunko," Patsy said. Bunko wasn't exactly stimulating. You sat a table and rolled three dice, trying to get certain numbers. "But I find out lots of good stuff—like who's planning on moving and might need a realtor."

"Mom, Kyle took my cornbread," Chelsea screamed. Patsy stared as the two of them fought over the piece of bread. Kyle finally returned it to Chelsea.

"Oink, oink," he said.

"Shut up." Her mouth was full of yellow mush.

"I don't understand why you two fight all the time," Patsy said, irritably.

"That's what siblings do, hon," Tom said.

"Not all of them," she said, walking out of the room. She and her sister had never fought, she thought as she climbed the stairs to the bedroom. Then another thought struck her as she stood in her bedroom doorway. Of course, they didn't fight. They didn't have that luxury. They had to take care of each other because no one else would. Her shoulders slumped. Even after all these years, there were still things she didn't understand about what it means to be a family. She brushed the hair from her face and went to her closet.

Patsy dressed in beige capris and a dark green knit pullover. Green looked great with her red hair and brown contact lenses. She stood in the bathroom and checked herself out as she inserted a diamond stud into her left earlobe. Not bad for forty-five. She didn't have to get Botox yet. Were diamonds too much for a bunko night? Well, they were small. She ran a mascara wand over her pale lashes. She took the eyebrow pencil to her blond eyebrows. Softly, she said to herself, never overdo it.

Patsy decided to walk to the bunko party. It would probably take all of five minutes to walk to Debra's house, where it was being held this month, but she knew that most of the women would pile into their SUVs and drive. As she stepped outside, she was amazed at how light it still was. She loved the long days. She had on a pair of comfortable flats and five bucks in her back pocket to get in the game as she strode along the street.

Debra's house was gorgeous, of course. All the women in the neighborhood seemed to have a natural ability to make their houses look lovely. It must be something they picked up from their own mothers. Patsy was inept when it came to decorating, and as much as she'd read Martha Stewart, she didn't get how to make a place look nice. She'd had to hire a decorator for their place.

When Patsy arrived, Debra was busy showing off her new wood floors in the kitchen.

"Hi, Patsy," Debra smiled and pointed to the counter. "The wine's over there, hon."

Most of the women were already there, and the room was noisy with their laughter and catching up. Patsy took a bottled water. She never drank with other people. "Loose lips sink ships," she had always heard. The only time she ever drank was when she was completely alone—when the kids were at Dad and Mom's condo and Tom was out of town. And then she didn't drink wine. But those were rare occasions.

On the kitchen counter, Debra had spread out the finger foods—chicken wings, spinach and cream cheese roll-ups, carrot sticks and celery, chips and three-layer bean dip, tiny pimiento cheese sandwiches and other goodies.

Finally the ringleaders sent everyone to their tables. She was at table two—a card table set up in the living room. She sat down with her next-door neighbor and two women from the next cul-de-sac. Patsy generally identified the women by their houses.

"Hi there, Patsy," Sue, gray two-story with black shutters, said. "Haven't seen you in a while. No, wait a minute. I saw you in your tai-bo class at the Y the other day. You were kicking butt."

"How are the kids doing?" This was Linda, two-story red-brick with a recent addition.

"Chelsea's still ice skating all the time. She came in second place at the state competition, and Kyle's doing great. He's taking driver's ed. It's hard to imagine my little boy driving a car," Patsy said, dipping into the peanuts and M & Ms bowl by her side. "Seems like last week he was demolishing matchbox cars. Now, he wants to drive one!"

"They do grow up," Sue said and rolled the dice. She got two ones and a three. "Two!" she said and picked up the dice to roll again. Patsy realized she was sitting by the pad and pencil so she wrote down "Us" and "Them" and made two marks under "Us."

When Patsy's turn came around she rolled a binko—three threes—and then a bunko—three ones—on her first two rolls.

"Lord, have mercy," Sue exclaimed. "This might be your lucky night."

After the break for dessert—a red velvet cake with cream cheese frosting, brownies and fresh peanut butter cookies—Patsy sat down at table one. She had actually won a lot of games in the first two rounds. Maybe she'd be going home with some money tonight. It had never happened before, but somebody had to win. Winner took home the pot except for five dollars for the loser and ten bucks that went to the person who'd gotten the last bunko. With twelve women chipping in five bucks each, that meant she'd get forty-five dollars if she won.

They were on fours in the third round. Debra was also at table one and getting pretty tipsy, laughing and talking about her crazy brother and his girlfriend. Linda was Patsy's partner on this round.

"So Patsy, do you have any brothers or sisters?" Linda asked.

"A sister," Patsy said automatically. Good Lord, what was she thinking? "Well, she wasn't really a sister. She was a foster sister, I guess. Stayed with us for about a year. Not really a sister."

"Your parents took in foster kids? That was sweet of them," Linda said.

"Crazy if you ask me," Debra said, rolling her eyes as she waggled her big bleached blond head. "I mean, what if one of them was a psycho? They've had rough childhoods, those kids. You could be letting the Son of Sam in your house."

"It was just one kid that one time," Patsy explained. "And she died later."

"She died?" Linda asked, leaning forward with an open mouth.

"Yes. Of meningitis."

"Oh, that's terrible," Debra said and seemed to have sobered instantly.

Patsy smiled grimly and rolled the dice. Why the hell had she said that? Meningitis? Could you even die from meningitis? That visit to Rebecca was probably a bad idea. She was getting confused. Who was she? She had to remember. She was Patsy Palmer, the only daughter of Nan and Jim Wofford. She was the real-estate lady who sometimes played tennis with prospective clients.

"So, I saw that the white house on your cul-de-sac was being listed with Century 21, Sue," Patsy said, heading back towards familiar territory.

Patsy was not the winner. She rode back to the house in Linda's Suburban. She felt tired and wired at the same time. Too much red velvet cake.

"Bye bye," she said as she climbed down from the front seat. Good grief, you needed a step ladder to get out of these damned things. She walked up to the house. Of course, the door was unlocked. They almost never locked up during the day. This neighborhood is like never-never land, she thought. But it was night time now, and so she locked the door behind her and went upstairs to Chelsea's room. Chelsea was in bed, reading the first Harry Potter book for the third time. Patsy sat down on the bed beside her.

"How come you're not asleep, bugface?"

"I'm not a bugface."

"Bumble bee."

"You're the bumble bee," Chelsea said, giggling.

"No, you're the bumble bee."

Patsy leaned in close and nuzzled Chelsea's cheek. Chelsea laughed and squirmed. At ten years old, Chelsea could still be teased and cuddled and kissed. Kyle had been a little more stand-offish at this age, but she noticed he still seemed to need affection even if he didn't admit it.

"Okay, you need to get to sleep. You've got skating practice early in the morning," Patsy said. "You're such a busy thing."

"Mommy, what did you do when you were my age? Did you do sports?"

"No," Patsy said. There had been no dance lessons, no sports, no arts programs, nothing after-school except TV if they were lucky. In the afternoons, she and Fancy Lee used to watch soap operas. When Randall would get home, they had to turn off the TV. Then at night she used to make up stories for Fancy Lee and pretend they were princesses. Patsy pushed the hair off Chelsea's forehead and said, "I acted."

"Like in school plays?"

"Yes," Patsy said. "Sort of like that. Not exactly. More like for family."

"You don't act anymore," Chelsea observed.

"Yes, I do," Patsy said. "I'm acting right now. I'm not really your mother. I'm really the Queen of Prussia."

Chelsea laughed and then began talking in what she thought sounded like a foreign language.

"Goodnight, Bumble Bee," Patsy said and kissed her on both cheeks and both eyelids.

"Goodnight, Bumble Bee," Chelsea replied.

Patsy stuck her head in Kyle's room next. He was lying in bed, playing with a small black gadget.

"What is that? The communicator with the mother ship?" Patsy asked.

Kyle held it out to her.

"It's a GPS, Mom," he said. "Global positioning satellite. You can tell exactly where you are when you've got one."

"I've heard of them. But, Kyle, honey, don't you know where you are?" she grinned at him.

"Yeah, I do now, but when I have a car, I'll want to know where I am."

"Really? Why don't you get one hooked up so your dad and I will know where you are." Patsy took the GPS from his hand and studied it.

"That's easy to do. You just connect it to a cell phone. Virtually, I mean," he said.

"Hmm. Very handy." She returned the GPS to him.

Kyle had Tom's gentleness, but he was more serious than Tom. He would be successful someday. She leaned over him and could smell his clean soapy scent as she whispered, "Goodnight."

He glanced up at her, his chin jutting forward, his pale eyebrows—pale like hers—relaxed. "Goodnight, Mom," he said.

She started to walk out of the room and noticed a pile of clothes in the corner.

"Kyle, I thought I asked you to pick up your clothes from the floor."

"Those don't fit," he said with a shrug.

"Well, then, throw them in the car and I'll drop them off at the Goodwill," she responded. That's when she remembered Lois's jacket, still in the trunk of her car. She'd have to figure out what to do with it one of these days.

Chapter 14

Lanelle and Rodney sat in the chief's office. A large window to the side looked out on the parking lot. A cabbage palm stood in the small patch of grass beside the window. Chief Carmichael had been hired out of Miami a few years back, and Rodney had never really been won over by the guy's style, but he seemed proficient at his job and funding for the department continued to grow so that they could do their jobs. Not all departments in the state could say that. The tax-cutters under the president's brother in Tallahassee were generally making sure their rich friends got richer, and if the poor people killed themselves for whatever was left over, they didn't care. They were still eating cake.

"How ya' holdin' up, Rodney?" Carmichael asked, looking up from the arrest report of Terrence Moore.

"I'm fine," Rodney said, "but I got to tell you I've got some reservations about the Jackson case." Lanelle looked over at him quizzically.

"Looks nice and tidy to me," Carmichael responded.

"Yeah, but things aren't always what they seem," Rodney said.

"No, only 99.99 per cent of the time. What makes you think this is any different?"

"The guy just doesn't seem like a killer," Rodney said. Rodney didn't mention the reverend's revelation to him about Willie's impending death. That wasn't what had convinced him anyway. There were too many things that just didn't add up. For one thing, Moore seemed way too smart to hang on to the murder weapon for a week. But the jilted lover story rang sweet with the press and kept them off the chief's back.

"Neither did Ted Bundy," Carmichael said. "Jesus, Rodney, you been doing homicide for how many years? And you still think you can tell a killer by the way he looks?"

"That's precisely why. And it's not how they look or what they do for a living. It's the way they act. It's everything about them."

Carmichael had large caterpillar eyebrows, and he raised them now as he stared at Rodney.

"Maybe you should take a couple weeks off," Carmichael said. "This thing with Willie was hard on you. You got some vacation time coming, don't you?"

Rodney took a deep breath. Yeah, he did have some vacation time coming. And he was feeling pretty tight in his arms right now, like they wanted to bust loose and punch Carmichael's lights out. But he didn't feel like getting pushed out just because Carmichael didn't want him to do his job.

"I don't need any time off," Rodney said.

"Sure, you do," Carmichael said with a tight-lipped grin. The two men stared at each other, and Rodney realized it was no longer a suggestion.

"Well, if you insist," Rodney said. "Think I'll go surfing."

Lanelle cleared her throat. She had something on her mind, Rodney could tell, but she wasn't going to bring it up in front of Carmichael.

"That's probably a good idea," she said to Rodney. "Don't worry. I'll manage without you—for a while."

Rodney forced a smile and looked Carmichael square in the eyes, and said, "Thanks, Chief. I'll start right now."

He got up and walked out of the room. Let the bastard fire him if he felt like it. Rodney had enough income from his rental houses that he could make it all right. His kid was grown, his house and truck paid for. Somehow the older he got, the more cynical he got. He just wanted to do his job and make the world a little bit safer, but nobody really wanted you to do that, especially the people who signed your paychecks. They were only looking to cover their asses.

Lanelle caught up with him in their office, more of a large cubicle actually.

"Rodney, I don't think Moore is guilty either. I can't be sure, but my gut says something is wrong here."

Rodney stuck his hands in his pockets.

"Ever hear of a working vacation?" he asked.

"You can't," she said. Then she crossed her arms over her rather ample chest and said, "But I knew that's why you agreed to it. Just be careful, okay."

He winked at her and said, "No problem, cuz."

Some vacation, Rodney thought as he drove along the green tunneled roads to the women's prison at Lowell. The surf was supposed to be great today off Ponte Vedra, four to five foot swells, the weather report said. But the ocean would have to wait till another day. Before he sent another man to spend his days fending off butt-fuckers at Raiford, he wanted to make damn sure the man belonged there.

Double fences topped by razor wire surrounded the prison. An administration building stood just outside the fences. Rodney walked in, showed his badge and asked to speak to the assistant superintendent. A petite white woman with jet black hair and a large smile came out momentarily and shook his hand.

"I'm Evelyn Doukatkis," she said. "How can I help you?"

"I'm working on a homicide in Gainesville. My partner spoke to you about it last week, I believe," he said.

"Yes, Thelma Jackson was murdered, wasn't she? I remember Thelma. A good inmate. Didn't cause trouble. She had a bump here and there, but it's tough to be locked up as long as she was and not run into something occasionally. Overall, though, she kept her nose clean."

"I was just wondering if there were any inmates—you know, real long-timers—that might have gotten to know her?"

Evelyn shook her head. "We transferred most of them out of here to Broward. We're not a maximum security unit, but I can check and see if there might be one or two who stayed here for medical reasons. Come back to my office."

"Thanks," Rodney said.

Joan Spivey was a three-time loser. She was about five foot eight with straight brown hair and slightly buck teeth. She was fifty-three years old, about the same age as Thelma, and yet she could have passed for thirty-three.

"You don't look fifty-three," Rodney said to her suspiciously.

"I figure all the time I've done in the penitentiary doesn't count," she said with a grin.

Rodney was looking down at Joan's file.

"All your busts have been for drugs?" he asked.

Joan nodded.

"Yep. That's why they keep sending me here. I don't belong with those murderers and child abusers. The only things I kill are brain cells," she laughed.

"You like being here?"

"I don't care. I go both ways if you know what I mean and at least when I'm locked up I'm not killing myself with cocaine or junk."

Rodney just shook his head.

"You're a piece of work, aren't you?"

Joan crossed her legs in an attempt to be seductive and flashed her eyes at him. Rodney studied the ratty-looking tennis shoes she had on.

"Hey, there's a lot worse than me out there. I just happen to love drugs."

"Enough to commit armed robbery of a drugstore, I see," Rodney noted.

"Dope ought to be legal. I don't like sticking a gun in someone's face, but if they're standing between me and a fix, they deserve it."

"Aren't you scared of killing someone and getting sent to the chair?"

She sneered and said, "That gun's never loaded. Once it wasn't even a real gun." Then she looked away from him. "Besides, death is death. Why should I care how it comes?"

Rodney glanced at her early history. Her father had committed suicide, and her mother died of alcoholism.

"Have you ever thought that maybe you should just try antidepressants?" he asked.

"Are you a shrink or are you here to ask some questions about your case?"

"Sorry," Rodney said. It wasn't his life, after all. "Okay, you were here in the seventies, right? You knew Thelma Jackson?"

"They called her 'Godfather' back then," Joan said smugly.

"They called a woman 'Godfather'?"

"We don't make nice little distinctions in here between male and female," Joan said, leaning on her knees. "They called her Godfather because she could get things taken care of. The shit-eaters trusted her, let her go work in the administration building. If you had a disciplinary report or something, she could make it disappear. It was little stuff like that."

"Did you know Vera Lee Gifford when she was here?"

"Yeah, I remember her. Pretty girl. Had all the studs in an uproar, but they were kinda scared of her, too. They called her 'Killer.'"

"So were Killer and Godfather friends? Were they lovers?"

"Not lovers. I don't think either one of them homosexed. But they knew each other. I think they respected each other. They say that Godfather helped Killer escape. Sylvia Black had just gotten sent here. Now, she was a bad bitch. And she was out for Killer's blood 'cause Killer had offed her old man. I mean, with all Godfather's access to the front office, she could have helped her get out. I don't know how they did it, but I don't think Killer went over the razor wire to granny's house though it has been done."

"What else do you remember about Vera Lee?"

Joan stuck out her feet and crossed them while she thought.

"I used to go in and play Scrabble with her and her cut-partner in the rec room. She was a good Scrabble player, played a mean game of chess, too. She was no dummy. She and her friend were always pretending they weren't really in prison. They'd call the canteen the mall and pretend that the field was the beach. Her friend was all broke up when Vera Lee left."

"Who was her friend?"

"I don't remember her name, but I do remember that she was one of those nice middle-class girls that you never expect to see in prison. She was in for vehicular manslaughter. Those kind are always a little different than us regular criminals. They get here by accident, and they're like lost sheep. Vera Lee took this girl under her wing, but the more they hung out, the more Vera Lee became like her friend and less like one of us. Vera Lee, she was a chameleon, you know. That's why most of us knew she wouldn't ever get caught. I've been in and out twice since then and never seen her back in here. I did meet her sister though."

"What?" Rodney asked.

"Yeah. This is some wild shit here, Detective, and I'm thinking I ought to get something for all this valuable information."

"Like what?"

"Like a little money in my account. I can't even buy a soda at the canteen 'cause there's no one outside to take care of me."

"I'll put fifty bucks in your account. That ought to last you a while. Now, tell me about Vera Lee's sister."

"She was a nurse, and she used to work in the prison system. Long after Vera Lee was gone. Only a few of us knew she was related to her, but I knew 'cause one time she asked me what I knew about Vera Lee. I told her the same thing I told you."

"When was this?"

"A few years ago, I guess. I haven't seen her in awhile. She must've quit."

Rodney thanked Evelyn and stopped at the front to leave a

check for Joan's account. What a convoluted mess this was. But the beautiful thing, he realized, was that he didn't have to answer to anyone about what he was doing. He could follow these threads wherever they led. He should take more vacations, he decided.

Chapter 15

Patsy spent the morning at the closing of a house on Lake Wylie. It was a big five-bedroom house, and her commission would help pay for the kids' tuition next year. Private schools were ridiculously expensive, but her kids were happy in private school and Tom thought it was the right thing to do. Of course, as a career counselor at a community college, it's not like he made enough to make a dent in their tuition and their trips to chess tournaments and ice skating competitions. His salary about covered the mortgage and one car payment. But Tom had other attributes. He was good and kind, and he respected her privacy.

She had met him in Chapel Hill at a basketball game—the only time she ever went to a game. He was in graduate school and she was a junior majoring in psychology. She was sitting in front of him on the bleachers when she felt him watching her. She turned around and glared at him, wanting to snap at him and ask him what his problem was. But then he smiled and said, "Want some popcorn?" He held a bag towards her. She looked into the popcorn bag and then reached in, grabbed a few pieces and said, "Thanks."

She'd only gone on a few dates in college. It never felt safe to her. She was lonely, but she made a few friends who would get together to go to movies or study. She wasn't close to anyone, but she didn't worry about that. She had spent most of her life in hiding. She did well enough in her classes not to be noticed. She liked psychology but she had never managed to unlock the key to her own mind. What had made her turn out the way she had?

The day after the basketball game, she was walking back to the apartment that she shared with two other girls. She took a short cut behind a big brick building and found herself walking past the track. She stopped a minute to watch the runners, jumping over hurdles. She was mesmerized by their pumping arms and the way they threw their legs out and leapt over the barricades. For a moment she felt as if she were one of them, always running, always flying over the obstacles in her path. Her books in her backpack suddenly felt heavy. She wanted to fling them to the ground, but she knew better. She turned to go home when someone called to her, "Hey! Hey!"

She saw a gangly young man with sandy brown hair and big round eyes approaching her. She felt a smile tug at her mouth so she looked away.

"Hi there," the young man said when he was just a few feet away.

"Hey, Popcorn Man," she said with a laugh.

"This is kind of like fate, isn't it?" he asked. "My name's Tom."

"Hi, Tom," she said and she felt warm inside, like she had stepped close to a fire. She was someone brand new, a clean slate, and together they would write her story.

Patsy's cell phone chimed at her. She flipped it open as she drove away from the office and looked at the number—Mom and Dad's condo. It was noontime and hot as the dickens. Summer was already staking its claim.

"Hi, Mom," she said.

"Are you free, Patsy? Jim and I want to know if you'd like to come over for lunch," Nan said.

"You're inviting me without the kids?" Patsy joked.

"You're always invited and you know that," Nan admonished her. "But there's somebody here I want you to meet."

"Oh, okay," Patsy said. Nan was always trying to get her to meet someone from her church. Patsy didn't mind it. She liked

Nan's friends. They were a little strange, talking about meditating and spiritual awakening workshops. Nan and Jim had left their old Methodist church and been experimenting for the past few years. Tom made fun of it, but their seeking seemed to make them happy.

Patsy drove past the golf course and turned into the condominiums where Jim and Nan lived. She parked beside Jim's Jetta and went to the door. It was unlocked, so she went inside and walked into the living room. Jim, Nan and a dark-haired woman sat at the wrought iron table outside. Patsy slid the glass door open and stepped onto the garden patio.

"Here she is," Nan said cheerfully and stood up to hug Patsy.

"I'm lucky to have the afternoon free," Patsy said and turned to see the guest. You would think that when you hadn't seen someone in twenty-six years it might take a while to recognize the person. And in fact there were a few surreal moments as Patsy registered the shape of the face, the ski-slope nose, the straight-across eyebrows and the brown hair cut just at the top of the neck.

The hand came out.

"Hi, I'm Mandy Danforth."

"Oh, my God," Patsy said, slowly taking the woman's hand. Mandy. She had aged and not entirely well. There were lines on her face, around her eyes and mouth. But her eyes were bright and her voice strong, confident.

"Do you know Mandy?" Jim asked.

"I don't," Patsy said quickly. "But I saw pictures of her and . . . and your daughter."

"Mandy was our first Patsy's best friend from the time they were six years old," Nan said. "She was in the accident with her."

Nan reached over and took Mandy's hand. A glance passed between them. Then Mandy turned to Patsy.

"Yes, it was such a surprise to learn they had adopted another daughter, another Patsy," Mandy said and looked Patsy over from head to foot.

"God brought her to us, Mandy," Nan said. "There was a void in our lives. I know that Patsy, our Patsy, is happy in heaven that we're so blessed."

"It just seems such a coincidence," Mandy said.

Patsy smiled nervously and sat down at the table next to Jim, a hollow feeling of fear in her chest. Surely Mandy had recognized her. They'd been so close for that year. Perhaps it had been foolish to seek out Nan and Jim, to try to convince them to take her in, but she knew that people like the two of them didn't have much contact with the law. Police looked for fugitives in the old places they were known to frequent, not in the home of a nice church-going couple. At the time she hadn't worried much about whether Mandy found out or not. She had trusted her. But that was a long time ago. Could this new, updated version of her old friend be trusted?

"So what brings you to Charlotte, Mandy?" Patsy asked, gazing level into Mandy's eyes. A long pause ensued before Mandy broke off the gaze and turned to Jim and Nan.

"Well, I came up to attend a conference on youth theater at the university, and thought I'd stop by before heading home," she smiled and looked at Patsy again. "I really needed to see Jim and Nan. You see, I've been in AA for about seven years, but there's one of the steps where you make amends to those you have harmed. I still needed to make amends."

"No, you didn't," Nan said earnestly. "We forgave you a long time ago. Yes, losing Patsy broke our hearts. And not a day goes by that I don't miss her. But you should not live in hell for the rest of your life. We all make mistakes. Holding on to anger at you would have been like toting around a sack of rotten potatoes all our lives."

"I know that," Mandy said. She tilted her head and ran her fingers along the condensation on the outside of the glass. "But I had to do this for me, Nan. I hadn't forgiven myself."

Jim cleared his throat and sat forward.

"You have to learn how to forgive yourself before you can ever forgive anyone else. That's what we learned," he said. "When you get to a certain level spiritually, you figure out there never was anything to forgive."

Patsy turned to Mandy and explained, "Mom and Dad are spiritual seekers. Some of the ideas are a little wacky, but they're generally harmless."

"Hey, there's nothing wrong with being into crystals or whatever," Mandy said and shrugged her shoulders. "If it makes you feel better."

Nan served sandwiches and salad for lunch. Mandy told them about the work she did in Florida with at-risk kids. She lived in Gainesville and worked with a theater group there.

"It's great for the kids. They can try on new identities and learn how to stretch outside of what they've known their whole lives. And it's really amazing the work they can do. I've seen complete transformations. I mean, they don't all change, but some of them do."

Nan wanted to know if Mandy had married or had any children. The answer to both was, no.

"I saw from the pictures on the entertainment center that you have kids, Patsy," Mandy said to her.

"Two. A boy and a girl. They're the loves of my life," Patsy said.

"I'd like to meet them," Mandy said.

"Well, umm," Patsy paused and then said, "I have to go get Chelsea from ice skating in a little while. Do you want to come?"

Mandy smiled. Oh, she had the same heart-shaped face and the same smile.

"I'd love to."

"Why don't you girls run along then?" Nan suggested. "Patsy can show you around Charlotte. She knows the town like she's got one of those GPS things in her head. She's a realtor, you know."

"Really?" Mandy said, observing Patsy curiously.

Suddenly, getting Mandy out of there seemed like a good idea. Patsy helped Nan clear off the table, kissed Jim on the top of his nearly bald head and led Mandy outside to her car. A couple of clicks and the doors of the Honda unlocked. Mandy got in the passenger side and Patsy got behind the wheel and started the car. Nan waved to them and then shut the door.

They drove in silence out of the development and turned right toward the golf course. As they passed the manicured green hills and sand traps and another development, Patsy felt her heart racing. Words flew around in her mind, but nothing came out.

Finally Mandy said, "You owe me ten dollars."

Patsy remembered the morning she left the prison. She had taken ten dollars from Mandy's little change purse and left a note in its place. Then she told the CO she was sick and was sent to the infirmary. When the night shift left, she had walked out of the prison with them using a stolen ID and stolen street clothes. From there it was long a walk through the woods to the interstate.

"Yeah, I guess I do," Patsy said. "I wondered if you knew it was me."

"I would have known that voice anywhere. I can't believe how much you've changed. It's not just the hair and the eye color. It's like your whole face is different."

"Well, I got a nose job for one thing, and I'm older and wear contacts. You look different, too, Mandy."

"I know. Being an alcoholic will put the years on you."

"You mentioned being in AA."

"When I got out of prison in 1980, I moved to Gainesville and started going to school. But I partied too much. Partied until it was no longer any fun. In fact, I don't think it was ever fun. You know what I didn't do though?"

"What?" Patsy asked.

"I never got another driver's license until about three years ago when I knew for sure I could stay sober. I had decided I'd rather give up driving than drinking. And I didn't want to kill anyone ever again."

Patsy glanced over at her. "Hell, I was gonna suggest we go get a drink. I sure could use one." She laughed nervously and Mandy smiled.

"I'll bet you could. Am I the first person you've ever run into? From your past, I mean?"

"Unh huh. I've been undercover for so long I don't even know the person I used to be." She paused. "I've got a wonderful life, Mandy. And I've got it because of you. You used to talk about your life, growing up, and it sounded so good. Everything about middle-class America sounded wonderful. It wasn't just money, it was the love, the things you did together as a family. I wanted that so bad my whole life. And I finally said, why can't I have that, too? Besides, you know if I'd stayed locked up, I wouldn't have lived all that long."

Patsy drove past a shopping center and turned toward town.

"Listen, I have to be honest," Mandy said. "I had a feeling I would find you here. Do you remember the note you left me?"

Patsy nodded. "But I don't remember what it said."

"It said, 'I'll always be your best friend.' But see, Patsy was my best friend. And you knew that. When I got out, I went back home and people at church told me about this mysterious girl who looked like Patsy and she showed up just a few weeks after you left prison. I knew it was you."

"Why now? Why have you shown up now, Mandy?"

"Maybe we should go get that drink," Mandy said. "Don't worry. I'll have a ginger ale."

"Well, I was just kidding about getting a drink. When I drink alone, I prefer to be by myself."

Mandy laughed, but it was a dry, frightened laugh.

Patsy pulled into a neighborhood of McMansions, each one gaudier than the one before.

"You live in one of these?" Mandy asked.

"No," Patsy said. "Oh, I know there's plenty of status here, but I don't care about status the way these people do. People think I send my kids to private school because I'm trying to be so high and mighty, but that's not it. It's just that when I had my kids, I realized I wasn't going to let anyone ever push them around the way people pushed me around. When I was a kid, I actually had teachers ask me why I wore the same dress to school every day for a week. I didn't have a mother, Mandy. And my father hated me. He said I was just like her, and promised I'd wind up just like her. For some reason that scared me so bad. It felt like a dark cloth being put over my face whenever he said that."

She pulled into the driveway of a large stone house with a "for sale" sign planted in a tiny lawn in front of a large gate.

"Isn't this the most outrageous place?" Patsy asked. This time when Mandy laughed it was genuine. "Wait till you see the inside."

"God, it's like we've never been apart," Mandy said.

Patsy looked over at her. It had been so long since she'd had a friend other than Tom and the kids. She smiled and reached her hand out. The two clasped hands.

"Come on. Let's go inside," Patsy said.

"Really?"

"Yeah. I've got the combination to the lock box. You are interested in buying this little cottage, aren't you?"

"Oh sure," Mandy said.

Chapter 16

Mandy gazed in awe. The double front doors looked like they belonged on an old fortress. Patsy opened one of the doors and waved an arm as if she were Vanna White and this was Mandy's grand prize. An enormous foyer of marble and iron stood before them.

"This is what we call a transitional house," Patsy said, going into her spiel.

"I don't get it," Mandy said, looking around at all the stuff—statues of swans and elephants and too many things to take in all at once. "Why is there an iron gate inside the house? And why is it still full of furniture? Does someone still live here?"

"Actually, she's leaving all the furniture here for the next occupants if they want it. She's a decorator, and she designed the house with the builder. Check out the kitchen."

They passed through the open iron gates into a living area that stretched into a dining room and a kitchen. Mandy tried to absorb what she was seeing. It was so foreign to her life as a "starving artist." Kat did pretty well as an assistant prof at the university, but she also had to support her invalid mother. And even the wealthiest of their friends didn't live like this. It was absurdly ostentatious, and yet as they wandered through the two master bedrooms on either side of the house into the gigantic bathrooms with glass-block walls and open shower areas, Mandy could see the attraction. She wouldn't really mind a little of this luxury. It was seductive.

"Let's go out on the deck," Patsy said. "I'll grab a couple of cokes from the refrigerator. I like to keep it stocked for potential buyers."

Patsy walked over to a pale beige cabinet and opened it.

"That's the refrigerator?" Mandy asked. She felt as if she were some rube from the country who was seeing the big city for the first time.

"Yeah," Patsy smiled. "She had it made so that all the appliances just blend into the wall here. So the kitchen doesn't really look like a kitchen."

"Cool," Mandy said. "Or 'that's really tight' as my kids would say."

After Patsy grabbed a couple of cans of Coke, they wended their way past the ornate glass dining table where probably no one ever ate and sat outside on the deck beside a concrete-swan-bedecked swimming pool.

"What do you think?" Patsy asked.

"You have some kind of life," Mandy said, laughing as she gazed around.

"Well, my house is much more modest. But it's fun to go into these houses and get to know the people who live here. This woman here is a real hoot. She's a charmer. She invited Kyle and Chelsea over to swim with her kids before they went to Europe. They had a blast."

Mandy stared at Patsy. How could this possibly be the tough little cracker she knew in prison? Some things hadn't changed, but other things were so different. Of course, she had seen it back then. She had seen Vera Lee's potential. She knew in her gut that Vera Lee had the toughness and strength to handle any situation and the smarts to adapt. And she'd been right.

"It's pretty ironic," Mandy said. "You got the good life I should have had. But for some reason, I threw it away."

Patsy reached over and touched her as she said, "Mandy, helping kids like you do, that's a good life, too. And now you've been sober for seven years. That's wonderful."

Mandy took a sip of her cola. Like most former alcoholics she loved the sugary sweetness and the caffeine buzz.

"You're right. I love working with those kids. They've saved me."

"You haven't answered my question yet. Why now?" Patsy asked her.

Mandy put her purse onto an iron table beside her and opened it. She pulled out a newspaper clipping from the *Gainesville Sun*.

"Someone killed Godfather," she said, handing the paper to Patsy.

"No," Patsy said and looked at the small article. There it was in black-and-white newsprint. Thelma Jackson killed by an unknown assailant. Patsy put a hand over her mouth. Then she put it down.

"But what makes you think this has anything to do with me?"

"I don't know, Ver . . . I mean, Patsy," Mandy said. "It's just that she had called me a few days before, asked if we could talk. She sounded nervous about something. I said, sure, but then rehearsals for a new show kept me busy and I guess I just forgot about it. Then I saw this article. And I thought maybe it had something to do with you."

"Why me?" Patsy asked, sounding surprised and hurt.

"I thought maybe that woman whose husband you killed . . ." Mandy began.

"Sylvia Black? Well, she is capable of just about anything. She'd never forgive me for shooting Lorenzo," Patsy said.

Mandy studied her old friend. The Patsy façade had mysteriously disappeared. And it was as if all the pretty surroundings disappeared as well. Instead of a golf course stretching out beyond the perimeter of the yard, there might as well have been the green baseball field by the bleachers where they used to sit after dinner in the prison cafeteria.

"Why did you do it? Why did you kill them?" Mandy asked. She had always wondered what could have driven her friend to such a horrific act.

Patsy shook her head, thinking. Her brow was furrowed.

"I don't know. Lance kept me in that motel room so drugged up I can't hardly remember anything except him showing me his guns. He was so proud of those guns. He had a couple Walther pistols from Germany. One of them was really rare. The P38. He even taught me how to put on the silencer. Then he drove me to the club and he gave me some angel dust. I snorted it and then for some reason I just felt this crazy rage. I just wanted to kill. My memory is fuzzy. Sometimes I'll have little glimpses of it—you know, before and after. I can remember kneeling down in that cramped little office and putting my hand in the blood. But I don't know why I had to kill them. It's so dark . . ."

A flock of geese flew past them, and Mandy stared up at them in surprise. Geese never came as far south as Florida. Patsy paid them no heed.

"I don't understand. Why didn't this Lance person get charged with murder, too?" Mandy asked.

"I didn't tell the police. I didn't tell them anything. Just kept my mouth shut like I'd been taught all my life. I pray every night for God to forgive me."

"I thought you had three charges," Mandy said.

"I did. But to be honest, I don't remember anything at all about the third one. They say I killed Lance's wife. I used to have blackouts, I guess you'd call them. I don't remember anything from the year that my mom left us," Patsy said. "One thing both Mama and Randall taught me, the less you remember the better off you'll be."

Mandy understood the philosophy. She so often wished she couldn't remember riding in the ambulance to the hospital, knowing that she had killed her best friend, how she begged God to let her die; instead she was forced to live on with her guilt branded onto her heart.

Patsy continued, "I've been going to see one of Mom's spiritual friends, and she's trying to help me recall things, but I don't want to remember killing that woman. I'd rather just not know. I have enough nightmares without that."

Mandy sat quietly for a long moment. Then she said, "Maybe Sylvia Black knew Godfather helped you escape. I mean, everyone was pretty sure she helped you. Even I knew. She did help you, right?"

"Yeah, she helped me. But that's not all. As soon as I got to the highway, some Christian guy in a station wagon gave me a ride all the way to Perry. That's where I found Thelma's momma. Thelma had given me her address and a note, asking her to watch out for me. That's where I got the plan to become Patsy. I thought it was heartbreaking that this girl you described as so wonderful was dead. Remember how you talked about her parents? They sounded like the kind of parents I always dreamed about. Even back then, Mandy, they forgave you. Remember that?"

"Yes, I remember," Mandy admitted.

"Thelma's momma was good, too. Never judged me. Never asked me what I had done. She fed me and bought me some hair dye. I told her to get that copper color like Patsy's hair. Then she gave me bus fare. First I hitched a ride to Fort Lauderdale. I had some business to take care of. Then I caught a bus to Alachua, where you were from. You described it so well—a little old southern town just outside Gainesville. Went to your church and found Patsy's parents. You know, if you don't take a risk you'll never have an opportunity. The first part of my life was so awful, Mandy. My daddy Randall was scary and Mama was always off with some other man."

Mandy felt a chill pass over her as Patsy talked about her real mother.

"Maybe you should go away. I'm scared for you," Mandy said. "I didn't even know if I'd find you, but now that I have and I've seen the way you're getting along, I just don't want you to get hurt. It would kill Nan and Jim if something happened to you, too. Maybe you should leave, start over again somewhere else."

Patsy stared hard at her. She remembered the nights that Mandy cried in her bunk, missing the friend who had died that autumn night. Mandy had often said that Vera Lee was like Patsy. It was like she was planting the idea in her head, watering it and watching it grow. Sometimes they'd get together in the dorm bathroom where the COs couldn't see them and they'd brush each other's hair—a punishable offense that they were willing to take the risk for. No one had ever been as kind to her as Mandy had been.

"Is this about me or is this about your own guilt for killing their daughter?" Patsy asked quietly.

Mandy sighed. "A little bit of both, I guess."

Patsy reached over, wrapped her arms around her and said, "I can't go anywhere. I've got a life here. In fact, I've got to go get Chelsea from skating right now. Listen, let's just forget about this thing with Godfather, okay."

Maybe Patsy had the gift of forgetting, but it would not be so easy for Mandy.

"Promise me you'll be careful," she said.

"I will," Patsy said. "See, this is who I am now. I'm the mom, the wife, the real-estate lady."

Mandy was at a loss. Patsy seemed to think she was invulnerable in this picture-perfect little world. She had created a fantasy and believed in it.

"Patsy, how can I get in touch with you if I need to?" she asked.

Patsy pulled out a card with a picture of her smiling face and phone numbers and email addresses. The best way to hide was right out in the open, wasn't it? Mandy put the card in her wallet.

About fifteen minutes later, they pulled into the parking lot of a large indoor ice-skating rink.

"I practically live in this place. Tonight I have to make a chocolate cake for a party we're having for one of the teachers who's moving," Patsy said, handing Mandy a large wool sweater. "Wear this. It's freezing in there."

"God," Mandy said. "This is so weird. You are making a chocolate cake?"

"Nan taught me how to bake. I'm not much good at the other stuff, but, honey, I make a mean chocolate cake. Cream-cheese brownies, too."

They went inside and sat up on a set of metal bleachers, watching the kids skating back and forth. Patsy occasionally waved and smiled brightly at another mother. Her smile was the same completely disarming, utterly beautiful smile that Mandy remembered. She had one of those adorable overbites. It felt so weird to see her old friend like this—with the make-up and the red polished nails and the color-coordinated outfit. Her handbag was a Kate Spade, for God's sake. Mandy wouldn't even have recognized such a thing if it weren't for a few snooty lawyers' wives who patronized her theater.

"All these years I wondered what had happened to you," Mandy said. "Sometimes I'd dream about you. I remember one dream, we were on a boat and we were going to Japan or someplace like that."

"I haven't been on any boats, I can promise you that. I don't like boats," Patsy said and then reached over and touched her hand. "I thought of you, too, a lot. I mean, whenever I was in a weird situation—weird for me, anyway—I'd ask myself what would Mandy do? You were my role model."

"You're kidding. It's a good thing you turned out okay then," Mandy laughed.

"Well, Nan and Jim had saved all this money for their daughter, Patsy, to go to college. She was already accepted at Chapel Hill. And I don't know, it just seemed easier for all of us if I went in her place. I mean, the school didn't have to know that Patsy was dead. Do you think I'm terrible for doing that?"

Mandy looked at the small red-haired girl down on the ice, skating in figure eights.

"I don't think lying on a college application is too terrible."

"I guess not." Patsy turned to look at the skaters. Mandy studied her profile. She wore dark red lipstick. Her face was thin. She wasn't exactly beautiful anymore but she was striking.

"You weren't all that bad, you know," Mandy said softly.

"You don't think so?"

"No. In fact, I was in love with you."

Patsy was silent for a moment. Then she turned and looked into Mandy's eyes and asked, "In love?"

"I'm gay. I've always been gay. I loved Patsy when we were in high school though she never knew it, and then I met you and fell in love with you. You were so kind to me. And you were funny and not afraid of anything. That's what I wanted to be like."

"I didn't know . . ."

"Well, when you grow up in a nice Southern Baptist home, you learn how to keep your true feelings under wraps. That guilt I felt over being a lesbian is probably what killed Patsy. It's taken me a long time to accept myself."

"So, I guess you understand what it's like to live in hiding then."

"Yeah, I do. I finally told my parents and they accepted it as best they could. I think they thought prison did it to me, though. All the way up till they died, I could never convince them that I was born this way."

"They're dead?"

"My mom got cancer and Dad had a massive heart attack two months after her funeral."

"That must have been hard."

"It was." They were silent for a while, watching the skaters. Then Mandy said, "This world seems so right for you—the whole suburban mom thing. It fits you like a glove, girlfriend."

"I do like that part. Yeah, it's good. And Tom is a good husband. It's just all the other stuff. Sometimes I know those other women look at me and wonder, 'now what the hell ain't right about her?'"

Mandy laughed. She remembered how Vera Lee had been able to make her laugh, imitating the COs or the other inmates. She could still do it. She had so many feelings. It was the weirdest day she'd had in a long time.

"Listen, Mandy, don't worry about me. I'll be okay. Godfather had no idea where I am. I'm really, really sorry if Sylvia Black killed her, but it was probably just some strung-out crack addict. Why in hell would Sylvia Black come after me now?"

That was a good question, Mandy thought. She decided she may have been worried about nothing. She turned her eyes to the children on the ice, twirling and jumping as if nothing in the world would ever harm them.

Chapter 17

Rodney entered the duplex and surveyed the damage to the wood floor. Buddy came in behind him and sniffed curiously.

"Damn," Rodney said, looking at the rotted wood. "Why didn't you call me sooner?"

His tenant, a chubby college kid named Rick, rubbed his forehead and tried to explain, "Well, we had a rug over it, so we didn't notice it for a while. And then we had finals. Then I went to visit my folks over the break. Then summer term started."

"Okay, okay," Rodney said. "I'll get some wood and repair it myself."

"Good thing you're on break," Rick said with a broad, goofy smile. Rodney wondered if he had ever been so young. Of course, a couple years service at the tail end of the Vietnam War kind of made you grow up quick.

"I read in the paper the other day that they're thinking of reinstating the draft," Rodney said, hunkering down next to the rotted hole in the floor. It looked like there was a leak underneath. Hell, they'd have to tear up the floor to fix the leak anyway. That would cost a pretty penny.

"Yeah. That sucks," Rick said, frowning. Buddy had found a tennis ball and brought it in. He looked expectantly at Rick, who reached down and took it from his mouth.

"Well, if they do, don't you go, son," Rodney said. "Tell those bastards in Congress that you'll go if they go."

Rick chuckled. "I don't know how they'd feel about that, Mr.

Ellis, but I'll do my best not to get involved with it. Come on, Buddy. You wanna chase the ball?"

Rick took the ball out to the front yard with Buddy leaping excitedly behind him.

Rodney came outside. Buddy was dutifully bringing the ball back as if it were the most important assignment in the world.

"Okay, listen. I'm gonna call some plumbers to come in and fix this leak. Then I'm gonna replace the floor."

"Sweet," Rick said. "You sure have a good dog. Let me know if you ever need someone to look after him."

"Oh, he pretty much goes where I go," Rodney said. Rodney whistled, and Buddy bounded toward the car, forgetting all about the ball and focusing on his new mission—sticking his head out of the window of the car.

On Rodney's way back home, he stopped by the station to see Lanelle.

"Damn, I thought you were on vacation," Al said, passing him in the hallway.

"I am," Rodney responded. "Just come by to check up on my old partner."

"I am not old," Lanelle said, hands on her hips as she came out of the office. "Come on. Let's go to the break room and get some coffee. I see you brought your friend with you."

Buddy wagged at her and smiled.

"Yep. It's too hot to leave him out in the car."

Rodney followed her down to the break room. A Tupperware container of cookies sat by the coffee maker. Buddy sniffed them longingly.

Lanelle sat down at one of the break tables. Rodney sat down across from her.

"Aren't you supposed to be off surfing somewhere?" she asked.

Rodney glanced around. The only other person was one of the dispatchers and she was on her way out the door. When she left, Rodney admitted, "I went down to the prison and talked to one of the inmates who knew Thelma Jackson. She says that Thelma might have helped Vera Lee Gifford escape. And we know Thelma's mom helped her once she was out. I think there's more to this Thelma Jackson thing than meets the eye."

"I know you do. And you might be right. I wasn't so sure about it either. On the other hand, what if you're wrong? I've been thinking a lot about this. If Terrence Moore killed that woman, I don't want him to get away with it. You understand me?"

Rodney bit into one of the cookies and said, "I've been party once before to sending an innocent man to death row. I don't want to do that again."

Lanelle took one of the cookies from the container, bit into it and changed the subject.

"You remember I told you about my nephew, Gawain?"

"Yeah, the thirteen-year-old that joined a gang and got busted for stealing a car?" Rodney asked.

"That's the one. I tried talking to him, but he wouldn't listen. Then this past year he got involved in a theater program after school. Honey, you never saw anything turn a kid around so fast. They've got a summer camp and he's so excited. He's made me promise to come see him perform. You can come with me if you want."

Rodney said he'd love to.

"Who runs this program?" he asked.

"Some woman got a grant to do it. She's a former convict herself. Not all of them come out of prison worse than they went in."

"Well, good for her," Rodney said. He felt odd sitting here with Lanelle. He knew she had things to do. A detective never has to worry about finding work. Standing up, Rodney said. "I've got to go home and call the plumbers. That's all I'm going to worry about till I can get over to the beach."

"Must be nice," Lanelle said.

*

Rodney turned off the TV and heard a loud banging on the door. He opened it to find his daughter, Amy, standing on his screened-in front porch, talking on her cell phone.

"You know what? This is a problem I don't want to deal with right now. If he won't take the plea deal, then we just go to trial. It's his life. We can't force him to do the smart thing. By the way, if Merlyn Photography calls, please tell them the date of the wedding. Please get a commitment in writing. Listen, I have to go."

Amy folded her cell phone shut with a click and stared at Rodney. He figured he was in trouble.

"Hi, baby," he said. "Come to spend the weekend with your old man?"

"Daddy, where have you been all evening?"

"Right here, watching my favorite TV show."

"Did you forget we were supposed to have dinner? I waited at La Vecchia's for forty-five minutes before I realized I'd gotten stood up."

"Damn. I'm sorry. I'm sorry. I'm an idiot."

Amy ran a hand through her auburn hair. "Daddy, I'm getting married in six weeks. Please don't flake out on me," she said.

"I'm not gonna flake out, honey. I promise," he said and placed his hands on her arms. "I love you. Come inside. I'll make you something to eat. We can discuss your wedding plans now." Amy gazed at him petulantly, and he remembered all the times she should have been happy and he'd done something dumb that caused her to cry. Like her eighth-grade graduation when she'd just gotten her ears pierced and she was so damn beautiful that it scared the hell out of him. All he could do was criticize her.

"I don't understand how you forgot that I was coming up to see you. What's gotten into you?"

Rodney sighed. He went into the kitchen and opened the refrigerator. Good, there was a big jar of Duke's mayonnaise. He could make some tuna fish. He had chips, too.

"So something is bothering you," she said, leaning in the

doorway. She wore a pair of those pedal pushers all the women wore now and some sandals. Her toenails were painted a light pink. What a woman. And a lawyer to boot.

"I guess I'm just a little freaked out that my baby girl is all grown up and getting married," he said as he opened a can of tuna. "I mean, I'm happy for you, but you know, it means I'm getting old. I just don't know if I'm the chick magnet I used to be."

Amy sidled up beside him and slid an arm around his waist. He was dumping the tuna into a plastic bowl.

"I'm glad that's all it is because I have some news and you might not like it," she said.

"What?" he asked suspiciously. "Hand me that bread."

Amy handed him the loaf of wheat bread and said, "Mom is coming to the wedding."

Rodney fought the anger rising up inside him. He pulled down two plates, made the sandwiches and carried them to the Formica table. Amy sat down across from him.

"Are you okay with that?" she asked.

Rodney took a bite out of his sandwich and then said, "No."

Amy let out a long sigh.

"Dad, she's my mother. I can't keep her away from my wedding. It's not right."

Rodney finished his sandwich silently. Amy took a few bites and gave the rest to Buddy. Rodney looked up at her pretty pale face—the freckles of childhood now faded. Her eyes were dark, her teeth perfect, her cheekbones high just like her mother's.

"I'll tell you what isn't right. It isn't right that a mother just ups and decides to leave her family one day. Just says, 'I've got to find myself. I need space.' Hell, we all need space. But when you're a parent, you have to give something up. You have to sacrifice. She wasn't ready to sacrifice shit. Amy, you were only twelve years old. You hadn't even started your period yet. Do you remember that? What kind of mother leaves her daughter to find out about that kind of stuff from a man?"

Amy put a hand out.

"I'm not saying what she did wasn't wrong. It was really, really awful. But, Dad, I can't spend my whole life hating her. And you shouldn't either. She did the best she knew how. If I hate her, I'm just going to turn into an old, bitter woman. I want my children to have a grandmother."

"A grandmother? You have to be a mother before you can be a grandmother!" Rodney banged his fist on the table.

Amy put her head in her hands. Her thick hair fell over her fingers. The solitaire diamond engagement ring gleamed between a few strands. Then she looked up.

"I give up." Amy stood up and dumped her dish in the sink. "I've got to drive back to Orlando tonight."

"That's a long ways, honey. Why don't you stay here?"

"Can't. I've got to be in court in the morning. Listen, Dad, Mom is going to be at the wedding. That's a done deal. Now, I hope you'll take the high ground and be in the wedding like we always planned."

Rodney felt an unmovable boulder in his chest where his heart should have been.

"I don't know if I can do that," he said.

Amy sighed.

"I'm sorry," she said. "I hope you change your mind." She gathered her purse and walked out without giving him the usual kiss on the cheek. When the door shut, Rodney's anger felt like a solid thing. He stood up and paced around the living room. Then he noticed the scrapbook that Twyla made on the table. Only a crazy poet would turn a cop's exploits into a "memory book." He sat down and opened it. The stories went backwards in time. He turned to the last page—the story of Vera Lee Gifford's arrest. Twyla had found copies of two different articles. She must have spent hours looking at microfiche. He doubted this stuff was on the internet. The first article from *The Sun* told of the arrest. But the second article was from the *Jupiter Pilot*—and there was a feature story about the hometown girl gone bad.

His eyes scanned it for details. Grew up in Jupiter Beach, mother a waitress on Singer Island until she disappeared. Then the girl ran away from home, lived with her boyfriend in Fort Lauderdale, worked at a place called the Black Orchid. A few weeks after her boyfriend gets busted for marijuana trafficking, she goes on a killing spree, shooting the owner of the Black Orchid and his bodyguard and then going to Lance Underwood's house on the Intra-coastal and shooting Lois Underwood. Steals Lois's convertible Jaguar and flees. But what would make a girl pick up a gun and fire it? The reporter mentioned a few possibilities: an abusive home life, jealousy, insanity caused by drugs. Not enough, Rodney thought. He looked at the byline: Michael McMillan. Now where did he know that name?

Buddy came up and licked his hand. The fact was no one cared to know the truth about something which happened that long ago. But he wanted to know. And he had a feeling Willie would want to know, too.

"We're going down south tomorrow, Buddy," Rodney said. "They've got some great surf down that way. What do you think about that? Want to catch some waves?"

Buddy obviously thought this was a brilliant idea and beat his tail against the wall to indicate his wholehearted approval.

Chapter 18

The hardest part of the whole AA experience had not been making amends. It was that business about the Higher Power. Sometimes they got stuck on that God stuff. But Mandy had known that if she didn't do something she was going to destroy any possibility of ever having a life. In fact, the night before she joined AA she'd had a dream about the accident. Only this time, instead of dying, Patsy got out of the car and walked down the road. In the dream Mandy watched her walking into the night, still wearing her band uniform. And she had awakened with a feeling of peace. That was the morning she realized it was time to stop, time to regroup and pull her life together. She called a friend in AA and asked when the next meeting was. It turned out to be that morning at nine o'clock.

As she drove away from Charlotte there was one image that she couldn't shake from her head—the picture of Patsy's ten-year-old daughter skating across the ice toward them, an enormous smile on her face, her copper-red hair flying back. She had thudded against the side of the rink with a laugh.

"Hi, Mommy," she said. Then she glanced at Mandy, looked at her for a moment and said, "Hi."

"This is Mandy, honey. She's a friend of Grandma and Granddaddy."

"Oh, hi, Mandy. Watch this new trick I learned, Mommy. I can do a double Lutz! Watch me." The girl skated into the center of the ice.

Chelsea's teacher skated up to them and said to Patsy, "She's so proud of this. She's really good."

The three women watched as the little girl in the white satin skating outfit and dark blue sweater jumped and twirled in the air. Mandy swallowed hard. She was suddenly so frightened for this woman who called herself Patsy. What would happen if someone found out who she really was? What would happen to this little girl?

Mandy mused as she began the long drive home. Vera Lee Gifford had managed to disguise herself for twenty-something years as Patsy Palmer, housewife and suburban mom. There was no reason to think she might not stay hidden forever. But could anything be hidden forever?

Seven hours later she pulled into the driveway of the brick ranch house that she shared with Kat. She took her bags from the car and entered the house.

"Kat?" she called out.

"Out here." She dropped her bags in the living room. Kat had cleaned up. The rug looked freshly vacuumed, and she could smell a lemony scent that meant the kitchen floor had just been mopped. Mandy went to the back door and saw Kat in the garden, spreading compost.

"Hi there," she said.

Kat looked up at her and smiled, then came over and kissed her. Kat was a small-boned woman with enormous green eyes, short dark hair and a thin face. She was younger than Mandy by about eight years, but to Mandy she seemed to be wiser than both of their years combined.

"Did you get done what you needed to get done?" Kat asked and tilted her head.

"I did, I think. It was a weird trip. Brought back a lot of feelings. But I think it was good overall." She paused. "The house looks nice and clean."

"There's nothing worse than coming home to a messy house," Kat said. "Do you want to go inside?"

"I want to take a shower and get in bed—with you," Mandy smiled.

"That can be arranged," Kat wrapped her arms around Mandy and hugged her. "I missed you." Then her hands slowly unbuttoned Mandy's shirt, and her face gently rubbed against Mandy's skin. Mandy fell back against the wall of the house. They were outside but the bushes hid them from nosy neighbors. Kat's mouth found her breast and nibbled at her through the silky material of Mandy's white bra. For a moment, Mandy thought of Vera Lee, now Patsy. There was still something tantalizing about her. What would it have been like, she wondered. Then she erased the thought. Nothing could be better than Kat's sweet love.

"I can tell you missed me," Mandy said with a throaty laugh.

Mandy took her shower and came into the bedroom where Kat had brought a tray of hummus and warm pita bread. The hummus had pools of olive oil, a smattering of chopped tomato and three plump olives on top.

"Yum," Mandy said, scooping up some of the hummus.

"Hey, you got a phone call this morning. It was weird. Someone said they were from the FBI and wanted to ask you some questions about a Vera Lee Gibbons or something like that. Do you know what that's about?"

Mandy felt the breath leave her body in a rush. She had mentioned her past to Kat, but not gone into a lot of detail. Mandy looked up at the ceiling. Maybe this trip had been a bad idea, but then again maybe the world turned of its own accord and you just did what it told you to do.

"Listen, I need to unpack and get some rest," Mandy said. Suddenly she wanted to be alone. She certainly didn't want Kat to get mixed up in this.

"Okay," Kat said, hurt. "I've got some prep work to do for the semester anyway."

Mandy went in her office and shut the door. She took Patsy's card out of her wallet and put it in the drawer of her computer desk. She'd have to contact her but probably shouldn't do it from here.

Chapter 19

The sky was Carolina Blue with tall green trees brushing up against it, as Patsy took Chelsea home. Tom had taken Kyle to a technology convention in Raleigh and they wouldn't be back till the next morning.

"Let's order pizza," Patsy said as they pulled into the driveway.

"Yes! And watch *Pirates of the Caribbean*?" Chelsea asked.

"Good idea."

"Mom, you know that lady who came with you to the skating rink?"

"Yeah?" Patsy said.

"Why did she tell you to be careful?" Chelsea asked. She had a worried look on her face as if she could sense that something was wrong.

"Just a saying, honey. She didn't mean anything by it," Patsy said. They were in the garage now. Patsy pushed the button to the garage door and it closed, darkening the room. Something bothered her. Something nudged at her consciousness like a dog nosing its way through a pile of trash, but she tried to ignore it. They got out of the car and went inside.

While Chelsea ran to see if any of her friends had emailed her, Patsy picked up the cat and went outside on the back deck. A hawk lazily swam the currents above. A couple of angry crows cawed. She scratched the cat's neck. Through the thicket of trees she could barely see her neighbors' yards, but she could easily smell the food grilling. What a different life she had than the one the State of Florida had intended for her, a life she would never have had if it weren't for a woman she once called Godfather.

She remembered how the two of them became friends, the way they would sit in the cosmetology room and Godfather would show her how to manicure her nails. Godfather had quiet, hooded eyes and wore red lipstick on her thick pillowy lips.

"You got lots of bacon in here, girl," she said, digging the meat out from under her cuticles. Godfather was the only one she'd talked to about her crimes, the only one who understood what it was like to kill, when that was the last thing you'd ever intended to do.

Then there was the evening they were sitting next to each other watching a softball game, and she had asked Godfather what would happen if she got another murder rap on her.

"Why? You thinking of killing someone, Killer?"

"Sylvia Black's supposed to be coming up here from jail next week, and she swears she's going to kill me for shooting her husband. I'm gonna have to get her first."

Godfather shook her head.

"No, you don't. You just turned eighteen, didn't you? Girl, they'll send you to old Sparky, don't you know? You're not a juvenile anymore."

"What am I gonna do?"

Godfather sighed. "You're gonna leave, that's what you're gonna do."

"How?"

"Walk out the door. I'ma steal you some street clothes and a pass. You have to figure out some way to get out of the dorm round 'bout five o'clock in the morning. The guard at the front gate on that shift is new. You'll say you're sick and you're clocking out early so you don't have to leave with the others."

"That'll never work."

"You better make it work. I know you can act. I've seen you. Now, you got to put it to the test."

And now Thelma Jackson, aka Godfather, was dead. Patsy buried her nose in the cat's fur.

Chelsea came out of the house and put her arms around her. "Mom, can I go to Carowinds for my birthday?"

Patsy ran her fingers through her daughter's hair.

"I guess so. Who do you want to take with you?"

"Leslie and Jessie."

"Okay. We'll call up their moms and arrange it."

"I can't believe I'm going to be eleven," Chelsea said gleefully as they went back inside the house. Patsy shut the door behind her and stood there transfixed, watching her daughter dance into the living room.

"I'm coming up so you better get this party started," Chelsea sang in her pseudo-Pink voice.

That night Patsy tossed and turned, tangling herself in the cotton sheets of her bed. She always loved to throw birthday parties for her children, but for some reason every time she tried to think about Chelsea's birthday, her head felt like someone had a pickaxe inside. Finally, she dozed. As she did she saw her father looming above her, holding something in his hand. She tried to run but it was as if she were paralyzed. She woke with a start, her heart beating hard. What happened to her, she wondered. What had he done?

Patsy drove down to Weddington.

"I want to find out what happened when I was eleven," Patsy told Rebecca. "I think that's what's wrong with me. See, my daughter is turning eleven next week. I think that's why I'm having this anxiety. Something must have happened to me when I was that age. But it's all a blank now."

Rebecca filled a glass with cool water and brought it to her. Patsy paced around the cluttered living room. Candles lined a bookshelf. Books sat on the floor and on small antique tables. A few abstract paintings dotted the walls and seemed incongruous with the rough look of the place.

"Did you do these paintings?" Patsy asked.

Rebecca nodded. "When the spirit moves me, I paint."

"They're really good."

"Thanks." She paused. "Shall we start?"

Patsy looked at her. She regretted being here. She didn't want to uncover whatever was under the blank canvases in her mind. But she had no choice. Chelsea's birthday was coming up, and just thinking about it paralyzed her.

Rebecca brought her down easily and gently into a soothing trance-like state and Patsy felt as if she were looking down at her life. She could see herself standing on the dock.

"Summers were long and lazy. Daddy would slip on his white parka and wear his deck shoes early in the morning and head for the marina. Mama would lay up in the bed until we crept in and snuggled under the covers with her. Mama would tickle us and laugh and tell us to get up and go fix her coffee. We did everything for her. Mama worked the lunch shift at the restaurant at the resort on Singer Island.

"We would play on the beach all day. Sometimes big lumps of jellyfish would be all over the beach. We loved to get a sharp stick and try to puncture them. Daddy sometimes brought home marlin, sometimes swordfish, sometimes tuna There was always the smell of fish in the house. Mama sat and drank beer and smoked her cigarettes and watched him cook the fish.

"During the day while Daddy was gone, sometimes Mama wouldn't go in to work. 'Vera Lee, you are gonna be one beautiful girl,' she'd say in her low voice. 'Men are gonna go ape-shit over you. Now, listen, don't you chase them. You let them come after you. And don't ever like one of 'em too much. If you do, he'll use you like a doormat, something to wipe his feet on.'

"When the phone would ring, Mama answered it. Her voice would change and she'd laugh and tease. I knew there was a man on the other end of the line, and I knew it wasn't Daddy because Mama never talked like that to Daddy. I can still see Mama wearing a white tank top and a pair of tight-fitting jean shorts, her small feet in a little pair of high-heeled sandals. Mama going out the door and saying, 'Vera Lee, take care of your sister. I'm gonna be back in a little while.' Mama getting in her black Mustang and driving away. Then we knew we'd have all afternoon to play. We'd make mustard sandwiches and head for the lighthouse. Mama volunteered there, and so we had a key. We could go all the way to the top by ourselves.

"When Mama came home, she'd be smiling. She'd take me and Fancy for ice cream. Mama had golden brown hair and blue eyes. She wore Charlie perfume and was always laughing about something. When Daddy would come home, he would give her money and she'd kiss him and tell him he was the best daddy. But I found it hard to breathe. What if he found out? What would he do?

"Then one day she was gone. 'She run off,' Daddy said."

"How old were you when that happened?"

"Nine."

"What did he do later that scared you? What happened?"

Patsy fell deeper into the past; it was like falling down a well. Everything was dark and she was spinning, spiraling down, down.

I am in my bedroom, it is dark—night time. The walls are an ugly green color. Dirty. They haven't been painted in years. I am fifteen years old, and I cannot get a job yet. Randall has been drinking. I hear him in the other room, yelling at Fancy about his dinner. Then I hear a crash. Dammit. Has he hurt her? I feel my heart pounding all the way down to my feet as I jump out of the bed. I slip and fall on the cheap little rug. I get up. I open the door. He better leave her alone. She's only eleven years old. I go into the living room. Fancy is whimpering, saying it's not her fault.

Randall wheels around. His hands are huge. He has a big red Frankenstein head. When he sees me, his eyes seem like they turn white.

"You whore! So you were laying up with some scumbag in my house? In my house?" He moves all jerky like he's spastic. He looks

around, swiveling his big head and sees a hammer. His hands close around the handle and he comes after me. Fancy is screaming, "No, Daddy. Don't."

"Get out of here, Fancy," I tell her. "Run."

Fancy runs into the bedroom and slams the door. I don't know where to turn, where to go. He grabs my hair and then my face hits the floor. I roll over and the hammer is coming down toward my head. I slide out of the way and the claw of the hammer lands two inches from me, right where my forehead had been. I kick up at him as hard I can, feel my foot hit him square in the ribs. He tumbles down. And then I am running and running. I am gone into the night, flying down the street past the other houses. I can't stop running. The night is like my mother's arms, carrying me away, far away.

Patsy became silent. The memory had turned dark.

"Patsy, I'm going to call you back to the present. Now, as hard as this is, I want you to remember this. We have to bring it up into the light so that you can release it. Can you do that?"

Patsy nodded. A tear trickled down her cheek.

"I left her," Patsy said after Rebecca brought her back to the comfortable chair by the window. "That's what haunted me all the years. I abandoned her. I didn't protect her. It wasn't what happened to me when I was eleven. It was her. She was only eleven years old—my baby sister."

Rebecca took Patsy's shaking hands.

"We're going to pray right now, asking the Holy Spirit within us to put forgiveness in your heart. I know it's hard to do. You need to forgive yourself. You were only a child. It wasn't your fault. Now it's time for you to release it, to forgive it, to forgive yourself for being small and helpless. And Patsy, even though your father did something that seems so terrible, I want you to realize that it was a cry for love. It was his own fear and self-hatred that made him do this to you. Because whatever we do to another person, we are really doing to ourselves."

*

As Patsy drove home that evening, she felt lighter than she had felt in years. So much of what she had done in her past was a foggy blur, but somehow the guilt remained even if the memory didn't. Remembering it was helping her, she hoped.

After the kids had gone to bed, Patsy went into the master bedroom. Tom lay in bed with the television on. He was watching some show on PBS, but something about the way he lay there in the blue flowered sheets with the pillow tucked under his arm made her think he was waiting for her. His lean body had started to thicken, but she found that the extra weight made him more attractive. He wanted to make love to her, she thought. She had been so closed off to him recently. It wasn't fair to him, and he was too gentle to insist.

"I'm really tired," she said.

Tom nodded his head. He seemed to expect such a response. They kissed quickly before turning out the lights. Soon Tom was breathing slowly and deeply. Patsy felt her heart thudding inside her chest. She would never be able to sleep. She had recovered memories from her childhood, but it was the later memories, the ones she hadn't quite repressed, that came unbidden to her tonight. Now, the doors to all her memories seemed to open and a scent wafted through them.

Lance Underwood wore that scent—impossible to describe except in terms of color—dark blue—and sound—a bass guitar, a train whistle, wind howling. She saw herself, wandering through the tiled rooms in Lance's mansion. His wife was out of town, and he had let her wear his wife's string bikini. She could see him through the French doors of the balcony, sitting in a chair cleaning one of his precious guns. She felt as if she were under some kind of spell and he was a sorcerer. He seemed to know everything about her. How did he know that she hated watermelon, but loved mango? How did he know the way she liked to be touched, just there along her scalp? She was naked to him. She obeyed him, slept with the men he told her to sleep with. He had wanted to know everything. She couldn't help herself, she told him. She told him about the beatings from her father, she told him about how her mama supposedly ran off with another man, she told him about the little sister she worried about.

"I'll take care of everything," he whispered. The memory was like an ice cube slowly sliding inside her veins.

A few hours later, Patsy got out of the bed quietly. Downstairs in the quiet kitchen, the cat rubbed against her leg. She dished out some cat food and looked at the bottle of vodka she kept in the cabinet for those rare occasions when she was all alone. She poured some in a small glass and sat on the couch in the near dark, waiting for morning to come.

By the time it did, she had managed to close all the open doors in her mind. She stepped into her realtor's outfit. She was Patsy Palmer, wife of Tom, mother of Kyle and Chelsea, daughter of Nan and Jim and she had never been anyone else.

Chapter 20

The plane touched down at the Maui airport. Tom squeezed Patsy's hand.

"Finally," Kyle said, standing up to get his carry-on from the overhead compartment. Chelsea leaned against Patsy's arm.

"I can't believe we're really here," Patsy said as the four of them slowly filed out with the rest of the passengers.

"Oh my God," Chelsea said when they left the gate area. "There are no walls at this airport. There are birds in here, Mom! Look."

"Oh my gosh, Chelsea—not God," Patsy said, a reflex from her Charlotte training. Nice children did not use the Lord's name in vain.

Tom rented a small Jeep and they all piled in, tired but excited.

Maui reminded her of Florida. The air was velvety and the color green nearly drowned her. They passed a pineapple farm and drove through a small shopping area. Enormous colorful flowers bloomed everywhere they looked.

"I couldn't have imagined any place so beautiful," Patsy said as they pulled into the resort—the banyan trees like welcoming hosts lining the front of the hotel.

Patsy pointed to one of the trees with its great root structure that dangled down from the branches to the ground.

"Those are from India," she told Chelsea. "Banyan means

merchant and that's where the merchants used to sell their goods in the shade of the banyan tree."

"Cool," Chelsea said.

They had two adjoining rooms. Tom and Kyle took one room. Patsy and Chelsea took the other. It was still daylight, and the kids wanted to swim immediately, so Patsy and Tom rested by the pool while Kyle and Chelsea swam and played like much younger kids. Patsy thought this might be Kyle's last chance to be a kid. In a couple of years he'd be going off to college. And Chelsea would be a teenager herself soon. She felt wistful as she realized they were growing up. What would she do without them to anchor her?

"You want a drink?" Tom asked.

"No," she answered and glanced at him. She never drank at home. Not with him at any rate. Did he think she would suddenly tie one on? People did strange things when they weren't in control of their faculties.

"Just asking. We are on vacation."

Sure, she thought. But some of us can never go on vacation.

The next day they took the Jeep for a drive around the island and stopped at some waterfalls to cool off and take pictures. That evening they went to a four-star restaurant. They sat outside under the stars. A beautiful Hawaiian waitress took their orders and walked away with a swish of her flowered dress.

"I can't believe the money we're spending on this trip," Patsy said, leaning into Tom.

"Hey, you only have one twentieth anniversary, right? That's something to celebrate. Not everybody can make it that long," Tom said.

"Has it only been twenty years? Feels like forty," Patsy teased. "You're right, honey. I'm not going to worry about the money."

"You can always sell another McMansion, Mom," Kyle said. "And when the last tree falls in Charlotte we'll put it in a museum."

"Yeah, yeah, and charge all the people a dollar just to see 'em. Give your mom a break, son," Tom said.

"That's right. I don't build the houses. I just sell them to people who need somewhere to live," Patsy said. Kyle was always complaining about the rampant development in Charlotte.

"I don't see why everybody needs to live in the same place," Kyle said.

Tom waved a fork in the air.

"Listen, I've got an idea. Kyle, why don't you and Chelsea take that sunrise trip up to the top of the volcano tomorrow with the tour. Mom and I will stay in the room and get some rest."

"Cool!" Chelsea said.

Kyle nodded nonchalantly but of course he was dying to do something without "the parentals."

"Tom, are you sure . . . ?" Patsy asked.

"Yeah, it's fine. They have a tour that goes from the resort, and I already checked with the concierge. The tour guide will keep an eye on the kids."

Patsy took a deep breath.

"I don't like it," she said. "What if they fall off?"

"Mom," Kyle rolled his eyes. "We are not idiots. At least, I'm not an idiot. I can go to the top of a volcano without jumping into it like I'm some sacrificial virgin."

Chelsea immediately joined in the argument.

Patsy looked over at Tom. He raised his eyebrows.

"We have to trust them once in a while, Patsy. Let's order some macadamia nut pie. I hear it's wonderful."

The next morning while it was still dark, Tom walked the kids to the lobby where they joined the tour group. Patsy waited in the dark hotel room and felt a hollowness inside. Why was she so afraid? She pulled the covers up around her neck. The air conditioner hummed as pictures of Chelsea falling headfirst from ten thousand feet and Kyle screaming as he tried to clutch her leg rotated through her mind. She shook her head. Stop this, she thought. Worrying doesn't change anything, Nan had told her. It only makes you crazy.

"God," she said aloud. "I'm giving Kyle and Chelsea over to you. Please take care of them and don't punish them for my sins." That was her biggest fear—that somehow her children would pay for the lives she had taken. Kids weren't something she thought about when she was out there doing drugs and running around with men like Trent and Lance. Then these children came along in all their innocence and she wondered what she could possibly have been thinking as she sat there with a gun in her hand and a straw stuck up her nose.

She could hear her own heart beating in her right ear. It was a strange sensation. The hotel room door opened. Tom undressed and crawled into bed with her.

"Alone at last in paradise," he whispered.

"Did you pay the tour guide extra to watch the kids?"

"As a matter of fact, I did give him a twenty. He said he won't let them out of his sight."

"You should have said he gets more if he brings them back alive."

"Stop worrying," Tom said. His legs rubbed against her, then she felt his warm hands on her skin, his breath on her neck and then his lips on her face. Suddenly, it felt as if jolts of electricity were dancing just under her skin. She turned her mouth toward his and a warmth engulfed her. She felt as if she were suddenly unmoored. How many times had she held back from him? Afraid, afraid to let her guard slip even with him, this man who had taken her in and made a life with her.

When Tom brought her to orgasm, she moaned deeply. All the chains dropped away from her. Everything loosened. She was momentarily free. And then she settled back into herself. She ran her hand across Tom's chest, wet with sweat. Sunlight glimmered around the curtain edges. The room took solid shape around her again.

"Tom, I'm sorry," she said.

"For what?" he asked. "Having sex with me?"

"Not about that," she said. "I'm sorry for not paying attention to you lately."

"Well, we've both been busy," he answered.

"Tom?" she asked.

"Hmmm?"

"I need to ask you something."

He yawned and stretched. "Go ahead."

"Will you always love me? No matter what?" she asked, leaning up on an elbow.

Tom turned his head toward her. "Why do you ask?"

"If there was something from before I met you . . . ?"

Tom gazed at the ceiling and put his hands behind his head. "I don't care about anything that happened that long ago. Why do you ask these things?" She could tell that he was annoyed with her. The sex had been wonderful, and for the first time in a long time, she hadn't withheld anything from him. That session with Rebecca had set something free inside her. But now she was needing something from him, something that she didn't dare come out and ask for.

"I just need to know. I mean, there are things I haven't told you."

"I've got just one question, have you ever cheated on me in twenty years?" he asked.

Patsy shook her head.

"I didn't think so. Listen, I love you, the woman I married—not whoever you used to be."

Patsy moved her head to his shoulder.

"That's enough, right?" he asked.

She stroked his chest and said, "Yes, that's enough." He was hers. He was her husband, her good husband, and she was damned lucky to have him. The diamond on her finger glittered in the tiny shaft of light that slipped under the curtains.

Chapter 21

Mandy sat in the front row of the house seats, watching as the three teenage boys began their improv. These three were her troublemakers, and she secretly liked them the most.

"See, we're going to buy some drawers," Gawain said, using his hands like he was P. Diddy. "We only got enough money for one pair. But they is some fly pants so we're gonna share 'em."

Mandy nodded, and the boys started. The other twelve kids were seated on the floor on the side of the stage. They needed to come up with at least four really good skits for the performance, and she was hopeful that the boys would come through. The premise, of course, was ridiculous, but as soon as they started she knew they had something special. Soon she was laughing uncontrollably and the kids who were watching howled as the three boys mimed switching the pair of pants to impress various girls they met.

There was a vibrancy and spontaneity with these kids that Mandy never found with adults and rarely found with the more privileged kids she worked with in other groups.

"That's terrific!" she said when the boys finished their skit. What set them apart was that they knew how to finish up the skit as well. There was genius inside them, but not much discipline. How could she convey to them the success that could be theirs if they would just do the work, acquire the professionalism involved to turn this talent into a way out of a dead-end life? Well, it was her job to nurture these kids and water this talent the way Kat did with that garden of hers.

At the end of the afternoon, they had decided on the four skits to develop for the performance at the end of the month.

"Remember we only have five more days, so I want you all here every day and on time," Mandy told them.

"Right, Ms. D," Gawain said with his big smile and sly eyes. Jesus, she loved him. She loved all of them.

"Bye, Ms. Mandy," Syreeta said, shyly.

"Bye, honey. See you Monday afternoon."

The kids strolled out. Mandy turned off the stage lights and then went to the front of the building and turned off the house lights. Being back with the kids had helped her forget about Godfather's murder, about Vera Lee aka Patsy, about the phone call. But underneath her forgetting there was still a flicker of fear. Who could possibly be looking for Vera Lee? She didn't think it was really the FBI. When she tried to call Patsy, she found out Patsy and her family were on vacation.

A thought crossed her mind. She could turn Vera Lee in to the police. If someone had killed Godfather to try to find Vera Lee, then they might come after her. The only problem was that Mandy was incapable of betraying another friend. She had betrayed Patsy Wofford by getting drunk and killing her in a stupid accident. She wouldn't do that again. Mandy realized that the "new Patsy" had helped alleviate her own guilt. Jim and Nan seemed to be happy. They had a lovely, successful daughter and they had grandchildren, too. It was so odd how that little Chelsea looked so much like the first Patsy, the real Patsy. Maybe there was such a thing as reincarnation after all.

Mandy locked the front doors of the theater and walked along the sidewalk to the driveway beside the building. It was an old building, a former warehouse, and the area around was not particularly populated. She followed the driveway, past the fire escape to the back of the building where her car was parked.

She dug her keys from her satchel and pushed the key button. The parking lights flashed, indicating the car was unlocked.

"Hey, lady. Can I ask you something?"

Mandy turned around and saw a balding man dressed in jeans and a torn t-shirt. His face was unshaven, and his smile was artificial. He had several tattoos, including something that looked like a cockroach on the back of his hand. He wanted money, no doubt about it. Mandy composed her face not to show annoyance. He couldn't help his circumstances.

"My car broke down, and I could use some money to get a cab. Do you think you could help me out?"

That was pretty lame, Mandy thought. He could use a few acting lessons from Gawain.

"Let me see what I've got," Mandy said. She felt a shiver of discomfort as she peered into her black satchel for her wallet. She leaned against the Nissan for support and saw her wallet in among the materials she had brought for the kids and reached in for it. At the moment her fingers wrapped around the leather billfold, the man was suddenly on her. It happened so quickly she could barely get a scream out before he wrapped an arm around her neck. His other arm pinned her against the car, and his body smashed against her. Pain, confusion and fear banged around inside her. In those few seconds she tried to figure out what to do, but he was choking her and all she felt was a desperate desire to breathe. She clawed at his arm.

"Hold her still, damn it," a woman's voice said.

With his legs, the man pushed harder against her. She felt his belt buckle in her back, his jagged breath against her cheek. He smelled like something sour. A hand pushed up her skirt.

My God, she thought, they're going to rape me. Then she felt a sharp jab in her butt.

"That should slow her down," the woman said. The grip around her neck loosened. She twisted around and tried to scream, but nothing came out. The man stood there with his face inches away from hers. She slowly slid down the car, the ground rising up to meet her, but he caught her in his arms. The only thing she had strength for was to push the little red button on her key alarm. The car began to honk frantically, but the man pulled the keys from her hand and hit the button. The honking stopped.

"Get her in the back seat," the woman said.

All she saw of the woman was a pair of white nurse's shoes.

Chapter 22

The waves had flattened out. Rodney waded into shore, his six-foot-three custom-made Bruce Jones board wedged under his arm. The water fell in droplets from his body, his hair and the board. Buddy rose from the shallow water where he had been lying and trotted alongside Rodney, stopping once to shake sand and water from his fur.

"You're a freakin' sand flea, Buddy," Rodney said, brushing the sand from his legs. The dog smiled happily. Every spoken word was a reason to wag as far as he was concerned.

Rodney stopped to slide into a pair of the cheapest possible flip-flops. Hard to find the really cheap ones anymore. Like everything else in the world, they got fancier and more expensive without being even the tiniest bit more useful.

The day before he'd been by the offices of the *Jupiter Pilot* and asked about a reporter named Michael McMillan. The receptionist had gawked at him and said, "Mac hasn't worked here in years, love. He's a mystery writer now. Got himself a condo overlooking the ocean in Palm Beach. Haven't you ever heard of him?"

"Well, now that you mention it, I did think his name was familiar," Rodney acknowledged. "Could you tell me how to get hold of him?"

"Sure. He loves hearing from fans. But don't call him before noon."

"Hard partier, huh?"

"Worse. He's an exercise fanatic. Spends his mornings in the gym or working out with his personal trainer."

Rodney grinned. A personal trainer. People were getting more ridiculous every time he turned around. The receptionist had given him McMillan's phone number in Palm Beach. It was now shortly after noon, so Rodney went back to the motel and gave him a call.

"A former cop? Listen, you aren't calling to give me shit about some fact I got wrong in my last book are you? I mean, it is fiction. You understand that, right?"

"Actually, I'm not calling up about any of your recent writing. I'm interested in an article you wrote back in 1976 about a girl named Vera Lee Gifford."

The writer was silent for a moment. Then he said, "Okay, tell you what. Meet me at three today at Panda's on Singer Island. We'll talk."

"The good bars are all gone," Mike McMillan said, sliding onto a wicker-backed stool at the outdoor bar. The man had short gray hair, a small neat mustache and the physique of a long-distance bicycle rider. Rodney figured McMillan was edging toward sixty, and fighting it every step of the way.

"Good bars?" Rodney asked, taking a swig from a Red Stripe. McMillan eyed the beer thirstily.

"That looks good. I shouldn't, but what the hell. I'll have one of those," McMillan called to the bartender. She cracked open a bottle and slid it to him.

"Here ya' go, Mac," she said.

McMillan shrugged and turned toward Rodney. "They know me here. This used to be an old dive where we journalists hung out. But you can't find those kinds of places anymore. It's all catering to the young and moronically rich now."

"I hear you're not hurting," Rodney said.

McMillan grimaced. "I wasn't. But a few bad investments and

wham, you're stringing for the *Miami Herald*. So what is it you wanted to know, Rodney?"

"I'm interested in the case of Vera Lee Gifford. Remember her?"

McMillan did remember her, or at least her case. He had sat through the entire trial, he told Rodney.

"I was there for half a day," Rodney said. "I had to testify as to her condition when we found her. Stoned out of her gourd. And then there was the little matter of the gun in the trunk."

"A Walther P38, right?" McMillan said. "One of those little James Bond guns. Now, what kind of dumb bastard lets that get away from him? That's a good gun. Of course, the police knew it wasn't a mob hit. You notice how when a hired killer does someone in, he always uses a really loud gun and does it when there's as many people around as possible. Twenty eye witnesses all telling a different story."

Rodney agreed that was a familiar tactic.

"I don't get what would send a kid like that over the edge," Rodney said. "Why'd she turn into a killer?"

"What do you mean? Kids kill all the time."

"Not girls. Not back then. It was unusual."

"Well, you know, Vera Lee had a rough childhood. Like they all do. Her mother, now she was something else."

"You knew her?"

"Sure. She waited tables at the resort. When her husband was off fishing . . ." McMillan shook his head.

"Did you . . . ?" Rodney asked.

"Oh, hell no. Mari Lee might have only been a waitress, but the men she fooled around with were wealthy sons of bitches. Lawyers, surgeons, guys like that. She didn't have time for some low-rent newspaper hack."

"Like mother, like daughter?" Rodney asked.

"What do you mean?"

"Well, Lance Underwood was a lawyer."

"Yeah, you're right. I never made the connection," McMillan said.

"Whatever happened to him?" Rodney wondered. "How did he die?"

"About ten years ago, he took out his boat for a little solitary cruise. The bad guys must have got him because when the coastguard found that boat, there was no one on it. He owed everyone south of Delray Beach money, I hear."

So Underwood was gone. Vera Lee had vanished. Who was left? Joan Spivey had mentioned a sister, a nurse. Rodney couldn't find any Giffords in the phone book in any of the small towns that dotted the coast. So he visited the oldest high school he could find in Jupiter Beach.

Yes, both Vera Lee and Fancy Lee had attended, he found out. Fancy Lee had gone on to nursing school in Miami.

"If you want to find her, she works about two miles down the road at the Palms Assisted Living Home," the secretary told him. "She kind of keeps to herself."

Rodney thanked the woman and drove to the Palms Assisted Living Home. He didn't know what he expected to learn from Vera Lee's sister. Surely, Vera Lee had not come back home for any visits. And if she had, her sister probably would not be inclined to share that information with him. But he was following his curiosity now, trying to see where it would lead.

About four little white-haired ladies watched him from their rocking chairs on the veranda. He smiled at them, and they all smiled back and said, "Hello."

"I'm looking for a nurse named Fancy Lee Gifford," he said.

"She doesn't go by Fancy Lee, mister," an old lady with a Boston accent said. "She's just Fancy. Plain Fancy." The other ladies thought that was especially witty and giggled.

"So she does work here?"

"She used to. I haven't seen her in a while, have you?" another said, turning to the first one who spoke.

"She's on a leave of absence," the first one said. "Told me she had things to take care of and might be gone for two or three weeks. Maybe more. I'd hate to lose her."

"Not me," a third one spoke up. "She stole my Demerol."

"No, she didn't."

"She sure did."

"Oh, you're always accusing someone of stealing something," a little red-haired lady entrapped behind a metal walker said. She frowned at Rodney and said, "Don't pay any attention to us. We're just a bunch of old birds."

Rodney checked inside. A receptionist sat at a desk in the lobby. In here, more old people sat and watched him curiously. Fancy Gifford had indeed taken a leave of absence, the receptionist told him. And no, she didn't have a home address for her. He could leave his name and number if he liked and when she returned she could contact him if she wanted to.

"Sure," he said, and handed the woman a card.

When he came back out on the porch, he noticed a man in his seventies watching him. The old man had a white beard, small black eyes and thick shoulders for an old man. He wore a captain's hat.

"Did you find out anything?" the lady in the walker asked, wavering in front of him.

"No, ma'am, I didn't find out where Miss Fancy Lee has gone," Rodney answered.

At that moment the man in the captain's hat began singing, "Merrily, Merrily, Verily, Fancily, life is but a dream." Then the man laughed and slapped his knee, looking at Rodney.

"Don't pay attention to the captain," the walker lady said. "His boat is still out to sea, if you know what I mean."

"Well, Buddy, I think we've hit a dead end," Rodney said, getting back into his truck. The dog licked his face. Maybe this whole thing had been a stupid idea. He didn't know what he'd do if he found Vera Lee Gifford anyway. He doubted she had anything to do with Thelma's murder. It was probably just as Chief

Carmichael said, the most obvious guy was the guy who done it. I bet he thinks OJ's innocent, too, Carmichael had quipped to Lanelle when he thought Rodney wasn't listening.

On the other hand, the department shrink would have said this was all his way of coping with Willie's death. Maybe so. Anyway, he'd done some good surfing. He'd head back home and let Vera Lee haunt someone else.

Chapter 23

As soon as he turned onto the street, he saw the silver Camry in his driveway. A herd of clouds passed across the sun and cast a pall over the flowerless azalea bushes.

"Damn, now who is that?" he asked Buddy. The dog seemed thrilled to have no answer.

He got out of his truck, unloaded his board from the back and found a woman sitting on the plastic folding chair on his porch. She looked up at him with a distraught expression. She had short dark hair; there was something delicate about her features. Her eyes had dark circles under them, and her clothing was rumpled.

"Detective Ellis?" she asked.

"Yes," he answered. "And you are?"

"Kat Lovatt." The woman stood up. She was not very tall, but her thin frame made her seem taller. Her nails weren't polished and she didn't wear make-up, so she probably didn't work as a professional. No, she looked more like an academic—intelligent, healthy, dressed in comfortable but not cheap clothes. He had spent a long time on the police force of a college town, so he knew the type.

"What can I do for you, Ms. Lovatt?" he asked as he slid the board into its rack on the porch.

"My friend is missing," she said, wringing her hands together. "My girlfriend."

Rodney picked up a towel that was lying on the wooden bench in the corner and wiped sand off his shoulders.

"I went to the police," she said. "But they said they can't really do anything without proof that there was foul play."

Rodney placed his hands on his hips and looked down at his gut. He needed to start lifting weights or something.

"So how do you know she didn't just run off for a few days to have some fun? Maybe she's gone to visit family. Maybe she's gone on a bender?"

"Mandy has been in AA for years. She has no reason to suddenly go off the deep end."

"It doesn't take much. You know what they say. Hey, you want some coffee? Come in. I'll make a pot."

He opened the door to the house, and Kat entered and sat at the wood table in the kitchen while he fixed a pot of coffee.

"Look, I think someone took her. It's not like her to just disappear. She's got a show coming up and she would never disappoint those kids. She's not like that."

"Show? What kids?"

"She directs plays for the Heartfelt Theater. It's a grant-based project that works with underprivileged and at-risk kids. She would not just not show up. She loves those kids, and she loves her work."

Rodney poured two cups of coffee and sat down across from her. Now, someone had been talking recently about a theater program for kids. Then he remembered his conversation with Lanelle about her nephew, Gawain.

"What's her name again?"

"Mandy. Actually, it's Amanda Danforth."

"You're pretty worried, aren't you?" he asked.

The woman nodded and looked down, tears trickling down her cheeks. Rodney had never been comfortable around gay men—Amy called it homophobia—but gay women were somehow different. He'd known a few over the years and always gotten along fine with them.

"Well, Ms. Lovatt, what makes you think I can help? How did

you even hear about me? I know no one from the department sent you to find me. I'm s'posed to be on vacation."

"You're pretty well known in Gainesville. I do read the papers. But also, I feel like I probably know more about you than other people. You see, I teach English at the university, and your daughter was one of my students."

"Oh," Rodney said and took a sip of coffee.

"Almost every paper she wrote in my composition class was about you or your work. You sounded like Superman. I mean, I know part of it was just ordinary 'father-worship'. But not all of it. You came across as not only really smart, but compassionate, too. I've kept up with Amy over the years, and I called her. She's the one who told me I could probably find you here."

Rodney shook his head. He noticed the woman's small hands. They were calloused, hard-working hands.

"You garden, Ms. Lovatt, or is it Dr. Lovatt?"

"It's Kat. Please call me Kat. Yes, I do garden. How did you know?"

"I'm a detective," he said with a wry grin. "Kat, I still don't know what makes you think there's been some sort of crime committed here."

She blinked up at him. Buddy came up, sniffed her and whined. He hated to see anyone in distress.

"Well, right before Mandy decided to go to this conference in Charlotte she was very upset about a murder she read about."

Rodney's ears pricked. "What murder?"

"This Thelma Jackson woman. See back in the late seventies, Mandy had been in a car accident and killed her best friend. She got sentenced to five years in prison. While she was in prison, she met this Thelma Jackson. She never mentioned her to me until she saw the article in the paper. Then she got so distracted. Later I saw the paper in the recycling bin and she had cut out that article. I asked her about it, and she said it was nothing. But I can tell you this, she had a couple of sleepless nights. Then when she came back from the conference she seemed okay."

"Do you know the name of the girl she killed in the car wreck?"

"Yes. Her name was Patsy Wofford. Mandy went to see Patsy's parents up in Charlotte while she was there for the conference. She needed some sort of closure."

Rodney nodded. Now it all came back—the dead girl in the band uniform, her friend unconscious, the blood, the crumpled Chevelle, Willie's heavy breath beside him as they waited for the paramedics and stood looking helplessly at these two young lives ruined. The girls were from a high-school marching band out in the county and had been playing for a big game with Bucholz. Seems they went to a party after the game. He shook his head.

"Let's go take a look around your place. I'm not promising anything. She's probably just gone off to see some friends or something. But I'll come look around, see what I can find."

Kat put the key in the lock of the brick ranch house's front door and turned it.

"That's really weird," she said. "The door wasn't locked."

"Maybe I should go in first," Rodney said.

Kat stepped back and let him pass.

He walked into the house, quietly. He passed through the foyer into the living room and glanced around. There were book shelves against the walls, a table by the window, some paintings that looked like they were Mexican or Haitian, and a coffee table strewn with magazines.

Rodney stood quietly for a moment. It was an old trick of his. He had found he could somehow sense when a house was empty. Like Willie, he knew that sometimes his intuition was his most reliable partner. It had even told him when Cheryl was gone. He had walked in the house and gone directly to the closet and opened it. Nothing but a few wire hangers looking forlorn and ghostly. Women tend not to leave their clothes behind. He followed the hall around the L-shape of the house, stuck his head in the kitchen and checked out a bedroom which had been made into a study. He heard Kat behind him. He passed a bathroom and a media room. At the end of the hall he entered the master bedroom. Large floor-to-ceiling windows were covered by mini-blinds, but plenty of light leaked in. He saw a king-size bed and a chest of drawers. The drawers were all opened, clothes spilling out on the floor. He opened the closet door. It was full of clothes.

"This her closet?" Rodney asked.

"Yes," Kat answered. "Rodney, someone's been in here. Those drawers weren't open when I left."

"Okay, look around and see what's missing," he said. "Maybe she just came back for a change of clothes. Check the bathroom and see if her toothbrush is there."

Kat went into the little bathroom and came out.

"Her toothbrush is not missing," she said.

"She get email here?" Rodney asked.

Kat nodded. "On the computer in the study. Come on."

Kat turned on the computer and clicked into Mandy's email. It was possible that Mandy could have another email address, one that Kat didn't know about. This account wasn't even covered by a password. Kat just clicked on the Outlook icon and Mandy's account was opened.

"See, it's just theater-related stuff. And here's something about the conference she went to in Charlotte."

"When was that?"

"A couple weeks ago. She went up there for this conference, and then she stopped at the house of Patsy's parents. She wanted to ask for their forgiveness."

"Well, they're good folks," Rodney said.

"How did you know that?" Kat asked.

"My partner and I were the first ones at the scene of the accident. I hadn't been on the force too long. We had to drive up to Alachua and break the news to them. Kind of made a lasting impression," Rodney said and scratched his cheek. He could remember exactly how it felt, pulling into the driveway of their small farmhouse out in the country, the way the gravel sounded under the tires of the car and the headlights panned across a weeping willow in the front yard, the way the mother collapsed to her knees at the news of her child's death.

"When Mandy came back from Charlotte, something was different. Something happened. I don't know. It's like she was happy, but she was worried, too. She said that Patsy's parents were wonderful to her. They completely forgave her, I guess. She seemed to feel good about that, but something else bothered her. I didn't know what it was. But something strange happened here while she was gone."

"What?"

"Well, I got a phone call from the FBI. This man said they were investigating a prison escape and wanted to talk to Mandy. I told Mandy about it, but as far as I know they never called back."

"A prison escape? But Mandy has been out how many years?"

"About twenty-three, I think."

"Did he say who the escapee was?"

"They did, but I don't remember it."

"Shit," Rodney said, sitting down. He wasn't the kind of person to get goose bumps, but he looked on his arms and saw the hairs standing on end. "Kat, where would Mandy keep really old papers. Really old letters or anything from her years in prison?"

Kat looked up and bit her lip as she thought about it.

"She's got a couple of boxes of old stuff in the garage."

"Show me."

They brought the boxes into the house and sat down at the table. It took about an hour of sorting through the boxes, but finally Rodney hit pay dirt. There was a Polaroid picture of Mandy Danforth and Vera Lee Gifford in their prison dresses. Vera Lee's smile was wide and friendly. Mandy looked shy but happy.

"Good Lord," Rodney muttered, Mandy must be the friend that the dope fiend Joan Spivey down at Lowell had mentioned.

"Who is that?" Kat asked.

"That is Vera Lee Gifford, a triple murderer back when that was a big deal. She was sixteen when she committed those murders or else she surely would have gotten the death penalty."

Kat sighed and looked at the picture.

"She's gorgeous."

"Yeah, she was something else. Funny. I was in on this case, too. Never dreamed they'd be somehow connected." He paused. Kat was still staring at the picture, transfixed. "Kat, do you think that Mandy and Vera Lee were girlfriends?"

Kat shook her head. "I don't think so. Mandy tried to repress her sexuality until she was in college."

Rodney pondered the situation. Mandy and Vera Lee were friends. Mandy also knew Thelma Jackson, who must have been in prison the same time as both of them. Thelma was dead. Mandy was missing. And Vera Lee had disappeared in 1978.

"Have you got a road atlas?" Rodney asked Kat.

"Yeah, somewhere."

"Would you find it for me?"

Kat went into another room and came back a few minutes later with a large Rand McNally's Road Atlas. Rodney turned to the page with the Carolinas on it.

"Isn't this interesting?" he muttered to himself.

"What?"

"Charlotte, North Carolina is right near Rock Hill, South Carolina. Looks like they're less than an hour apart. Let me use your phone, okay?"

Kat handed him a cordless phone and he dialed a number. He got Lanelle's voicemail: "This is Detective Lanelle Thompson. I'm out of the office right now. If this is an emergency, please hang up and call 911. Otherwise push zero and you'll be connected to the operator."

Rodney dialed another number.

"Grimes, it's Rodney Ellis. Let me talk to Al."

"Dude! Surf's up. Are the waves gnarly or what?"

"You're a riot, Grimes. But don't quit your day job. Leno isn't retiring any time soon. Where's Al?"

"Not here. But you can call him on his cell phone."

Rodney hated cell phones. You couldn't hear anything on them, and some asshole was always standing in line at the supermarket, yakking it up. He dialed the number.

"Al, here."

"Hey, man. It's me, Rodney."

"What's up, man? Can't stand a little R and R? Or are you just missing me too much?"

"You and Grimes should form a team, you know. You're just about the funniest jokers on the planet. Listen, I'm at a young lady's house. She's a college prof. Seems her friend has gone missing, and no one at the department is willing to take a look into it. You know anything about it? The missing woman is Mandy Danforth."

"Look, Hot Rod, the chick's a dyke. She probably ran off with another girl and they're off rubbing uglies or whatever it is they do at the No-tell Motel."

"You know, it's guys like you give the rest of us a bad name," Rodney said.

"Well, I'm sorry about that. It's just that I got a stack of cases on my desk and so does every other swingin' johnson in the department, and a missing lesbo just ain't a top priority. I got child molesters and mother-rapers on the loose. Man, it's an ugly world. Or have you forgotten?"

"I haven't forgotten."

"Rod, if you're not on duty, you better leave it alone. An off-duty cop is just another word for civilian, you know."

Rodney hung up the phone. Kat had left the room. He went into the family room and saw that the sliding glass door was open. Outside Kat was pulling up some weeds. A few rose bushes lined the wall of the house, and there were wild flowers in the middle of the yard, surrounded by long green blades of monkey grass.

"Nice garden," he said. A bush of big blue flowers bloomed by the gate. He saw them everywhere and still didn't know what they were called. "What are these?"

"Those are hydrangeas," she said, coming to stand next to him. "They're very common, but so pretty."

Kat was a gentle person and he felt comfortable with her. She was sincere in her belief that something had happened to Mandy. And she was no dummy.

She had a drawn, worried look around her mouth.

"Look, I'm going to check with the FBI and see what's up with this so-called investigation of Vera Lee Gifford," Rodney told her. "Then I think I'll take a drive up to North Carolina and visit Patsy's folks. I've got sort of a personal interest in seeing how they're doing anyway."

Tears began to trickle down Kat's pink cheeks. The father in Rodney came out. He couldn't help himself. He pulled her into his arms and let her weep.

Chapter 24

Rodney had called every number he could find with the FBI, and on the few instances when he got an actual human on the line, he learned that no one was investigating Vera Lee Gifford. One woman was so scornful it liked to burn his ears. "We have terrorists wanting to blow up buildings in every major city in America. We could not possibly care one iota less about some fugitive woman from a Florida prison."

Rodney thanked the woman, got in his car and drove to the theater where Mandy worked. Kat told him that Mandy always parked in the back in the space by the wall. He decided to look around. It was empty now. A couple of cardinals flitted about in a dogwood tree. He wondered that they could even fly in this humidity. He methodically paced over the tar. He found an empty drink can, a few cigarette butts, a dead half-decomposed bird, a quarter and two pennies. He stopped a few feet away from Mandy's parking spot and leaned over. A small white square with red letters. He picked it up. It was an unopened alcohol pad—something a nurse or doctor might use. He slipped it into his pocket. He found nothing else of any interest, so he figured it was time to go to Charlotte.

About seven hours later he knocked on the door of a condominium in Charlotte, North Carolina. A woman in her sixties answered.

She looked at him with bright eyes, silver hair and a warm smile. She had an attractive elfin look.

"Hi there," she said with a question in her voice. "Is there something I can do for you?"

"Yes, ma'am. My name's Rodney Ellis. I'm a detective from Gainesville, Florida. I'm here to find out if you happen to know what has happened to a woman from Gainesville who's gone missing."

The woman tilted her head.

"Who?" she asked.

"Amanda Danforth—Mandy," he said. "She's been missing since Friday evening about six or so."

"Oh my word," the woman said. "Jim! Jim! Come here. My husband's outside with his bell peppers. Come on in. I'm sure he'll want to talk to you."

Rodney followed the woman inside. The living room was bright and airy with a pale green carpet and an oval mirror over the sofa that captured his tired expression. Damn, he sure looked his age, and it was always a bit of a shock.

"Have a seat, please," she said and indicated the sofa. "Would you like some iced tea?"

"Yes, ma'am," he said, glancing toward the patio. "I'd love some."

"Call me Nan, please. What did you say your name was?"

"Rodney Ellis."

"Well, that's a name I'd never forget," a man's voice broke in. Rodney wheeled around and saw a nearly bald man carrying a basket of large bell peppers, coming through the sliding glass door. He was tall and lean-looking, and Rodney suddenly had a very clear image of him twenty-eight years earlier. Even then his hair was thinning. He had one of those long faces that make some men look particularly wise and gentle.

"What do you mean, Jim?" Nan asked as she brought Rodney his glass of tea.

"Rodney Ellis was the name of the police officer who came to us the night Patsy died. He was the one who found her."

Nan turned toward Rodney with wide eyes, her mouth shaped in a silent "Oh."

"I didn't recognize you," she said, and he heard a deep pain submerged below her words. She collected herself quickly and turned to her husband, "Dear, he says Mandy Danforth has gone missing."

Jim raised his eyebrows and placed the basket of peppers on the table.

"That's right," Rodney explained. "I'm actually off-duty, doing a private investigation for Mandy's roommate on my own time." He didn't want them calling the department.

"So what's happened to Mandy?" Jim wanted to know.

"Mandy didn't come home from work on Friday evening. Her roommate hasn't seen her and is worried sick. Apparently, this is unlike Mandy. But there's not enough to warrant a full-blown police investigation."

"Mandy was just up here to see us last month. It was the first time we'd seen her since the night she picked up Patsy to go to the game. We didn't go to her trial, you know. We just couldn't bear it. Her parents were good friends of ours. They went to our church until the accident. Then after Mandy went to prison, they moved to Lake City."

"Well, that's why I came by. You see, her roommate mentioned she had been up here to see you. And I wondered if anything happened or if you noticed anything about her or she said something . . . I need to rule out the possibility that someone abducted her. Maybe she met someone while she was up here."

"Well, anything we can do to help you find her, we will. Have a seat, please," Jim said.

Rodney sat down on the plush sofa. Nan sat down in an easy chair, and Jim stood by the mantle of a gas fireplace.

"She said she came to make amends for Patsy's death. Poor girl. She never really got over it."

"How did she seem to you? Happy? Worried about anything?"

"No, not really worried," Nan said, thoughtfully. "She

seemed settled, I suppose. She's doing wonderful things with those kids down there."

Jim nodded his head.

"She seemed as if she was finally coming to some sense of peace with her life," he interjected. "I think that's why she came to see us. I got the sense she was happy with her life though she didn't talk about it a lot—I mean, her personal life."

"How long did she stay?" Rodney asked, taking a sip of the iced tea. It was sweet tea like he had grown up drinking in Palatka.

"Just a couple of hours. She had been to some sort of academic conference at the university and she stopped here, had lunch, talked with us a while. Then she left to go back home."

"She didn't mention meeting anyone unusual at the conference?"

"Oh, no. She said she felt it was a complete success."

"Well, maybe I'll go talk to the folks at the university."

Rodney stood and looked around the room. It was tastefully done with pictures of the grandkids on the wall. He leaned toward one of the pictures on the wall—it was of a little red-haired girl on a pair of ice skates, her arms outstretched and one leg behind her.

"This isn't Patsy, is it?" he asked.

"No, that's her daughter Chelsea," Nan answered.

"Her daughter?" Rodney asked surprised.

"Well, not that Patsy. . ." Nan began.

"We adopted another daughter," Jim said. "Her name is also Patsy."

Rodney looked at the picture again. "Wow. That's quite a coincidence."

"She's blessed us with two wonderful grandchildren. Kyle is an honor student, and Chelsea is a champion skater."

"The next Tonya Kwan, right?" Rodney said.

"Michelle Kwan," the older man corrected.

"She is pretty good," Nan said. "We go to all her competitions."

"Well, they're beautiful kids. How lucky you were to get a . . . a second chance. When did you adopt this girl, their mother?" Rodney pasted a look of benign curiosity on his face—a look that for some reason got people to tell him just about anything.

"About a year after Patsy's death. She showed up at our church one Sunday morning. She was homeless and scared. Our hearts went out to her. And well, we still had an extra bedroom and all of Patsy's clothes and things. We knew the Lord brought her to us so we could help her."

Rodney felt like a dog that smells steak in the air but hasn't zeroed in on it yet. He let his eyes rove across the room for other pictures. There it was—smaller than the ones on the wall. It was a five by seven in a gold frame on top of a bookshelf. He walked over to it and picked it up. The kids were younger by about three years, he'd guess. The mom wore pearls. The dad had on a suit. Quite the well-heeled couple of yuppies.

"Is this her? She looks a bit like your daughter looked. Same color hair, same build even."

"Yes, we thought so, too, when we first met her," Jim said, moving next to him and gazing at the picture.

"But she must have been older than a normal adoptive child. I mean, she looks like she's in her thirties here."

"She was about Patsy's age," Jim said. "I know it's not typical, but she needed a home and a family, and we had one to give. We would have taken her in even if we hadn't lost Patsy."

"Was she orphaned?"

"Yes," Jim answered abruptly. Rodney sensed this was a subject that wasn't discussed much. They might not know a lot about this woman before she came into their lives—and fate had handed her a gift. But naturally law-abiding people—not to mention proud grandparents—were averse to telling you to mind your own business. Because, of course, they had nothing to hide.

"You know what can happen to girls if they're out on the streets," Nan said. "We couldn't bear to see anything bad happen to her."

"So you took her in and . . . supported her?" Rodney asked, careful to be non-judgmental in his inflection. The slightest vocal variation could clam people up.

"Well, till she got out of college," Nan smiled. "Now she doesn't need any help from us. In fact, she gave Jim and me a cruise to the Caribbean for Christmas last year. It was fabulous."

Nan reached her arm around her husband's waist and looked up at him wistfully. It was obvious they were very much in love. Not easy to maintain after the loss of a child.

"I guess her husband must be rich," Rodney conjectured.

"No, he isn't. He works for the community college," Jim said. "That women's lib stuff really paid off for some of these guys. She makes probably twice as much as he does."

"She sells real estate," Nan confirmed.

"A realtor? No kidding. What's her last name?" Rodney asked.

"Palmer. Patsy Palmer."

Rodney looked again at the picture. A very pretty Patsy Palmer if you liked the type. Interesting timing on her part to arrive in their lives a year after Patsy Wofford died and just around the time that Vera Lee Gifford escaped from the Florida Correctional Institution for Women. She didn't exactly look the way he remembered Vera Lee, but that had been a long time ago and people change.

"Well, you must be proud," he said, setting the picture back in its place.

"We are," Jim said as if daring anyone to deny it. "Very proud."

Rodney took his keys from his pocket and jangled them.

"Too bad Mandy didn't get a chance to meet her."

Jim and Nan exchanged a look. People were really pretty easy to read—people who weren't used to deception. And what Nan's slightly pursed lips and Jim's softly hooded eyes told him was that they had the slightest notion that they shouldn't be talking to him, but they couldn't think of why not and they were just too used to telling the truth to do anything else.

"Oh, Patsy joined us for lunch that day. We wanted Mandy to meet her. Please don't think that we just found someone to replace our daughter," Nan said. Ah, there was the source of their misgivings, he realized—a sense of guilt that they had found some measure of happiness in spite of the awful tragedy. "There's a hole in our lives, in our hearts, that no one else could ever fill. But being able to help this young woman and to have grandchildren to call our own, it gave us a reason to keep living. Honestly, before she came to us, I thought Jim was going to die. And God knows, I prayed that I would." Her lips fell downward at the corners and tears gathered in her eyes. Jim squeezed her and said, "Shhh."

"Well, thank you so much for talking to me," Rodney said. "I don't suppose I could talk to Patsy? Maybe she noticed something?"

"Oh, they're in Hawaii. Their first real family vacation in a couple of years. Tom and Patsy's twentieth wedding anniversary. Quite a feat these days."

"Yes," Rodney agreed, and even now he thought of the empty closet and the note that Cheryl left: "I can't do this anymore. Not even for another second." And she was gone.

"I hope you find Mandy," Jim said, offering his hand. Rodney shook Jim's hand and then Nan suddenly reached out and hugged him.

"We'll be praying for her and for you," she whispered. "We'll call you if we think of anything."

"Thank you," Rodney said.

It wasn't too difficult to find out where Patsy Palmer worked or even where she lived. At the public library he simply went on-line and found Patsy Palmer by Googling Charlotte Real Estate. Tom Palmer was easy, too. He worked as a Career Counselor for the local community college. There was even a picture of him. Rodney shook his head. How could this woman possibly be Vera Lee Gifford? How could she possibly have buried herself so well, so completely transformed herself? Of course, when you're facing life in prison that could be a powerful incentive not to screw up, but screwing up seemed to come naturally to most criminals.

It was late in the day by the time he found out as much as he could. He wasn't even sure this would yield any information about the Danforth woman, but he had to follow every lead. He called Patsy's office and got her voice mail.

"Hi, you've reached the voice mail of Patsy Palmer. I'll be on vacation until August tenth, so if you need to speak to someone immediately, please dial zero for the operator. In the meantime, Aloha!"

Good God, she sounded just wholesome as all get out. Well, August tenth was in two days. Maybe he should hang around. On the other hand that would be two days wasted. He went back to his room at the Clarion. It was late in the day and he wondered how he could find out anything now. He hated to sit around. Then it came to him—the most obvious answer.

He started dialing.

"Twyla, it's Rodney Ellis," he said.

After he talked to Twyla, he called his house to check his messages. Maybe Amy had called. What a mess he had made with this whole wedding thing. Maybe this wasn't about Cheryl at all. Maybe the idea of his little girl getting married just scared the hell out of him. There was one message. It wasn't from Amy.

"Mr. Ellis, this is Rick. Um, I don't know how to say this, but there's been an accident. Buddy got hit by a car. He's not dead but he got hurt real bad. I took him to the emergency vet. Anyway, I'm real sorry about this. I had him over at the park and well, when I threw the frisbee for him it kind of flew over the street. Like I said, I'm really, really sorr . . ." the message clicked off.

"Damn," Rodney muttered. He got in his car and drove straight through the night.

Chapter 25

At the Indian restaurant on Maui, Patsy watched Kyle eat his paneer. She still marveled at how he had grown.

"How did this happen?" she turned to Tom and asked, nodding toward Kyle.

Tom looked up from his plate and studied Kyle for a minute.

"Fairies did it. They came and kidnapped our baby boy and put this big hulking man in his place." Tom dipped his nan into the tikka masala sauce.

"Jeez, you guys," Kyle said. But Patsy thought there was a flicker of pride in his eyes. Hell, at sixteen she'd certainly thought she was a woman. She had strapped on a pair of high heels and pranced into the Black Orchid like she owned the place. They didn't even ask for ID. Chuck had hired her as a dancer on the spot. She could remember everything about that place—the smell, the sticky floors, the little dark tables scattered about, the private booths for the highest-paying customers, customers like attorney-at-law Lance Underwood. She remembered the look on his face when he first saw her. Half of his mouth curved into a smile, and his eyes narrowed. "My, my," he had said. "I hope they broke the mold when they made you, beautiful. Because you are positively lethal."

Patsy lowered the fork to her plate and stared down at the white tablecloth. She had forgotten those words—the exact words he had said when he met her. "Positively lethal." That bastard. He was the one who had made her lethal.

"What's wrong?" Tom asked, solicitously. "Isn't it good?"

She turned to look at him. The gentle eyes, the soft sweet mouth, lips pink and full. Why was she remembering Lance again? He was out of her life. He was dead.

"I love you," she said.

"Well, darlin', I love you, too," he answered with an exaggerated drawl.

"Please!" Chelsea said, and rolled her eyes. "Can you save this for some other time?"

Patsy turned and stuck her tongue out at Chelsea. "You're just jealous."

"I am not."

"Chelsea," Kyle said in a syrupy voice. "I love you."

"Oh, bite it," she responded.

"You've been watching way too much Bart Simpson, young lady," Tom said. His voice had shifted just slightly but the disapproval was unmistakable. Patsy admired the way he could do that. When her voice changed, it went dark and scared the hell out of the kids. She sounded almost like her father with his belt tapping against his leg. Tom's admonishments were so much gentler and yet still effective.

"Sorry," Chelsea said.

After dinner they went back to the resort and walked down to the pool. The kids had to have one more swim.

"I'm gonna have a beer," Tom said to Patsy. "Want anything?"

"You know what? I think I'll have one of those pina coladas," she said.

"Really?"

"Really. We are on vacation, right? Now that your conference is over, anyway." Tom had been required to go to a few meetings and seminars, but it was worth it, since it paid for at least his airline ticket.

"Yes. And a pina colada is *de rigueur* for any tropical paradise," Tom said with a smile. She didn't know what *de rigueur* meant, but she got the gist. Living with Tom had improved her vocabulary immensely. He was such a bookworm. Her body remembered their private morning in bed without the kids the other day and a warmth glowed inside her. She had to stop worrying. She had to stop thinking that it could all come crashing down. No one had ever suspected a thing. And Mandy would never tell.

The cool, frothy drink was delicious.

Patsy kissed Tom goodnight at the door which adjoined their rooms. Chelsea was already in her pajamas, sitting on bed watching television.

"Goodnight, Daddy," she called to him and turned her attention back to the TV. Kyle was in Tom's room with a chessboard set up in front of him.

"I thought I'd let him beat me in a game before bed," Tom told Patsy. "Keeps me humble."

"Goodnight, Kyle," Patsy said and blew him a kiss before shutting the door. She went into the bathroom to brush her teeth. They had figured out long ago that family vacations went smoother if the kids didn't share a room. The drink had made her feel good. A little light-headed, different—like she had just stepped out of a pressurized room. It's okay to relax, she told herself. When she came back into the room, Chelsea was already fast asleep.

Patsy crawled into her bed and turned out the light.

Chapter 26

When Rodney got home from Charlotte, he called the emergency vet but they said there was nothing they could tell him except that Buddy was stable and that he would have to wait for more information till the morning when Dr. Chevalier arrived. He had this image of Maurice Chevalier singing "Thank heaven for leetle girls" as he operated on poor Buddy. Rodney slept for a few hours, awoke groggy and stupid, washed his face, changed clothes and then drove to the emergency vet office.

When he got there, the grogginess had worn off and his state of panic returned. He would like to wring Rick's neck. How could he be so reckless as to throw a frisbee into the street? He barged through the door and strode to the desk where a young woman looked at him brightly.

"I'm here about my dog, Buddy. He got hit by a car and brought here last night."

"Oh, yes. What a shame."

"What do you mean, 'what a shame'? Is he okay?"

"Um, I don't know. You'll have to talk to the doctor . . ."

Just then a woman's voice interrupted.

"I'm Katherine Chevalier. I took care of Buddy last night."

Rodney wheeled around.

"Is he okay?" he asked.

"Well, he will be okay. He broke a leg and cracked a couple ribs. He's going to need to take it really easy for a while. But he'll be fine. You want to come see him? I've got the technician bringing him to the examination room."

"Yeah, sure," Rodney said. He felt humbled by his relief and gratitude. Then he took a look at Buddy's vet. Dr. Chevalier had dark curly hair, clear green eyes and a curvaceous figure. For a fleeting second he forgot all about Buddy. What are you doing, dude? he asked himself. You don't need to be checking out the doc, you need to find out what happened to your Buddy.

Buddy lay on the metal table with his head between his front paws. His tail thumped the table when Rodney walked in and he grinned a doggy-grin. Rodney put his hands on either side of the dog's face and lowered his lips to the dog's forehead. Then he placed his cheek on his Buddy's head.

"What the hell were you doing, Buddy?" he asked. "You know better than to run out in front of a car."

The vet leaned against the table and gently scratched Buddy's ear. Rodney noticed there wasn't a wedding ring on her hand. This is ridiculous, he thought.

"He knows now," she said.

"I don't know how to thank you, Dr. Chevalier," he said.

"You can call me Katherine," she said with a smile. "I only make my students call me Doctor."

"Oh, you teach? What do you teach?"

"Nuclear physics."

"Really?"

She laughed. "No. I teach for the vet school."

"Oh, of course. Sorry. I drove all night from Charlotte. I'm a little out of it. I'm working on a case up there." What a dumb shit, he thought.

"A case?"

"I'm a detective. Except I'm supposed to be on vacation. Guess I'm a workaholic. Anyway, I'm doing some missing person work. That's how Buddy wound up in the hands of that knuckle-headed college kid."

"Well, don't worry. Buddy is going to be fine. But I want to keep him here for about a week for observation just to make sure his ribs heal. Would that be okay?"

"Sure, fine. Can I just spend a few minutes with him?"

"Of course. I've got some other patients to check up on this morning anyway," she said. Her dark hair swished as she exited the room.

Chapter 27

Kyle had been demanding to go snorkeling the whole trip. They were scheduled to leave to go back to Charlotte the next morning at seven-forty.

"You all can go," Patsy said as they were eating the room-service breakfast. "I'm going to stay here and shop."

But Kyle and Chelsea were adamant that she come along. Tom gave her a funny look.

"Why wouldn't you want to go, honey?" he asked.

"I don't like boats," she said. "I've always been afraid of water. You know that."

"But you were okay when we went to the Outer Banks," Chelsea said. "Remember when you came to the beach with us?"

"Yes, but I stayed on land if you remember. This is different," Patsy said adamantly.

"Look," Tom said. "Are you going to live in fear all your life?"

Patsy shook her head. Tom was right. She had no idea why she didn't want to go. When she was little she had gone on her father Randall's boat all the time. He had a seasonal charter fishing business and she could remember going on trips out into the gulf stream, sometimes as far away as Bimini. But something bad had happened to her mother out on a boat. You are not your mother, she told herself. Her mind was stronger than this.

"All right. I'll go. But we're taking the short trip." She donned her flowered one-piece and checked the polish on her toenails. She was applying a quick coat of red passion to her nails when the phone rang.

"Get that for me, Chelsea, honey," she said.

"Mom, you need to hurry. We're leaving in fifteen minutes to go to the boat," Kyle said.

"Hi Grandma," Chelsea said in surprise. "Yeah, sure, Mom's here."

"Shit," Patsy said. "I hope everything's okay."

"Don't cuss, Mom," Chelsea whispered.

"Hi," Patsy said.

"Patsy, honey, I don't want to bother you on your vacation, but I thought I should let you know. A policeman came by. Oh wait, Jim says he's some kind of detective." Patsy felt adrenaline flood her bloodstream. "He came by and said that Mandy had disappeared. We were just wondering if she might have said anything to you while the two of you were together that might help them find her."

"No," Patsy stammered. "She didn't say anything to me except, you know, small talk."

"Okay then. Jim said we should call you and ask. Listen, don't you worry about it. She's probably just off visiting friends and forgot to tell anyone."

The snorkeling trip was torture. Patsy felt pitched by the waves. The wide open space gave her a bizarre sense of claustrophobia. The worst part was that she couldn't stop worrying about Mandy. What had happened to her? Kyle and Tom and Chelsea immediately took to the water, snorkeling on the reefs while Patsy sat aboard the boat. The sun beat on her like a mallet. She stared down into the blue water. One time Sylvia Black, her face bright red like a Big Boy tomato, stormed into the dressing room at the club and slapped her across the face and told her not to get near her husband. Sylvia's eyes narrowed and her voice was low and ugly. "Stay away, slut, or I'll shoot you a new asshole." Patsy remembered the whispers, the threats, other inmates taunting her, saying Sylvia Black, who'd gotten busted for various extortion schemes after Lorenzo met his untimely demise, was going to stick a shank in her back. Messages flew fast between the Broward County Jail and the prison until she found out that Sylvia Black had been sentenced and was on her way to the prison. That was when she knew she had to escape somehow. Now, in this pristine life she'd been living, people like Sylvia didn't even exist.

As she stared at the water, it seemed as if she saw someone just below the surface. Was that Mandy's face? She felt a rising panic choke her. A head suddenly burst up through the water. Patsy screamed.

"Hi, Mom," Chelsea said with a grin.

"Oh, my God. You startled me," Patsy said. Chelsea dove back under the water and Patsy moved away from the edge of the boat. She would close her eyes and pretend that she was back home in her office. She tried to imagine real-estate deals. She hated to be away. That life gave her security. People knew her as Patsy Palmer. They knew her as a mother and a real-estate agent. Without the constant reminders, she felt her identity slipping, dropping from her fingertips. She needed her house, her work, her routine. Otherwise time seemed to do a dance and she might forget who she was.

Finally, the snorkeling trip was over.

"That wasn't too bad, was it?" Tom asked as they got off the boat at the marina.

"No, it was fine," Patsy said, hiding her eyes behind her sunglasses and hoisting a flowered beach bag over her shoulder.

"You look green, Mom," Kyle observed.

Patsy shrugged. "Maybe I'm a little seasick."

Her picture-perfect life was shattering, and there was nothing she could do.

Chapter 28

Rodney sat at the Java Hut drinking a latte.

"What happened to plain, regular coffee?" he asked Twyla.

"Well, it's boring," she answered. "But it was so exciting to get your call yesterday. I stayed in the office till about eleven, researching your questions. And this morning I made a few calls and found out even more."

"So, let me have it, baby," Rodney said, leaning forward.

"Okay, this is what I was able to dig up about Vera Lee Gifford. Born in 1959, she's an Aries, by the way."

"That's useful," he said, sarcastically.

"Well, that means she's a fire sign. Volatile, but also clever. Can be extremely generous—but ferocious when someone she loves is in danger."

"All right, Twyla. Tell me something I can use. Please?"

"Okay, she grew up on Jupiter Inlet. Her father ran a charter fishing boat and did construction work. Her mother disappeared when she was nine years old. At around fifteen or sixteen she left home and moved in with Trent Lewis, a marijuana cultivator. She was working as a dancer at a club in Fort Lauderdale until Trent got busted for possession of twelve pounds of pot."

Rodney knew most of this. He remembered his one night at the Black Orchid well, but thought he wouldn't share that with Twyla.

"At this point, Vera Lee is suddenly on her own. So she hires Lance Underwood to represent her boyfriend. But then inexplicably she goes on a killing spree. She guns down two men—the man who manages the club where she's a dancer and the bouncer. She uses a gun, stolen from Lance Underwood's collection. Now, looking over the transcripts of the trial there's an interesting piece of information. It turns out Underwood owed $80,000 to the manager of the club. Vera Lee's PD tried to make an issue out of this but he didn't try too hard."

"Those lawyers—always protecting their own," Rodney said, shaking his head.

Twyla's eyes flickered up at him.

"Bastards," she whispered.

Rodney laughed. He hadn't known that Twyla had a sense of humor. "Careful, my daughter's one of them now."

"It's okay. We'll let her slide."

"What about the third murder charge?"

"Lois Underwood. Lance Underwood's wife. The prosecution alleged that Vera Lee was a jealous psycho and killed the wife in the belief that Lance would then marry her. Lance's testimony was pretty damning. I guess the jury bought it."

"I was at part of the trial, and I remember a lot of this except the part about the $80,000. You know, I felt in my gut that Underwood was dirty," Rodney said. "I couldn't figure out why he didn't get any charges in this whole thing. It just didn't make sense that she would kill another woman over someone like Lance Underwood."

"Maybe she thought Lance would share the life insurance policy with her," Twyla said.

"Life insurance?"

"Back then a million bucks was a lot of money, so I hear," Twyla responded and tapped her fingers on the table. "The society pages of the *Sentinel* are full of him the next year—going to this function and that, always with a different rich babe on his arm. I'm not sure where he is now."

"I know. Some writer down in Jupiter told me that Underwood is MIA. He disappeared from his boat about ten years ago, but apparently the body was never found. By the way, he was bankrupt at the time."

"So Lance Underwood is dead?" Twyla said.

"It looks like it. No one has seen him since. I think if someone is working with Vera Lee Gifford it's probably her old flame, Trent Lewis. Twyla, do me a favor, check with North Carolina and South Carolina records. See if they turn up anything, especially anything recent, on Trent Lewis."

"Okay," she said. "I can get on it as soon as I get back in the office."

"Good. I need to get with Lanelle too and find out if she's gotten Terrence Moore to confess. Somehow I doubt it."

"Okay, Rodney," Twyla said and grinned.

Rodney sipped his coffee and pondered his next move. Should he tell any of this information to Carmichael or just ask for another week's vacation? He was sure he was owed more than two weeks, considering it had been five years since he'd taken any at all.

Chapter 29

The day after they got back from Hawaii, Patsy dropped Kyle off at driver's ed and Chelsea at the ice rink, then drove to Jim and Nan's condo in a daze. She hadn't slept the entire night. Her esophagus felt as if it was twisted in a knot somewhere about the middle of her chest. Her hands felt weak. She pulled into the guest parking space and fumbled for the car door handle. She'd held it together in front of the kids but now she felt as if the earth were rocking below her feet. The trees bent a little too low, the air felt too thick to breathe. She knocked on the door. Nan answered it.

"Hey, sweetie," Nan said. "Come in. You don't look so good. Are you okay?"

Patsy stepped inside and followed her into the living room. Jim was up already, watching the golf channel.

"Jim, turn that off. Patsy's upset," Nan said. Jim pushed up the recliner and clicked the television off.

"Patsy, sit down, sweetheart. What's wrong?" Jim asked.

"It's Mandy," she sobbed. Her shoulders shook as she sank onto the sofa. "I just can't believe what happened to her."

Nan came back in with two glasses of tea.

"Here, drink some tea. I know. It's terrible, isn't it?"

Patsy felt tears on her face. Her nose was running. She couldn't breathe. She picked up a cushion from the couch and held it over her face. She had taught herself not to cry when she was about five years old, and here she was, weeping and she could not stop.

Nan sat down beside her. "Listen, Patsy. I know it's frightening. But I wonder that you're this upset. I've never seen you like this."

Everything inside Patsy was cracking, breaking apart. She was like some iceberg breaking into pieces. She had to talk to someone, someone who would help her figure out what to do. These two people had been with her, had supported her and cared for her all these years. They loved her as if she really were their daughter.

Jim put an arm around her.

"Patsy, talk to us. We need to know what's going on." His voice was so kind. He was so much the father she had always wanted. And she knew she would tell them now as much as she could. It wasn't fair to them, but perhaps they would understand.

"Oh, God," she moaned. "Oh, God. This is my fault."

"How on earth can this be your fault?"

"I knew her," Patsy said. "I knew her before. I'm sorry I lied to you."

She felt both of them watching her. They were waiting, had been waiting patiently all these years. They had to have known something was strange, the way she appeared in their lives a year after their daughter was killed.

"I met Mandy before I met you. I met her in prison. She's why I came to you. Mandy was my best friend, the best friend I ever had. She told me about Patsy, about you, and when I met you, I tricked you into taking me in. I'm so sorry. I just wanted a family like you had, and I thought with your daughter gone, maybe you'd take me in if I looked like her and took her name. And you did. God, you believed me."

Jim took a deep breath. He was silent for a moment. Patsy was afraid she had just destroyed the very thing that had once saved her. He gazed into her eyes and finally said, "Honey, we took you in because you were a girl in trouble. We didn't know what your trouble was, but we knew God brought you into our lives for a reason."

"He's right," Nan said. "I never thought of you as a replacement for Patsy. No one could ever replace her. Just like no one could ever replace you. We love you for you. We always have. We always will."

"No, you won't," Patsy said. "You won't love me when you know the truth about me."

"Try us," Nan said.

"I can't." She had hurt them enough, she thought. She couldn't tell them that she was a murderer, a stupid girl who had recklessly taken lives and now a woman who had been living a lie. Nan folded her hands on her lap. Patsy sat in the wreckage of her grief and stared at her adopted mother.

"It won't do any good, Mom. Everything's falling apart."

"That doesn't matter. We're here for you."

"I just have to carry on. Chelsea's birthday is Wednesday and I'm taking her and her friends to Carowinds for the day. I can't fall apart. I can't let her down, don't you understand?"

Patsy's mind was racing. She couldn't seem to focus, but she couldn't allow herself to break down. What would Tom say if he found out the truth? Why hadn't she told him in the beginning? Then she realized how foolish that thought was. He would leave her surely and take the kids. Maybe that would be the best thing. But without them she'd die. She had to try to keep her world afloat. She had to hold on. She had to pull it together if it took everything she had.

"Listen, I'll be okay," she whispered and hugged Nan. She stood up and kissed Jim on the cheek. "I'm sorry if I've hurt you."

"We're tougher than you might think," Jim said. His eyes reminded her that he had lived through the ultimate sorrow—the death of a child—and survived.

Patsy smiled gratefully and wiped the tears away. She had

made it this far. She had to be strong. But how was she going to hang on? And was it Sylvia Black who had Mandy?

It was night time when Patsy went to see Rebecca again. Tom had taken the kids to a movie. Patsy sat down in her customary chair. The place looked different at night. Outside the darkness seemed to lurk at the window.

Rebecca made cups of chamomile tea but Patsy didn't find it soothing. She felt nervous and on edge.

"Is there anything special you want to try to cover tonight?" Rebecca asked.

"I don't know. I'm scared. A friend of mine is missing. Another woman I knew was killed recently. It feels as if my life is coming to pieces."

"Okay," Rebecca said calmly. "Let's go to another time that your life was falling to pieces, okay?"

"Okay."

"See, we repeat these patterns in our lives. At some point you can choose to stop repeating them. So, let's do a little relaxation and I'm going to take you down to that familiar place. Then you can choose what area of your life you need to revisit."

I am in the lighthouse, playing with my sister. She is up in the lamphouse and I am hiding in one of the niches in the wall of the tower. Fancy calls to me, there's a car outside. Stay hidden, I tell her.

The door to the lighthouse opens. I hear voices—a woman and a man.

"We could have gone to my hotel room, you know," the man's voice says.

"But isn't this more exciting?" the woman says and giggles. It is my mother's voice. We'd get in trouble if she finds out we're here. I don't make a sound.

"Let's go upstairs," mama says.

"No," the man says. "I want you right here, right now. Where's the blanket. Lie down on it."

There's some shuffling and then other sounds as if the man is hurting her, but I know he isn't. After a while the sounds stop. Now there is talking, but it's low and soft. A bright square of light appears on the wall and disappears when they open the door to leave. I run up the steps to the window and see a big white car driving away.

"Where are you now?"

At home. It's time for dinner. Daddy comes back. He smells like fish. He's been on his boat. He loves his boat. Its name is "Daddy's Baby." Mama has made hamburgers. I put ketchup and mustard on the table. Fancy takes out a bag of chips. Mama is singing "I can't get no satisfaction." She's laughing and dancing. She says to Daddy in her laughing voice, "Do you love me?" And he says, "More than anything in the world."

"What do you think about that?"

Love is a dangerous thing.

Chapter 30

Mandy felt as if she were swaddled in a thick sticky web. She lay on the floor of a small room, duct tape around her hands and feet. But she could not have gone anywhere even without the duct tape. Her muscles were like jelly, and her head felt like it had swelled to three times its normal size. It felt like a boulder was blocking her breath, as if the air had turned to granite.

A plump woman with eyes that looked hard as concrete gazed down at her and said, "Just a little bit of Ativan and Haldol, honey. It won't kill you."

Mandy had no idea where she was or how long she'd been out.

The woman sat on the floor by an old phonograph. A record was playing. Mandy recognized the song—Led Zeppelin's "Stairway to Heaven." She didn't want to go to heaven. She wanted to stay here on earth where she had finally found love and some measure of happiness.

"We've got an old friend in common," the woman said, tapping her feet together. "Miss Vera Lee Gifford. Remember her? I do. Daddy always liked her best. Sure, he beat her sometimes but he just didn't want her to turn into some kind of slut like Momma. Momma was bad. So was Vera Lee."

In a whisper, Mandy asked, "Did you kill Thelma?"

"What?" The woman turned down the record player.

"Thelma?"

"Oh, her. Couldn't be helped. She was going to go to her parole officer. Didn't care that we knew all about that preacher she was havin' sex with. Besides, I thought it would send a message to Vera Lee. Once she heard about the hammer, she'd know her turn was coming. Trent said she used to wake up screaming about that hammer. Of course then the paper didn't even mention how she died. But that's okay. You delivered our message for us, didn't you?"

Mandy heard the creak of footsteps on the floor.

"We got what we need," the man said. "I been doing some checking and I swear the woman on this card has got to be Vera Lee. You gonna dispose of this one?" He kicked Mandy's foot.

"No," the woman said. "We might need her later. We'll take her to Daddy's. Did you get rid of the car?"

"It's in a thousand parts by now."

"Good. Bring my bag. She's due for another shot."

Mandy could smell them close to her. An image of Kat in her garden came to her mind. The thought soothed her and broke her heart at the same time.

"How about me? I'm due for something myself."

"Aren't you always?"

"This is nasty work. I don't like killing people."

"I don't *like* it either! What do you think I am, some kind of sociopath? You're the one who wanted to find Vera Lee so bad. Give me that needle."

Mandy felt a sharp prick in her hip. The fog in her head thickened and she dreamed she was in prison again. But this time Thelma and Vera Lee were playing Russian Roulette. She begged them to stop, but they kept passing the gun back and forth, and placing the muzzle to their temples, pulling the trigger, click.

Chapter 31

The three girls piled into the car and Patsy threw a couple of bottles of sunscreen into her large flowered tote bag. Chelsea sat with her two friends, Leslie and Jessica, in the back seat of the Honda.

"Mom, play Avril Lavigne, okay?" Chelsea said.

Patsy obediently pushed the button for the CD player, and all three girls began singing about the skater boy. Patsy was glad they were distracted. She couldn't stop thinking about Mandy. Gainesville was a college town, full of drifters and transients like Chapel Hill had been. What if someone had killed her? Who would ever know? She felt a tightness in her throat and a creeping sensation on her skin. Patsy knew she needed to be here in this moment, taking care of her children, relishing this second chance she had at life. And yet the uneasiness lurked in her mind. Had Mandy somehow paid for mistakes that Patsy had made—in another life?

Theme parks weren't exactly Patsy's idea of entertainment, but Chelsea and her friends loved roller coasters. They walked down into the "County Fair" section and the girls raced to ride Top Gun, a roller coaster that would turn them upside down and hurtle them through the air at a million miles an hour. They would stand in line for forty-five minutes just to get three minutes, maybe less, of screaming thrills.

Patsy sat near the exits and waited patiently. Before she left Rebecca's, Rebecca had given her an assignment. "Don't judge anything or anyone for a day or two. See if you can do it. It will help you be less judgmental of yourself once you learn how to stop judging others."

Carowinds was a lousy place to try, but it was a good place to take your mind off your worries, temporarily. The hordes of enormous, sweaty people trudging back and forth in their unthinkable outfits boggled Patsy's mind. She watched the women pushing their baby strollers and smoking their cigarettes, their legs tattooed and their brood of children swarming around them. During the girls' expedition to the Thunder Road ride, Patsy sat on a concrete slab that was part-bench part-wall with other people waiting. A few feet from her sat a grandmother, dutifully puffing on a cigarette, with a toddler in a stroller.

Then another woman—short with tattoos on her arms, frizzy red hair and a too-tight halter top—walked by, folds of her belly showing. She looked exactly like the kind of women she saw in prison. Rebecca was right. Best not to be judgmental. "There but for the grace of a woman named Godfather, go I," Patsy said to herself.

The best place she found to sit was at a red concrete table underneath a Coca-Cola umbrella by the water park. The girls had donned their swimming suits and shorts and were playing in the "wet zone." But the table was just far enough away that the screams of people who were suddenly doused by an overhead water spray and the grinding of various rides was buffered and she was out of the way of the stream of people. She pulled a book from her purse—a paperback novel that the librarian had recommended.

She was well into the fourth chapter when a shadow fell over the book. Patsy noticed a man's legs. He was wearing black Nikes and a pair of jeans. He seemed to be wanting something. She looked into the face. He was balding. He hadn't shaved in a day or so.

"Excuse me, do you have a light?" he asked. A tattoo of a cockroach adorned the back of his hand.

The skin around the eyes was wrinkled and weathered. But

those eyes were the same pond-water green she remembered from almost thirty years ago when he first walked up to her after school and asked her if she wanted to go for a ride in his GTO.

She shook her head, no. She would not let her voice give her away again.

"Don't smoke, huh?" he asked.

She shook her head again.

"Do I know you? You look familiar."

Again, she just shook her head. He shrugged and smiled, "Oh well. I guess I'm mistaken." He winked at her and turned away. Patsy went into the nearby restroom and threw up. Then, shaking, she went to find the girls.

"Chelsea, honey, I'm sorry. I think I've gotten some kind of flu. I just got sick in the bathroom. Would it be okay if we went home now, and I brought you and the girls back another day?"

Chelsea looked at her friends, and Patsy looked around at the crowd to see if he was still there, watching her. She was suddenly terrified, but she couldn't let it show. She didn't see him anywhere.

"Sure," one of Chelsea's friends said, a gleam in her eye at the thought of another day at the theme park. "We can come back next week."

Chelsea smiled. Chelsea was the sort of kid who wanted to make everyone happy. She took her mother's hand. "I'm sorry you're sick," she said.

"I'll be okay, but maybe we should go now," Patsy said. The smell of chlorinated water and sunscreen was overwhelming. The crowds of screaming kids. She needed to get out now.

That night he called her at the house. She was in her office when the phone rang. She knew before she picked it up that it would be him.

"I miss you, baby," he said. "I've thought about you every single day for all these years."

Bullshit, she thought, but she didn't say anything.

"I know it's you, darlin'. Don't try to pretend it ain't."

"I'm sorry. We're not interested," she said and quickly hung up the phone. How had he found her? What did this have to do with Mandy? She unplugged the phone and turned on the computer. The least she could do was try to find something about Sylvia. Maybe she and Trent were in on this together. She couldn't believe that Trent would kill Godfather or snatch Mandy. He had to have someone behind him, someone manipulating him. She went to Google, typed in Florida Department of Corrections. Home page. That was easy enough. She found a link to a list of offenders. She clicked on the link and typed in Sylvia Black. Damn, there she was—a big color photo. She had aged considerably. Her strawberry blond hair was now yellow and sticking out around her head, her cheeks sagged and her lips were so pale you could hardly call them lips. Her release date was Nov. 11, 2020. What had she done this time? Instead of feeling happy to see her old nemesis locked away, Patsy felt strangely sad. Something—compassion, perhaps?—settled inside her. They were all so messed up. Sylvia and Trent and all those other lost souls. Even Randall. Randall. No, that didn't make sense. Trent and her father wouldn't be working together. Then she remembered how sweet, how utterly charming Randall could be when he wanted something. She took a couple of Tylenol PMs and slept downstairs with the television on.

Tom came down the next morning and kissed her.

"Babe, what's going on? You didn't come to bed all night."

"Sorry," she said. "I had a restless night."

She showered and dressed and got the kids to their respective activities and went into the office. She didn't want to be at the house. But of course, he knew where she worked. The phone was ringing when she entered.

"Patsy Palmer," she said in a tight voice.

"Vera Lee, baby, I'm not trying to give you a hard time. But if you hang up on me, I will make a phone call. I got one of them phone cards and it would be real simple to call the Florida

Department of Corrections and give them your forwarding address."

Patsy's heart thumped hard; she could see the pulse jumping in her wrists. She didn't say anything but she didn't hang up either.

"That's better. Hell, you'd probably be worth a movie on one of them women's channels. You know what I can't believe is how you ran around on me with my own lawyer. Did you really love him so much you had to kill his wife?"

There was nothing she could say. If she said anything at all, it would destroy her, but she was probably dead already. She felt her life slipping away—Tom, Kyle and Chelsea, her red-brick house, the friends she'd made at work. It was all fading away.

"You aren't gonna say nothing to me? After all these years?"

"What do you want?" she finally asked.

"Okay. That's a good question. I want you, Vera Lee, but since it's obvious you don't want me, I'll settle for something else."

She held her breath, waiting. How much, she wondered.

"Come to the Main Library. Lots of guys like me hang out in the library. We're a very literary group. We get together and talk about Oprah's latest choice. Now, Oprah's got great taste, baby. That woman knows a good book. Why don't you join us for our little book club, say around seven o'clock tonight. I'll be upstairs in the non-fiction section because, sweetheart, this here is the real deal. Bye, bye."

Patsy slowly put the phone back down. What a fool she had been. She should have left. She shouldn't have put her family in this jeopardy. What if he hurt one of them? And what had he done with Mandy? Had he tortured her to get her to talk? Then she remembered that she had given Mandy her card. How stupid could she have possibly been?

Chapter 32

Rodney had three women to see today and, as usual, none of them were dates.

He drove to the Krispy Kreme and saw that Lanelle was already there.

"Now, why did you want to meet here?" Lanelle asked. "I gain about ten pounds just smelling these donuts."

"Aw, come on. You know you love 'em," Rodney said, sitting down with a cup of coffee and two fresh glazed donuts.

"Well, I do. That doesn't mean they're good for me."

"Listen, Lanelle. I got to talk to you about this missing woman, Mandy Danforth. Something is definitely twisted about her disappearance."

"Yes, I know. Gawain and the other kids are just devastated," Lanelle said. "She doesn't seem like the type who would just walk out on everything. Then again, you never know, do you?"

"Well, I think Vera Lee Gifford, the woman who escaped from FCI back in '78, is somehow involved."

"That seems like a stretch, Rodney. Do you have any proof?"

Rodney shook his head. "No. I think she's hiding out in Charlotte, North Carolina. I'm heading back there today, and I'm going to check her out. If this woman is Vera Lee, I'll let you know."

"What do you want me to do?"

"Check out Vera Lee's family. She's got a sister lives down in Jupiter. Try to find out anything you can about her. And whatever happened to her old man?"

"Okay. That's the least I can do. You let me know about this Vera Lee woman as soon as you know something, you hear?" Lanelle gulped the last of her coffee. "I've got to get to work. A high school kid shot himself last night. Looks like he was trying to impress his friends, and killed himself in the process."

Lanelle patted Rodney's shoulder and then remembered something.

"Oh, Twyla gave me something for you," she said.

"What's this?" Rodney asked.

"It's a ray gun, Rodney," Lanelle said. "What do you think."

"I think it's a cell phone. She's giving me a cell phone?"

"Yeah, I think she wants you to call her. Anyway, I hope you and Nancy Drew find your escaped killer. Let me know if there's some connection with the Jackson case. Terrence Moore is sticking to his story."

The next stop was on campus. He walked across the green lawn toward the English Department. Big trees draped with Spanish moss shaded the green. The red-brick buildings looked stately. He felt a buzzing in his pocket and remembered the cell phone. He answered it.

"Ellis here," he said. It was Twyla with information about Trent. Seems he had a lead foot and the South Carolina Highway Patrol had noticed it. You'd think he'd be smart enough to use fake ID.

"Thanks, Twyla," he said. He clicked the phone shut and stuck it back in his pocket.

He remembered walking across the green with Amy when she was a senior in high school, and she told him she wanted to be a lawyer. She was so excited about coming to college. She couldn't stop smiling and talking excitedly. Of course, Cheryl hadn't been here for that, but now Cheryl would be at the wedding. He hadn't seen her in all these years, and he was afraid what he might do. You weren't supposed to smack the snot out of a woman, but he couldn't think of anyone who deserved it more.

He walked down the hallway and found Dr. Kat Lovatt's office toward the end. Her door was open.

"Hi," he said, peeking in. Bookshelves lined the wall. A curtained window looked out on the green. She had a tiffany lamp on the desk and piles of paper everywhere.

"Hi," she answered and beckoned him inside. He sat down in a wooden armchair. "I'm trying to get prepared for the semester. I've got a brand new course I'm teaching. It's hard to concentrate with Mandy missing, but on the other hand, I was going crazy just staying at home."

"No, it's better to keep busy," Rodney agreed. "I take it you haven't heard anything?"

Kat shook her head. Her eyebrows furrowed and lips trembled. She pulled them inward. "Have you found anything?"

"I'm not sure," Rodney answered. "I may have found her friend from prison. I'm going back up there today. And my research assistant has learned that Trent Lewis, Vera Lee's old boyfriend, got a ticket for speeding in Columbia, South Carolina. That's just a couple hours south of Charlotte, so I'm thinking I might find him up there, too. Maybe they can lead me to Mandy."

"She's still alive, Rodney," Kat said, leaning her elbows on her knees. "I know it. I can feel it."

Rodney didn't say anything in response. Then he asked, "Did she ever, ever talk to you about her years in prison? Did she ever mention Vera Lee?"

Kat leaned back and thought. "Well, not by name. But she did say that she got interested in acting in prison. She said she thought that people could practice new identities through acting. So someone who had done really bad things could put on the persona of a good person and then by changing their externals they could eventually change internally as well. I know it sounds crazy but she believed that."

Rodney shook his head. "I'm not sure people can change who

they are. Rot is rot." But he wasn't thinking about people in prison. He was thinking about his ex-wife, Cheryl Ellis.

The last stop was at the emergency vet's office. It was just before lunchtime. The technician brought Buddy into the examination room again. This time Buddy was so excited he tried to jump up, but Rodney immediately commanded him to stay down. Buddy looked chagrined. He had no idea what he had done wrong. Rodney knelt down and nuzzled him.

"It's not your fault, Buddy, but you can't be jumping up till your ribs are healed, dude."

Dr. Chevalier walked in a few moments later, holding Buddy's chart.

Rodney stood up and smiled at her. But for some reason she looked pale and distracted.

"What's wrong?" he asked. "Isn't he getting better?"

The veterinarian put a hand on his arm, reassuringly. "Buddy is coming along great. He'll be ready to go home in a few days."

"Oh, that's good," Rodney said. He glanced at the woman's face. She turned away from him and seemed to brush something from her cheek.

"Katherine?" he asked, remembering she had told him to call her by her first name. She took a sharp breath.

"I'm so sorry. This is so unprofessional. I thought I was fine."

"What is it?" he asked.

She turned to face him. Her eyes were wet, but she tried to laugh it off.

"You know. I've been a vet for about fifteen years, but still sometimes when I have to put an animal down, it gets to me. I just put an old black lab down this morning. The whole family was there and they were so broken-hearted. It was like they were losing a child. I thought I was fine, but seeing Buddy must have triggered something. I'm really sorry. I'm supposed to be . . ."

"Hush," Rodney said. "It's okay for you to have feelings. I've been a cop for almost thirty years, and it still hurts when someone's child or sister or brother gets killed." She looked into his eyes. A moment of understanding passed between them.

He would never know what prompted him to say what he did next: "Listen, isn't it almost time for your lunch break? How about you let me take you to lunch?"

Her mouth opened slightly in surprise, and she looked down as she thought about it.

"I brought something for lunch today," she said and then she grinned. "But who wants an old brown bag lunch? I'd love to go out."

Chapter 33

Patsy drove uptown and took the interior beltway to College Street. Tom and she had joined the board of a non-profit organization to aid the homeless a year earlier and the meetings were always held in the conference room at the library, so she knew it well. What an idea that had been, that somehow doing something good for the less fortunate might wipe out some of her debt. It would never end. The guilt would just pile up like interest on a credit card. For a second she wondered if it had been worth it, living with this constant fear. If she'd stayed in prison, she wouldn't have to worry about anything except for someone possibly stealing her shampoo. But then she thought of her children. She remembered Kyle as a little boy, snuggling into her arms, clutching his stuffed Big Bird. She thought of Chelsea as a baby, nursing at her breast. She would never have had those experiences, never have known what it felt like to truly love another person. She had known hate and fear, but never unconditional love. And so she had to face Trent Lewis. She had to find out what he wanted and see if she could buy some time.

She pulled into a space by the library, crossed the street and walked along the columned walkway. Literary sayings were posted on the square pillars. Usually she read them, but not today.

The library was a haunt of homeless people. A rail-thin black man sat outside on the steps, staring at the sidewalk. A grizzled white man leaned against the wall. Patsy strode past them quickly. Her heart was going like an oil derrick, pump, pump, pump. She had a sick feeling in her stomach.

The library was beautiful and rather austere inside. She loved the place, but tonight she felt only dread as she walked past the large circulation desk and the racks of popular fiction.

She took the elevator to the second floor. It was six-fifty-five. She glanced around nervously and headed toward the non-fiction section. Bestsellers were displayed on shelves. She passed them and slowly began to walk past the stacks. Where was he? What if it was a trap? She should have told Tom. If they arrested her now, what would happen to the kids? How could they stand to see her on television or read about her in the papers? They would be stared at and laughed at by their school friends. But she saw no cops. She turned around and suddenly bumped into a man. She looked down and saw the cockroach tattoo.

"Hi, baby," Trent said. "Long time no see."

She looked into his eyes. When he was nineteen and she was fifteen, she thought he was the cutest guy in the world. Now, he was weather-beaten and scary looking—not ugly, but devoid of something he'd once had, a heart maybe? She felt a shiver of revulsion and pity at the same time. This is what his life had come to. But for some reason, the fear dissipated. She had never been afraid of Trent. He never hurt her the whole time they were together. Compared to Randall, he was Peace Corps material.

"Let's sit down," she said. They found a table at the far end of the hall and sat. "Trent, I want to know if you had anything to do with Mandy Danforth's disappearance."

He looked down at his hand and self-consciously covered the cockroach tattoo.

"I looked her up and I asked her about you," he said. "She told me where you were, but she said she was scared you might hurt her. Said she was going to lie low for a while—something about going to visit Daddy's. That's all I know. I didn't do nothing to her, Vera Lee. You know me better than that."

Patsy winced at hearing her old name. Over the years in the real-estate business, she had come to be able to read a liar, but Trent was practiced in the art of deception and she couldn't pick up on any cues. Would Mandy really be afraid of her? That was probably a lie. But it was difficult, impossible, to imagine Trent hurting someone.

"Trent, tell me what you want," she said.

"I want you," he said. "All these years I've dreamed about you. I love you. I promise I'll do whatever you want me to. You don't know what prison was like for me. All for a stinking marijuana charge. I was doing that for us, baby. And I paid with years of my life."

"Trent, I was just a kid. You can't lay this on me. You made your choices and I made mine. I'm not going to leave my husband and kids for you. Now, tell me what it is you really want," she whispered.

"Okay. That's how you're gonna be. Give me a hundred thousand dollars and I'll be out of your life. I know you ain't no millionaire, but I figure you can get up enough to make it worth the years of my life that were ruined, trying to make a life for you."

The sum was a big one. Patsy's hands curled into fists. She started calculating quickly. If she sold the house in Ballantyne, depleted the savings account and cut her expenses, she could probably manage. She could even get a loan because her credit was pretty good. But she knew that even after she paid him, that wouldn't be enough. Eventually he would want more. But maybe it would buy her some time. And maybe she'd sell more big-ticket houses. All she had to do was get her kids raised. Then if she needed to run again, she could. She'd have to leave Tom and Nan and Jim. No, she couldn't follow that train of thought any farther. She would break down.

"I can get the money. It will probably take a couple weeks, but . . . I'm not giving you a cent till I know that Mandy is alive and safe."

Trent shook his head. He was thinking about it.

"Okay. Here's the deal," he said. "You bring me ten grand tomorrow as a show of good faith. I'll get Mandy to contact you. Then we'll settle up the rest."

"I guess you think I just have ten thousand lying around my house," Patsy hissed.

Trent pointed his cockroach hand at her.

"No, but I figure you can get it. Hell, with your looks, baby, you could make it tonight by just laying on your back. Or if you want, we could negotiate something . . ."

Patsy leaned away from him.

"I'll get you the ten thousand dollars."

"Remember when you and I used to go to your house after school?" Trent said, wistfully, gently grabbing her arm.

Patsy sighed. "I remember."

"It wasn't all bad, was it?" Trent asked. "I did help you out when your old man tried to kill you, you know."

"I know," Patsy said. "Look, I've got to get going. Where will I meet you tomorrow?"

"The Holiday Inn on Woodlawn. Room 221. Be there by noon."

"It may take me longer to get the ends together," she said, slipping into their old street talk. "And I don't want to be seen going to a motel room. I'll be there after dark."

She was about to stand up and leave, but then another thought pulled her back down.

"Trent, what happened to Thelma Jackson?"

"Who?" His tongue wiped across his lip.

"Never mind," she said. She left Trent sitting at the table. Maybe she should turn herself in, she thought, getting into the elevator. And turn Trent in, too. But there was no proof he had done anything to Mandy or Thelma either—just that little tongue-wipe, erasing his words, and the emptiness in his eyes. Had he been turned into a killer? Had something happened to him in one of his prison spells? As the elevator doors opened on the ground floor, Patsy remembered her conversation by the pool with Mandy. She had said both her parents were dead—died within a few months of each other. Damn Trent. Mandy better be okay wherever she was.

When she got home, she found Tom and Chelsea watching some reality show on the television.

"Where's Kyle?" she asked.

"Upstairs."

She kissed Chelsea on the top of the head. Her darling child. Fear gripped her. Were her children safe? Whatever happened, she had to protect them. She couldn't fail them the way she had failed others. No, she wouldn't fail them, and she wouldn't fail Mandy either. Somehow she'd find her.

She went upstairs and walked into Kyle's bedroom. His science fair trophy sat on his dresser. Just beside it was the GPS. Kyle was intently looking at something on his laptop.

"Honey?" she asked.

"Yeah, Mom?"

"Remember you said you could connect a cell phone to that thing and you could know where someone went?"

Kyle tilted his head toward her.

"Yeah."

"Could you show me how?" she asked.

Chapter 34

Fancy looked over at Trent, leaning back on the motel bed with the remote in his hand. He was a piece of work with his cockroach tattoo on his hand. What the hell had made him think that would be attractive? His teeth were a mess. How many times had she tried to get him to floss? He was too lazy to even brush them properly. But the thing about Trent was that he could be counted on to do what he was told, as long as you popped him a couple of pills. And Trent didn't discriminate. He took any kind of drug at all.

"Damn, she is one pretty woman," Trent said, staring at the TV. "She's still got it."

Fancy looked at the screen to see what scrawny, fat-lipped celebrity he was gawking at, but he had it on the weather channel.

"Who the hell are you talking about?" Fancy asked.

"Your big sister, baby. She's just as hot as she was thirty years ago when I first saw her coming out of school that day in her little blue jean mini-skirt. Mmmm. I will never forget the taste of that sweet thing."

Fancy's lip trembled in anger.

"You insect," she said with quiet rage.

"Ah, baby, don't be jealous. You know I love you. It's just that me and Vera Lee had a special bond. I was her first lover while you were just a runt hiding in the closet spying on us."

Fancy leapt up in a fury. "You bastard. I wasn't spying on you."

Trent laughed. "You sure were. I bet you're the one who told your old man on us, weren't you? I don't know how else he could have found out. Now, just think, Fancy Lee, if you hadn't told Randall about me and Vera Lee riding horsy in the afternoons, he wouldn't have tried to kill her and she wouldn't have run away. And those three people would still be alive."

Fancy was aghast. How did he suddenly have the nerve to bring any of this up. Yes, she did tell Daddy about Vera Lee and Trent, but that was because Vera Lee was doing just like Mama had done. Fancy studied him, lying there on the bed with that smug expression on his face. He didn't ever treat her like this. He was always too busy wheedling drugs out of her. Then it hit her like a two by four upside her head.

"You think she's gonna get back with you, don't you? Why, you ignorant son of a bitch. She doesn't want you. She's got a husband. She's got children. What the hell would she want with someone who can't even hold down a job?"

"I don't think she's going to have much choice," Trent said. "And why would she care if I had a job? She's got plenty of money. You ought to see that nice little car she's driving."

Trent met Fancy's eyes.

"Damn, girl. Can't you tell when I'm teasing you? I'm not going to get back with Vera Lee. I'll admit when we talked at the library, there was a little bit of that old feeling. I think she felt it, too, but I wouldn't leave you. You're my everything."

Fancy's eyes narrowed.

"I'm your medicine cabinet is what you mean," she said.

Trent chuckled. "That does add to your appeal, babycakes. Listen, you gotta go get another room. You can't be here when she gets here."

Fancy got up and went into the motel room bathroom, taking her medicine bag with her. She couldn't trust him alone with her drugs. There was a small bar of wrapped soap on the sink. She sat down on the toilet to pee and played with the soap nervously. She had rarely seen Trent so arrogant. She could tell by the way he said those things he did plan to leave her. He thought Vera Lee would ditch her husband and kids and take up with him. And why not? Vera Lee was capable of anything. Every bad thing in her life could be laid right at the feet of her big sister. But she could have forgiven her all of it if Vera Lee hadn't abandoned her. If she'd come back like the man promised she would if she'd just let those men do those things to her. Now Trent was planning on doing the same thing—leaving her high as Mount Everest and dry as the desert.

She went back into the room and opened her medicine bag.

"Well, since you don't have to see her till tomorrow, maybe we should celebrate," Fancy said, holding up a bottle of white pills.

Trent smiled. "God, you're an angel."

Chapter 35

Rodney got into the Charlotte airport at eight in the morning, rented a car and drove to Patsy Palmer's real-estate office. He wore a baseball cap and shades. He was not exactly incognito, but he thought it better to be able to change his appearance if he needed to. He walked inside and told the receptionist he was considering moving to Charlotte.

The receptionist got super-friendly and handed him a booklet with some of their recent listings and the names and pictures of all the agents.

"Would you like to see someone now?" the receptionist asked.

"No, thanks," he said. He didn't want to get stuck with some other realtor. He had Patsy's address. Maybe he'd drive by her house and see if she was home. He walked out the door and got back in his car when a black Honda Accord zoomed into the parking space next to his. A striking red-head stepped out of the car and strode quickly into the office.

Within minutes she came back out, holding a stack of printed brochures. She didn't notice him as she backed out of the parking space and sped off. Rodney took off behind her. It wasn't too difficult to keep up with her. She drove fast and zipped through traffic, but she stayed within the mainstream speed. She hadn't made it this far by being stupid—if Patsy was who he thought she was. Just glancing at her profile hadn't been enough to tell him.

She turned into a ritzy subdivision where the big new houses all looked like they cost about five times as much as his house and his rentals combined. He wondered what all these people did to make so much money. Maybe Amy would have a house like this one day. It was a different world. When he was coming up, no one needed to live like this and the only ones who aspired to were criminals. Now everyone was an American Idol star or a professional basketball player or some damn thing. Either that or poor as spit.

She drove down what looked to be a dead end cul-de-sac. From the corner, Rodney saw her stop the car in front of an enormous gate and put the brochures into some kind of holder. She was obviously doing fairly well if this was the kind of house she was selling.

Rodney pulled into a driveway down the street and watched for her to come back out. Soon enough the Honda pulled into the street and headed back out of the winding subdivision. At that moment, a woman came out of the mini-mansion where he had parked in the drive and stared at him. He waved at her and pulled away, following Patsy Palmer. He saw the car pull onto the main road. He followed it again. Next stop? She turned at a traffic signal. She could either be going to the gas station or, he looked to the left, the bank.

She turned into the bank parking lot, parked the car and went inside. This was curious. Why not just go through the drive-through? He waited until she went inside and then he went in. Another receptionist greeted him with aggressive friendliness as he came in. These Charlotte people were sure eager for your business.

"Welcome to American Bank," she said with a smile bright as neon.

Rodney glanced around and noticed that Patsy was in an office talking to some kind of manager. She held a large black purse in her lap.

"Could I get some information on opening an account here?" he asked the receptionist.

"Sure," the receptionist handed him a folder. "This describes our free checking account, our check card services and our on-line services. Would you like to see one of our customer representatives?"

"No, thanks. I'm just doing a little investigating right now," he said and walked outside. He got back in the rental car and waited. Patsy walked out shortly after, clutching her large purse to her side.

"You look like a woman on a mission," Rodney said under his breath. Either Patsy Palmer had too much caffeine in her system or she was a woman in trouble. He continued to follow her. By now it was eleven-thirty.

She drove to a shopping center and went into a cell phone store. He wished she would go somewhere to eat. He hadn't had breakfast and his stomach was starting to growl. But she seemed to be buying a cell phone. He wondered why. Didn't she already have one? Was she getting ready to run? What had spooked her?

Eventually, she went back to her office. He parked across the street and ate at Jack in the Box. He could see her car from the parking lot where he sat eating a greasy taco. Finally, she left again. He followed her to an ice-skating rink. Well, so far, she wasn't doing anything particularly suspicious. She stayed in the rink for about thirty minutes. Then he saw her come out with her arm around the little girl he had seen in the picture. This sight stunned him. The smile on Patsy's face was warm. Her every gesture seemed loving. Even from this distance, he could see the way she cared about that kid. They got in the car and drove off.

Her next stop was outside a high school. She drove around back. He lagged behind a couple of cars that followed her in the lot. Coming around the high school, he saw a trailer and several late-model cars in front. A blond teenage boy came out of the trailer with some other kids. Patsy smiled and waved to him from her car. Rodney took out his binoculars and looked at the boy. Well, Patsy might not be the spitting image of Vera Lee Gifford, but this kid was. Except where Vera Lee Gifford had looked angry, this boy's expression was entirely different. He smiled warmly at his mother. The grandparents had said he was an honor student. How could Vera Lee Gifford possibly have raised two kids like this? He was beginning to think he was on a fool's errand. And there was no way this woman was leaving those kids. He'd been with a woman who ran away. He knew what they were like. Just watching Patsy with her children told him she'd never leave them. She wasn't like Cheryl.

Patsy's neighborhood was a well-maintained upper-middle-class enclave. He liked this neighborhood better than the one where her mansion-for-sale was. It seemed older and to have some character. Each house looked a little bit different and there were tall trees in spacious yards. Patsy pulled into her garage. Rodney realized he was going to look conspicuous in this neighborhood. There was only one entrance to the neighborhood. If he waited by the main street, he could see if she left the subdivision, and the neighbors weren't as likely to notice him.

It was after dark. Rodney had watched cars pull into the neighborhood, and a few come back out. But not the Honda. Usually, he had a sixth sense about people. But this Patsy woman was a cipher. She just didn't seem like a criminal. She seemed like a loving mother who sold real estate. On the other hand, he felt a pull toward her that had nothing to do with the business at hand, a pull he hadn't felt in a long time. Was his old obsession with Vera Lee Gifford surfacing? Sitting behind her in that Fort Lauderdale courtroom he had wanted to go up to her, to take her in his arms. The truth is he didn't want to comfort her. He wanted to have sex with her, and he figured that a lot of men had wanted to, and that was probably what was wrong with her. Some women were like that. With Cheryl it had been different. Cheryl was his high-school sweetheart—the girl who slid notes to him during math class. She'd waited for him while he served in Vietnam and had even waited when he went back a couple years later to try to get his buddies back. He thought she'd be part of his life forever. That had been his mistake. He kept asking her to wait for him, and she must have gotten tired of it at some point.

She must have realized she'd never had a life, never done anything for herself.

He looked across a field at a row of tall pines waving in the moonlight. It was the first time he'd thought of it like that, the first time he hadn't blamed her. It still wasn't right that she left her bewildered twelve-year-old kid behind. Then again, maybe she knew that without Amy, his life would have been completely meaningless. Sitting by the side of the road in the dark, he thought of Cheryl without a burning rage for the first time in at least a dozen years. Suddenly the idea of Amy standing at the altar without him pierced him like an ice pick to the heart.

Just then a pair of headlights came out of the neighborhood. It was the Honda. Rodney waited till it passed him, and then he turned on the engine and followed. She drove on to the interstate where he needed to stay close by so he wouldn't lose her in the dark. But for a few minutes a car got between them and he couldn't see her. He was searching frantically when he noticed her car taking an exit. A few minutes later she was pulling into the Krispy Kreme. Just like back home, he thought. She must have had a pretty strong craving to drive all the way up here for a donut. But then he noticed she kept driving. He pulled in front of the donut shop and watched. Patsy parked down in front of some offices and got out of her car.

There was a Holiday Inn next to the closed offices. Rodney slipped into the shadows of a building and saw her disappear into a stairwell at the motel. He hurried down. Looking up at the second floor, he saw her walking purposefully along the exterior hallway. He ducked behind an SUV and saw her stop in front of a room. She knocked on the door. She looked around impatiently, nervously. No one answered the door. She knocked again, this time harder. Finally, she opened the door and walked in. He waited. In a moment, she walked back out without the bag. She hurried down the hallway. He heard her footsteps echoing in the stairwell. Moments later she came out. She walked on the other side of the SUV and kept walking to her car. Her movements were stiff as she got in the car. Then she drove off. Rodney ran back to his car and followed her back out to the road and onto the interstate. She seemed to be going back home in a hurry. Rodney followed till she got off at her exit. Then he turned around and decided to pay a visit to the motel.

Chapter 36

Rodney knocked on the motel room door at the Holiday Inn. The night sky was filled with clouds that were a weird orange from the city lights. He wondered how the waves were back home. How did anyone live this far away from the ocean? There was no answer at the door. He wasn't exactly sure what to do. Up till now there had always been a partner to back him up. Now, he was on his own.

He walked past the window and noticed a crack in the curtain. That was the thing about motels. You could never get the curtains to close all the way. He swore someone was in there. He got a creepy feeling, and turned back to look at the door. He reasoned with himself. He couldn't go barging into places, but then again, he hadn't exactly been playing by the rules these past couple of weeks. He turned the knob and gently cracked open the door. A television played on the dresser across from the bed. He pushed the door further open and stepped inside. He saw the black bag on the floor by the window.

A man was sprawled across the bed. Drunk?

"Hello?" Rodney asked. The man didn't respond. Rodney walked over to the television and turned the sound down. Without the TV volume on, he realized that the room was too quiet. The man was not snoring, not breathing, not making a sound. With a bad feeling, he came closer and turned the body over. Closer inspection showed a gash, a gaping hole, right between his eyebrows. The pillow case was steeped in blood. Rodney stopped in his tracks. No need to disturb the scene any further. Rodney noticed the cockroach tattoo. The body had belonged to Trent Lewis. And someone had not been happy with him.

He heard a sound and whirled around. Everything went black.

The waves on the Puerto Rican shore rose in perfect curls and he felt the sudden lunge of his board as it hung suspended in air. What was he doing back here? The wave gently pushed him toward the brilliant white beach. Up there on the mountain side was the hut he and his friends had built that summer. The last summer before Vietnam. There they were, waving at him: Dennis, Tommy, and Mike. All of them alive again. Now, he knew that Mike was still alive, but Tommy had been lost to drugs years ago and Dennis had kissed life goodbye in the jungles of 'Nam. But there they were, building a bonfire just like they had done all those years ago.

As his board got closer to the shore, he felt the water frothing on top of it, licking at his feet. Then he was off the board and in the water. He turned and looked toward the horizon. The biggest wave he'd ever seen staggered above him as if it would eat him. He saw his board twisting in the water and coming straight toward him. Damn, his head hurt. Good Lord.

The sun beat his eyes through the slice in a curtain. He squinted and tried to raise up on all fours. He looked down at the carpet. What the hell? He was holding onto a hammer. He looked up and saw the body of Trent Lewis on the bed. His head pounded, and he reached behind to feel the knot on the back of his skull. He wondered why they hadn't killed him. Of course, this was convenient for someone, he figured. He dropped the hammer and stood up. The floor was unsteady. Had to get his prints off that hammer. A towel from the bathroom would do.

He staggered into the bathroom and got a towel. Something on the floor caught his eye, a white envelope. He leaned down and picked it up and stuffed it in his pocket.

No time to look inside now. The clock beside the bed showed

seven o'clock. He had to get out of here. Maybe he could convince the Charlotte police that this was all a set-up, but maybe he couldn't. He thought about Terrence Moore, sitting in one of the pods at the Alachua County jail. Just as he and Lanelle figured Terrence was obsessed with Thelma Jackson, someone could think he was obsessed with Vera Lee.

He looked around one last time. The black bag was gone.

Rodney stepped outside and closed the door, wiping off his prints and those of Patsy Palmer in the process. Of course, if she had done the killing there would be other physical evidence to link her. You couldn't make that kind of wound without getting blood on you. It would be nice to have a coroner to confer with, but now he had bigger problems. Namely, who had conked him on the head and tried to set him up? Patsy sure seemed headed home last time he saw her. Who took the black bag?

Rodney had things to do, and if Patsy Palmer was going to be arrested, he wanted to find out what he could about Mandy and Thelma first. And he needed some caffeine and some Tylenol quick.

He rented a Mini Cooper at a local car rental place. He had a Rolex that had once belonged to a cocaine dealer and was sold at auction for a tenth the original price. He stopped at a department store and purchased some new overpriced designer khakis and a polo shirt. The Tylenol had started to kick in, but he still felt groggy.

"I'm going to wear these out of the store," he said as he paid for them. He checked himself out in the mirror on the way out. He could pass as a rich guy. The richer they were, the less they dressed up anyway.

He drove the Mini Cooper to the big country club development where he had followed her the day before. It took him a while but he finally found the house. It was a big mother, surrounded by a tall iron fence. He pulled the brochure from the holder. Twyla's cell phone gift came in handy now. He started dialing. It took him a moment to remember to push "Send".

"Patsy Palmer," he heard.

"Hello. My name is Rodney Ellis. I'm up here from Miami and I'm looking at one of your houses."

"Yes, Rodney. Which house has caught your eye?" He could hear a practiced smile in her voice. It was effective.

"The address is 10100 Belvedere Court."

"Oh," Patsy said. "Good choice. When would you like to see the house?"

"Right now."

He hung up the phone and waited for Vera Lee Gifford to show up. Then he remembered the envelope. He pulled it from his pocket and opened it. Inside were three old Polaroid pictures. A girl, naked, and two men. The girl looked to be about twelve or thirteen. She had a frozen, terrified smile on her face in the first picture. In the second you couldn't see her face. In the third, she was crying and one of the men was penetrating her. The other man was masturbating. Rodney felt a wave of pure revulsion. Was Trent into kiddy porn?

Chapter 37

Buyers are liars, Patsy reminded herself. She didn't want to get her hopes up that this house would sell this quickly. But it would be great if it did. Then she could give Trent more money. The thought of Trent made her shiver with revulsion. She pulled up in front of the house beside the Mini Cooper. That was a cute car. Better than one of those hulking Escalades that dotted so many of the driveways around here.

The man leaning against the car had an easy, relaxed air about him. Maybe too relaxed? Well, it didn't matter. It was always good practice to show a house. The more you showed it, the more you learned about it. She inhaled and focused her mind on the task at hand.

"Hi," she said with her warmest smile.

They shook hands and introduced themselves. He held onto hers a little too long, she thought. It seemed as if he were searching her eyes. Did she know him? Those eyes of his were like a hypnotist's.

"Come on in," Patsy said. They went through the open gate and walked along the stone driveway. "See the garage doors. Those big wooden doors? That's very popular now. That dark wood is such a warm color. It contrasts nicely with the stone, don't you think, Rodney?"

Rodney nodded.

She opened the lock box, and they went inside the house.

"What do you think?" Patsy asked, smiling again. Her eyebrows flashed up. It was an impressive place. The light wood floors spread out, revealing a large room with an open kitchen to the left.

"See these rounded window-walls. What a view! Come on. I'll show you the dining room."

In the dining room, Rodney stared up at the ceiling. It was designed into recessed blocks. A chrome chandelier hung in the middle.

"I like it," he said. "What's that room?"

"The butler's pantry," Patsy answered.

"Of course."

His answer was a little glib, she thought. Was he really in the market for the house? Maybe a condo would suit him better.

"Do you entertain much?" she asked. "What about your family? Any kids?"

Rodney nodded. "Two kids. When we entertain it's mainly birthday parties for six-year-olds. They're twins. Boys."

Patsy's eyes swept down toward his hand. He didn't have a wedding band, but then again some men didn't wear them. A flicker of fear passed through her. And why was she so attracted to him? The pull felt like invisible wires wrapping around the two of them.

"Is something wrong?" the man asked.

"Not at all. Wait till you see the lower level," she said. "Do you work out? You look like you do."

"Yeah, a little," Rodney nodded. "I've got a personal trainer." He had a set of weights on his patio that he lifted once in a while.

"There's an exercise room downstairs—big enough for a Soloflex and a Stairmaster, whatever it is you use." They walked down the circular staircase. For a minute, Rodney tried to imagine what it would be like to be rich enough to live in a place like this—three levels, six bedrooms, seven and a half bathrooms. Then again, what did anyone need all this space for? Besides, it was at least three hours to the ocean from here. Thunder sounded overhead. As they came downstairs, they entered another large room with curved window-walls overlooking an azure pool. There was even another entire kitchen with a bar.

"This is some place," he said. Rain began to fall and the empty room felt quiet, as they were shrouded in the sound of the rain.

"You can see the golf course and the pond from here," Patsy said. Her voice was quieter now. For a moment she had stopped selling. Her eyes gazed into the distance.

They stood in the large empty room as the rain fell and pocked the surface of the pool. Patsy opened the door, and the wet smell of rain poured in. Suddenly Patsy felt cold. Then she heard her mother's voice in her ear. "Run."

She turned to him. He was a nice-looking man, but lots of cops were nice-looking. And she knew clearly that's exactly what he was. Trent must have turned her in.

"You're not really looking for a house, are you?"

"Well, maybe not. Maybe something smaller would be better. One of those condos on the lake."

Patsy swallowed.

"No, you're not in the market for anything, are you? What do you want?"

Rodney's eyes narrowed as he studied her, but he didn't respond.

"Is your name really Rodney?" she asked.

"Yeah, it is. Is your name really Patsy? Patsy Palmer?" She turned away and walked over to the black granite bar. It was all unraveling. Fear trampled every cell of her body. She looked down at her hands. She'd just gotten a French manicure last week. Her fingers were trembling.

"So tell me," Rodney asked. "How did you know I wasn't a buyer?"

"It's an instinct," Patsy said, and then a voice she hardly recognized continued, "I knew you were a cop the second I saw you. It just took a while to register."

"Why? Do I smell like pork?" he asked with a mirthless laugh. He stepped closer to her. He was trying to scare her. She'd been so scared since the first moment she saw Trent Lewis that she didn't think she could get more scared, but there was something inside her, something like liquid steel slowly pulling her out of the fear.

"I'm the one who arrested you," he said quietly.

She turned back toward him. He was muscular and had a belly, but it wasn't a big gut. His face was tanned and his eyes were an inscrutable gray. His hair was thick and sun-bleached with a few silver strands. She was rarely attracted to men other than Tom, but this was a powerful, almost palpable thing, and she could tell by the way his jaw slackened slightly and his pupils dilated that it had hit him, too. He glanced away.

"I remember you, now," she said. "You came to my trial. You stared at me the whole time. When I looked at you, I felt like I was looking into a mirror."

"So, are you going to talk to me, Patsy?"

"About what?"

"About Amanda Danforth? Or possibly Trent Lewis?"

Tears sprang to her eyes.

"What do you know about Mandy?" she asked. "Has anyone found her? Jesus, I can't bear this." She paced across the length of the room and then turned back to him.

"I thought you might know something about what happened to her?" Rodney stared at her steadily. She closed her eyes.

"She came here a couple of weeks ago. We talked. I hadn't seen her in a long time."

"Not for twenty-five years at least?"

"Something like that," she said, tilting her chin up. What was the use of pretending? He must know the truth or why would he be here? The question in her mind was did he, like Trent, want something? Was there still a way out? She and Tom were not wealthy. She could deplete the kids' college funds, but then Trent would just want more and more. It would never end.

She sighed. "I don't know where she is. He said that she had gone to 'Daddy,' but her father is dead. So he must have been lying, trying to scare me."

"Who was lying?" Rodney asked. "Trent Lewis?"

Patsy nodded her head.

Rodney leaned his hand against the window frame. It was an encircling sort of gesture as if she could walk into his arms and find some comfort there. Perhaps she should. If she were going back to prison, she would probably never have another opportunity to be in a man's arms. Then she thought of Tom—his trust shattered. What would it be like to no longer have him in her life?

"Patsy?" Rodney said in a soft voice. "I followed you to Trent's motel room last night. I saw you go inside."

Patsy's composure evaporated.

"I wanted to buy some time. My son and daughter are just kids. I can't leave them yet," Patsy said, tears running down her face. "He wants a hundred thousand dollars. He said he wouldn't turn me in. He . . . he promised that he'd have Mandy get in touch with me."

Rodney looked into her eyes.

"I saw you go into the room. And I know what you saw. You saw Trent Lewis with his head bashed in. Unless you bashed it in yourself."

Patsy's knees buckled, and Rodney stepped forward and grabbed her. She felt his hands on her elbows as he raised her up.

"I need to sit down," she said. She dropped down on the stairs. Rodney sat beside her. She looked up at the ceiling, trying to collect her thoughts. "I thought he was alive. I thought he was sleeping. I was so scared. I just dropped the bag on the floor. I didn't want to wake him. Why would I kill him? I'm not a killer."

"But you were, weren't you? You killed Chuck Staples and Lorenzo Black. Then you killed Lois Underwood."

"Yes, I killed Chuck and Lorenzo—or at least Vera Lee killed them. I don't remember killing Lois Underwood, and I know I didn't kill Trent. I'm not that person anymore."

"Well," Rodney said, taking her hand and turning it over. "The cops are going to be all over that motel. If you killed him, they'll know."

Patsy pulled her hand away from him.

"Thelma Jackson was killed the same way, you know. The coroner said it looked like the claw of a hammer."

Patsy stood up quickly and held a hand to her mouth.

"A hammer?" she asked. "That wasn't in the newspaper."

"It took us a while to find it."

"Randall."

"Who?"

"Randall Gifford . . . my father. He's here. He did this. He's after me." The panic flooded through her. Her fears of being caught and going to prison were nothing now. Now Randall had found her. What would he do to her? What would he do to her family?

"How do you know?"

"Because he tried to kill me a long time ago just like that with the claw of a hammer." Then she remembered what Trent had told her in the library. "And when Trent said Mandy was going to Daddy, he didn't mean her daddy. He meant mine."

She turned to Rodney and said urgently, "You've got to find him and stop him."

"Okay, Vera Lee," he said.

"Don't call me that. Please. I haven't been that person for a long time."

Rodney came close to her. She could feel his breath against her cheek.

"I want to show you something," he said. He pulled the envelope from his pocket and handed her the pictures. Patsy stared and then it felt as if she couldn't breathe. That which was forgotten was now unfolding in her mind. Sitting in Lance's Cadillac, the burning sensation of the drug in her nostrils, the way he said, "Vera Lee, take a look at this. Let me show you what these guys are capable of," she remembered all of it. Then he handed her the gun and it felt like power. She was God and vengeance was in a bullet. Now she could see it so clearly, opening the door to the office, pictures of *Hustler* women taped to the walls, the rage turning everything purple, the look on their faces, first angry, then shocked. She had pulled the trigger again and again and again.

"Do you know who they are?" he asked.

Patsy nodded.

"This is why I killed them," she said in a weak voice.

"Who?"

"That's Chuck, the heavy one, and the other guy, the one who's masturbating, that's Lorenzo," she said, gripping the pictures tight in her trembling hands.

"Who's the girl?" Rodney asked.

"That's my little sister, Fancy Lee. I'd do it again. I'd kill them again if I had the chance."

"And yet you want me to believe that you didn't kill Trent Lewis? That you didn't set me up to take the fall for it? For that matter, how do I know you didn't come to Gainesville and smash Thelma Jackson's head in. Was she going to give your secret away?"

Patsy threw the pictures on the floor and glared at Rodney.

"I took Trent the money, and I left it there. I knew it wouldn't be enough but I thought it might buy me some time. I wanted to explain things to Tom," she said. Then despair took over. What was the use? "I knew it was over though. I should have known it was over when Mandy showed up. She told me about Thelma, but I can promise you that I never went back to Florida. On the day Thelma was killed, I was showing a house in Rock Hill. Then I stopped at a mailbox and dropped off some money for her momma."

Rodney thought back and remembered that the postmark on the envelope had been the day before he and Lanelle were called to the motel. If Patsy was lying about this, it would be easy enough to prove.

"Why did you give Trent money? Why not just turn yourself in?" Rodney asked.

"I don't want to hurt my kids. I don't know how they'll take this. How will they grow up without their momma? I don't want them to turn out like me."

Rodney walked to the windows.

"What's your husband going to do when he learns the truth?" Rodney asked.

Patsy shrugged. "I don't know. Divorce me? What else can he do?"

Rodney turned to her. "He can stick beside you. He can support you through this. You know, you might even get a new trial for the killings in Florida." He paused. "You admit doing those killings, don't you?"

Patsy nodded.

"I remember being really angry and shooting Chuck and Lorenzo. I did just like Lance told me to do. 'Just kick in the door and start firing, beautiful. Don't give them time to think about it.' But I don't remember killing Lance's wife. It's just a blank—like there's nothing there. I can't even tell you what she looked like."

"Well, she looked like a million bucks to Lance Underwood. That's how much he got from her life insurance."

Patsy leaned against the wall. All these years she had felt the pain of that woman's death. Chuck and Lorenzo were mean and dangerous men. Lorenzo and his wife Sylvia were known to have done killings for hire, and Chuck used and abused anyone who got in his way. Lance must have shown her the pictures in her drugged-out stupor. She could only remember a blind rage, a hatred that was like a tiger inside her. But she didn't feel anything like that for Lois Underwood. A little jealousy maybe, but not enough to kill her.

"When they found the gun in the trunk of Lois's car, when they found me, there weren't any prints on that gun."

"Yes, I remember," Rodney said. "Lance's dead now, so I guess we'll never know."

"So what are you going to do? Are you going to arrest me?"

Rodney shook his head.

"I'm not acting officially. I'm an investigator, trying to help Mandy's friends find her. The problem is, whoever killed Trent Lewis and tried to set me up for it probably either has Mandy or has killed her. And there's an innocent man sitting in jail right now for the murder of Thelma Jackson. I'm afraid if I turn you over to the courts now, we won't find out who that person is."

He took her by the arms and brought her face close to his.

"You have to remember, Vera Lee. You have to remember everything or we're not going to find her."

Patsy pulled free.

"I'm not Vera Lee."

"Yes, you are." Rodney's voice was hard. "What did you promise your daddy you wouldn't tell? When I arrested you in Florida, you said you were sorry. You called me 'Daddy.' And you promised you wouldn't tell. What is it, Vera Lee? What have you been hiding all these years?"

Patsy turned and reached for the door. He didn't try to stop her. She ran into the backyard past the curved lap pool, down the sloping green lawn. The rain fell hard on her, soaking her hair and her clothes. But still it felt as if she couldn't breathe, as if she were drowning. She heard her mother's laugh and could smell the cigarette smoke. Then the laughter turned into crying. The grass was wet under Patsy's feet as she ran toward the pond.

She stood by the water, taking deep gasping breaths. What was it that she had buried so deep in her psyche? Patsy's memory cracked open and she fell to her knees. Suddenly that day was as fresh as if it had just happened. It was late in the day. She smelled the fish in the sink. She ran a finger across their silver scales.

"You've made a fool of me, woman!" her daddy screamed. "You've been running around with some slick dick, and now you think I'm gonna take on one more young 'un that ain't mine? You damn cheap whore."

"Don't cuss at me," her mother had answered in a voice like hard steel. There was a long silence. Vera Lee stood poised over the fish, staring into its dead black eye.

"I got to do some work on the boat tonight," he said. "We'll talk about this then."

Briefly she came back to the present. She heard someone behind her. It was Rodney, but he said nothing. Just stood there in the drenching rain. And then she was gone again. The light of the day faded and it was dark night. The house was quiet, too quiet. Vera Lee got out of bed and went to her parents' room. The white bedspread was tucked over the pillows. Her parents were gone. She went back in the room and woke up Fancy.

"Come on," she said, "something ain't right."

Fancy followed her. The marina was only two blocks away. They walked barefoot along the cool road. Frogs and katydids sang at them. The stars were still and quiet. Vera Lee took Fancy's hand. The night was lonely and strange. She had to find her mother. They crossed the gravelly parking lot that led to the boat slips. *Daddy's Baby* was gone.

"We'll just wait for 'em," Vera Lee told Fancy. But Fancy had whined, so Vera Lee snuck onto another boat and took some cushions and towels off it. She made a little bed for Fancy and the child fell sound asleep. Vera Lee tried to stay awake, but she couldn't. She leaned down next to Fancy and soon Fancy's breath sounded like the ocean and she heard someone screaming, heard heavy thuds, heard the splash. Did she dream this? She couldn't remember.

Now she hears something, hears Randall Gifford picking up Fancy and taking her away. He has left Vera Lee there, thinking she is asleep. Vera Lee doesn't move until he is gone. Then she gets up.

"Mama?" She stands up and goes to the boat. She sees no one on the deck. A chill crawls along her back. She knows even before she steps on the boat that her mother isn't there. But she calls down into the hold anyway. "Mama?"

"What the hell are you doing?"

Vera Lee jumps, turns around and sees Randall glowering at her.

"Nothing," she whispers.

Randall comes close to her. He hunkers down right in front of her and says, "Your mama run off with one of those boyfriends of hers. It's up to me to take care of you. You don't want to go to the orphan home, do you?"

He was not a tall man, but he was powerfully built, muscles bulging from his sports shirt.

"No, sir," she said.

"Come on," he said. Then he turned and stepped off the boat. Vera Lee didn't look back.

The rain had slackened. Rodney stepped closer to her.

"I never went on that boat again," Patsy said. "He killed her. My daddy killed my mother. And I knew, but I didn't tell. I guess I was so conditioned to keeping secrets that I didn't know what else to do."

Rodney took her arm.

"Let's go inside. You're soaked," he said gently.

The rain had stopped, and steam wafted up from the road in front of the house like wraiths. She could almost see figures dancing—her mother, Chuck, Lorenzo, Thelma, and now Trent. But it was her mother who she saw the most clearly, and she wasn't dancing. She was sinking, slowly and eternally sinking through the blue waters of the Atlantic Ocean.

"Rodney," Patsy said. "I need to get my kids. I need to make sure they're safe. Do you understand?"

Rodney nodded.

"Okay, let's go get your kids and take them home. Then we'll figure out our next move. We need to find out where he took Mandy Danforth."

Chapter 38

She pulled into the parking lot of the Ice Palace.

"I'll wait here," Rodney said.

Patsy got out of the car, glanced up and noticed a crow watching her from the top of a pole. Something was amiss. She felt it. But then again it was a terrible day. She was afraid, but there was nothing she could do. She was heading down the chute into some unknown future. What mattered most was finding Mandy. No one else should suffer because of her.

She crossed the heat of the parking lot and entered the building, donning her sweater automatically. Inside the music blared at full tilt—some Britney Spears song that some little girl thought was so extremely cool. She was grateful that somehow Chelsea had skipped right over the Britney Spears phase. Patsy glanced around the rink, looking for Chelsea's pink skating sweater. She saw three pink sweaters but none of them were worn by red-headed girls. Then she saw her teacher, speaking to one of the other parents. The teacher, Toni, was a young black woman—a gifted skater and an even better teacher. Patsy approached her and caught her eye. Toni looked at her in surprise. Patsy's face tightened as she read Toni's surprised expression.

"Hi, you're all right," Toni exclaimed and skated toward Patsy.

"Of course, I'm all right. What do you mean?"

"Well, we got a phone call saying you were in an accident and someone was coming to pick up Chelsea. Next thing I knew, Chelsea was gone. I thought someone was taking her to see you."

"Chelsea left? Who took her?"

"I don't know," Toni said, her eyes wide and frightened. "Chelsea was so scared when she heard you were in an accident, she just grabbed her things and went outside."

Patsy turned and pushed past the skaters congregating by the side of the rink. This couldn't be happening. The low sound in her head, got louder. "Run," it said. "Run." She covered her ears as if that could drown out the voice as she fled the building and ran back to her car where Rodney waited.

"He's got her," Patsy screamed. "He's got Chelsea."

"Okay, calm down. We'll put out an Amber Alert right now. Don't worry, Patsy. We'll get her back."

While Patsy frantically drove out of the parking lot, Rodney dialed Lanelle's number and told her what had happened. As soon as he hung up, Patsy said, "Rodney, he's already killed two people! Don't you think he'll kill her, too?"

She felt a chaotic hysteria building inside her. The sun splashed around her and a suffocating feeling took over. "God, I can't breathe," she gasped.

"Stop at that store, Patsy. I'll get you something to drink. You have to calm down. We'll find her."

Patsy pulled into the gas station-convenience store. Rodney hurried inside. As she leaned toward the steering wheel gasping for breath, a cold chill moved up from the soles of her feet through her legs, her abdomen and settled in her shoulders. Suddenly, she could breathe again. She looked up and saw that everything was the same in its ordinariness. The red and white building with cars parked in front, the car vacuum and air machine, the black layer of asphalt. She remembered the gun, the weight of it in her hands, how she had stepped out of Lance Underwood's car and walked through the back door of the club. The hallway was cool and dark and smelled damp. "Just kick open the door and start firing, beautiful," Lance had whispered into her ear. And she had done it. She had gone through the lounge, past the pool tables and into the office. Two men sat across from each other, laughing. One of them held a green bottle of beer in his hand. The other smoked a cigarette. She raised the gun.

Suddenly Patsy wasn't afraid. She heard a voice like a razor blade cutting through the layer of time. Not her mother's voice this time. It was Vera Lee who told her to drive. She reached over to the gear shift and moved it from park to drive. She didn't even look back to see Rodney's expression. She knew exactly what to do. She would get her child back, and no one was going to stand in her way.

The first thing to do was to find an ally. There was only one person in the world she could trust. She drove to the high school and saw Kyle standing with some friends outside the gym. She noticed Rodney's cell phone on the seat and threw it in her purse out of habit.

"Hi, Mom," Kyle said.

"Hi, babe. I'm in a hurry, okay? So let's go."

Kyle got in the car.

"Where are we going?"

"I've got to get out of town," she said.

"What's going on, Mom?"

"I can't explain it to you, but I need you to show me how to work this thing." She thrust the GPS at him.

"Tell me what's going on first."

"I can't, Kyle," she practically shrieked. Then sitting at a red light, she began to cry. The fear shook her like an angry parent. "Someone's got Chelsea," she sobbed. She knew she shouldn't tell him, but he was the only person she ever truly trusted.

"Who?"

"I'm not sure. But they have the bag with the cell phone in it. The one you fixed up for me with the GPS tracker yesterday. So we can find them, right? We can find them, can't we?"

Kyle looked frightened but resolved.

"Yes, Mom. We can find them. But I'm going with you. You

are not going to do this by yourself. First of all, you can't track and drive. You need me."

"No, I can't endanger you," she said.

"You have to take me, Mom. I won't let you go without me." His jaw was locked and his eyes hardened like metal.

"Okay," Patsy said, giving in. She knew it was true. If anyone could help her get Chelsea back, it was Kyle. Besides, she knew what it meant to leave a sister behind.

"Show me how to read this thing," she said, handing the keys to Kyle. She got in the passenger side and locked the doors. "I'll navigate. You drive."

"Okay," Kyle said. "This shows how fast they're traveling. And right now, it looks like they're going east on 74. Mom, if we know this is them, why don't we call the police?"

"Because as soon as they see a cop car, he'll ditch that bag, and we'll lose them. And he might kill her. It's me he's after."

"Who is he?"

"My father, Randall Gifford."

Kyle drove in silence through the city traffic. It was five o'clock. "I'm scared. Are you going to tell me what's going on?"

Patsy swallowed. Kyle pulled onto the interstate. Two exits down and they could take 74 west to 95. Then it was south. Home. A vast blue body of water awaited her.

"He's taking her to Florida," she said quietly.

Kyle swiveled his head toward her. She saw the fear in his blue eyes. He looked so much like she did at that age, but he'd had such a different life.

"Okay," Patsy said. "I'm going to tell you a story. You might find it hard to believe, and you might not love me after I tell you this story."

"Are you crazy? I'll always love you. You're my mom."

"Well, yes, I am your mom, and yes, I'm also crazy. At least I used to be. See, Kyle, my life wasn't like yours. My momma left me when I was nine years old and I'm pretty sure she was murdered."

He sat stunned.

"There's a lot I haven't told you." Patsy looked out the window.

"How was she murdered, Mom?"

"Randall took her out on the boat and didn't come back with her," she said.

"Recently, he killed another woman, a woman named Thelma Jackson. I don't know if she told him where I was, but somehow he found me. I know it's got to be him. When he kills, he just likes to crack someone's skull right open. I used to see him kill fish that way."

"Why would this make me not love you, Mom? It's not your fault that your dad was a psycho bastard."

"Well, there's more to it. But I don't want to talk about it now. Let's just get to Florida."

"Mom, why don't we tell the police?"

"Because it's me that he wants. Randall wants me to come back so he can kill me, too. He'll keep her alive to lure me back."

"Can I at least call Dad? He's going to be worried."

Just then Patsy's cell phone rang. She looked at the number. It was a Charlotte area code. She didn't answer it. She would only answer it if she saw a Florida area code. Eventually Randall would call her. If he knew how to find her, he would know her cell phone number. It was posted everywhere.

"You can call your dad later," she said. "When we get out of the state."

Patsy closed her eyes. She didn't know who she was anymore or why she had gotten her son into this mess, but whatever was driving her was stronger than she was. When they reached I-95, she told him to go south.

Chapter 39

It was pure instinct that made Rodney slip Douglas Framingham's Velcro bug under the collar of Patsy's blouse when he had her in his arms, but he knew the range wasn't great, and he needed to get his own car fast. He'd heard the conversation with her son, but then they went out of range and all he heard was static. If they were on their way to Florida, then they were probably trying to find Randall.

The cab driver who gave Rodney a lift back to the empty mansion to get his car was the most annoying person Rodney had met in a good long while.

"Ha, ha, ha. See that truck there—Estes Trucking. I got in trouble as a kid for doing a little editing work with a spray paint can on one of those trucks. Ha, ha, ha. I added a 't'. Get it, 'Testes.'"

"That's hilarious," Rodney marveled dryly. Unfortunately the entire twenty-minute ride was a continuous prattle of similar witticisms, followed by the man's own raucous laugh-track. Rodney tried to think but it was difficult with this idiot's constant noise.

He told the man to excuse him, he had some calls to make, and slipped on the headset. Nothing. The thing about being a cop was that there were certain procedures you always followed. Not that he always followed them exactly, but they were there for you to fall back on. Now, he had to resist the urge to be a cop. He needed to talk to Tom Palmer and let him know what was going on, but of course, he'd left his cell phone in Patsy's car. He'd tried to call her from the payphone but she didn't answer, so he called Lanelle instead.

Lanelle had probably already alerted the Charlotte Police Department about Chelsea's disappearance. The Amber Alert should be in effect soon, and CPD would be at the Palmer residence. Rodney decided to go straight to the airport. He'd call Palmer at work. It would be nice if Patsy would call him first, but who knew what she was going to do.

So Rodney took the Billy Graham Parkway to the airport. It was not a religious experience. He left the Mini Cooper in daily parking. He called the car rental place from a payphone and told them he had an emergency and to just add the parking rate to his bill. The next flight to Florida was to Jacksonville. Rodney thought Orlando would be closer but apparently bad weather had caused all flights south of Jacksonville to be cancelled.

Next he called Twyla and asked her to drive to the Jacksonville Airport and meet him there.

"Twyla, look up any information you can on Randall Gifford. Last known address was Jupiter, Florida. I think he was some kind of charter fisherman. Find out if he still lives there. If he's got a record. Anything. Check him out with DMV—anything you can think of."

"Roger that," Twyla said. Rodney rolled his eyes.

"Also check with Lanelle for me. See if she got out the Amber Alert and if she has any info from the Charlotte PD on Trent Lewis's death."

Rodney had ten minutes before he had to board the plane. He called the community college information and got Tom Palmer's direct line.

"Tom Palmer here."

"Hello, Mr. Palmer. My name is Rodney Ellis. I'm a detective from Gainesville, Florida. I've got some bad news for you. I've been up here doing an investigation on a missing person—a friend of your wife's. Mr. Palmer, I need to let you know that your daughter is now missing as well."

Rodney heard dead silence. Then, "What are you talking about? Who did you say you were? A detective?"

"Listen. I know this is hard, but the Charlotte Police are going to show up at your house with questions, and I thought you should be prepared. We've got an Amber Alert out for Chelsea, and your wife . . . well, I believe your wife may know who took her. She's gone to try to get her back."

"Who was it?" the voice on the other end of the line was hysterical. "Who took Chelsea? How the hell is Patsy involved in this?"

"It may have been Patsy's estranged father. Police in Florida are checking up on him now. And Mr. Palmer, I should also let you know that your wife is an escaped felon. Now, this is not something you have to talk to the police about. But you need to be prepared. They will want to know where she is. And they'll figure out soon enough who she is. Look, I've got to go. I'm flying down to Florida and I'm going to try to find your daughter and your wife. Both of them are in danger. The best thing you can do is go home and wait to hear from someone. Patsy will probably call you. I'm sorry, sir. I know this is difficult."

It was a long plane ride, but it gave him time to think, and even with his aching head he couldn't stop his mind from racing. Randall Gifford? Who was this guy? Vera Lee seemed to think he killed her mother. What was the mother's name? He rubbed his eyes and thought back to his conversation with the mystery writer. That's right. It was Mari Lee. And the daughters were Vera Lee and Fancy Lee. Mari Lee, Vera Lee and Fancy Lee. Merrily, Verily and Fancily. His head felt heavy and he tried to lean back. Why did they design airline seats for crustaceans with these curved backs, he wondered. He closed his eyes. Merrily, Verily, Fancily. Life is but a dream. He sat up with a start. The old man at the assisted-living facility. He had sung that song, looking slyly at Rodney the whole time.

"Shit," Rodney said aloud and a bored middle-aged woman in designer jeans turned to him with a quizzical look.

"Just remembered something," Rodney said and grinned foolishly.

Twyla was waiting outside the airport in her trusty old Volvo. Rodney dropped into the passenger side.

"What did you learn about Randall Gifford?" he asked.

"Not much. He's retired. He gets his social security checks sent to a PO box in North Palm Beach Gardens."

"That's close to Jupiter," Rodney said. "Let me use your cell phone."

"What happened to the one I gave you?"

"It's gone."

Twyla handed him her phone and he dialed Lanelle's office.

"What did you find out about Trent Lewis?"

"The autopsy showed a variety of kinds of drugs in his system. High-grade pharmaceuticals like you'd get from a hospital or something."

"No shit. Hey, Lanelle. Vera Lee Gifford had a sister. A sister who was a nurse."

"Yeah."

"And here's something else. When I was looking around the parking lot where Mandy Danforth's car was last seen, I found a little packet with one of those alcohol wipes in it. The sister's last known employment was The Palms Assisted Living Home down in Jupiter. They wouldn't give me her address but I didn't have a real big reason to push for it."

"Rodney, did you know there's a hurricane heading straight for South Florida? It's all over the Weather Channel. The police there are busy getting everyone evacuated. You're not going to get any help from them right now."

"Damn." Rodney said. He doubted the hurricane would deter whoever had Patsy's kid.

Then it struck him who he should call. He looked through the notepad of phone numbers that he kept with him and dialed.

"McMillan here," a bored voice said.

"Mac, this is Rodney Ellis. I met you at a bar on Singer Island not too long ago. You gave me some information about Vera Lee Gifford."

"Sure, I remember you, man. The cop from Hogtown. That is what they call Gainesville, isn't it?"

"Yeah, some people do. Listen, I think Vera Lee Gifford's sister may have something to do with a kidnapping—maybe two kidnappings."

"That's interesting," Mac said. "What do you want me to do about it? There's a hurricane blowing this way. It's heading straight for our little town."

"How come you're not evacuating then?"

"Are you kidding? I love hurricanes."

"Listen, I got a question for you, Mac. Do you think that Randall Gifford killed his wife? You said she ran off and left the girls when Vera Lee was nine, but do we know that she wasn't killed?"

"Naw, Gifford was a mean, abusive drunk. But I don't think he was a killer. In fact, I ran into Mari Lee a couple of years after she left him. She was waiting tables down in Miami. I don't know what happened to her after that, but she was alive and kicking at least till then."

"Hmm, Vera Lee thinks he killed her mother. She also thinks he's got her kid right now."

"Well, she's mistaken about . . ." Just then the phone went dead. Rodney dropped it on the floor.

"You think it's Vera Lee's sister who took Mandy Danforth?" Twyla asked.

"Maybe."

"I thought she was the good one. By the way, where are we going?"

"To see an old man," Rodney said. He dialed Lanelle again. "You're not afraid of hurricanes, are you? How about meeting me down in Jupiter? And stop by my place and get my board, the waves are probably awesome."

"You're joking, right?"

"Yeah. Is it that hard to tell?"

Lanelle ignored the question. "Where in Jupiter?"

"The Palms Assisted Living Facility."

"I'm gonna need to call in a favor to get jurisdiction to be doing work there, Rodney. You know you'll probably lose your badge."

"Lanelle, I'm not sure I care anymore. Working on your own has its drawbacks, I've discovered, but there's a helluva lot less paperwork and bullshit to put up with," he said. "Maybe I'll go private."

"To follow cheating wives so you can snap their pictures doing the Monica on some guy in a parking lot?" she asked.

"Laugh if you want. But there's a lot of people who need help, and as a cop I don't have time," he said. "I'll call you back later."

The sky was orange from the city lights reflected off the clouds. A steady rain began to fall.

"Fortunately that hurricane is only a category two right now, but the storm surge could be huge," Twyla said. "And it's heading right toward Palm Beach."

"That's just our luck," Rodney said. The windshield wipers beat a steady hypnotic rhythm. Rain water ran in rivulets along his window and headlights came at him and zoomed past. He remembered the night they had arrested Gavin Worthy. The man was drunk and had passed out in the back seat of an old Ford Fairlane. As far as they knew he didn't even have a home. He had pulled Gavin from the back seat, and Gavin took a swing at him. That was all it took. He'd swung back with his flashlight and sent Gavin sprawling to the ground, the pictures of a mutilated twenty-year-old pregnant woman's corpse vivid in his mind as he kicked Gavin in the ribs. Willie pulled him back before he did it again, but Rodney remembered the mindless rage he had felt, the rage for things that had nothing to do with Gavin Worthy or even the girl they thought was his victim. He was angry because Cheryl had left him, because his government had betrayed him, because he'd seen too many children die in Vietnam. And Gavin Worthy went to prison. He spent thirteen years on death row before the real murderer was arrested, his identity confirmed with DNA testing.

"Twyla," Rodney said. "Do you think the good a person does ever outweighs the bad?"

Twyla didn't answer right away.

"It's up to the judge," she said.

"God?"

"Well, I don't believe in God, per se," she said. "I think you're probably your own judge. So you can sentence yourself to hell or you can show yourself a little mercy."

Rodney thought about it. He hadn't known Twyla to be a particularly wise person but she was a poet after all, and they were supposed to know something about the human soul.

The rain was horrendous in Jupiter and the wind laid down the trees in its path. On the plus side, traffic was practically nonexistent. A tree toppled in front of Twyla's car on US One and blocked her path about a block before the old folks' place.

"Turn around and go around the block," Rodney said. Twyla kept her cool and wheeled around. Rodney thought she seemed glad for the extra obstacles, as if that made the whole enterprise more exciting. Eventually, they made it to the small white building. The roof on the terrace was caved in at the corner, but otherwise the place looked all right. Twyla waited in the car while Rodney plowed through the wall of rain and ran to the front door. It was unlocked and he went inside.

The old people sat in the lobby of the place, their eyes frightened and wide.

"They left us," the red-haired lady in the walker said, clomping toward him. "All the staff. There's just one nurse's assistant.

All the rest of them took off. Can you believe it? That's what happens when a corporation out in California owns your place. No one cares. No one cares what happens to us."

A tall white-haired lady agreed. Rodney looked around him. Staring out the window was the man in the captain's hat. He looked at the red-haired lady and asked, "What is that man's name?"

"He's Captain Gifford. I think he's related to one of our nurses," the woman added.

Rodney sighed.

"Has he been anywhere in the past week or so?"

"Oh, no," she answered. "He's always there at the window or outside on the porch with the rest of us. Sometimes he makes sense. Other times, well, you know, a lot of us don't have all our marbles."

Rodney thanked the woman and walked over to speak to Vera Lee's father.

"Did you find Fancy Lee?" the man looked up at him and asked. For someone with dementia, he had a pretty good memory, Rodney thought.

"No, Mr. Gifford, I didn't. You are Randall Gifford, aren't you?"

"One and the same." The old man nodded and gazed at the rain running in rivulets across the porch.

"Mr. Gifford, I really need to find her. I believe she has your granddaughter."

Randall Gifford looked up at him sharply. "I don't have grandchildren."

"Yes, you do," Rodney said. "Vera Lee has two children—a boy and a girl."

Randall's mouth dropped.

"Vera Lee? I don't have a daughter named Vera Lee. That was Mari Lee's girl. Not mine. She was just like Mari Lee, running with boys, cheating on me. She deserved everything she got."

Rodney stuck his hands in his pockets.

"Where would Fancy go? Where would she take a little girl?"

The captain grinned up at him. "A little girl?" He shrugged and gazed out at the sky. "Who knows? Life is but a dream."

Rodney stared at the bright pulse of light from a lighthouse in the distance.

Chapter 40

Kyle pulled off the interstate. It was almost midnight. Patsy had been quiet for most of the trip. They had turned off the cell phone so that Tom couldn't call them back. The rain fell on them in torrents and gusts of wind nearly blew the car off the road.

"We're in Florida," he said. "I always wanted to come to Florida. Never thought it would be like this—in the middle of a hurricane."

"Are you tired?" she asked.

"Yeah. And I'm worried about Chelsea. Do you think he'll hurt her?"

Patsy just shook her head. "I don't know."

She wanted to change the subject, to try to get him calmed down. Perhaps to calm herself down as well.

"So whatever happened with Alessandra?" she asked.

Kyle shrugged. "She's dating a soccer player."

"Oh," Patsy said. "Sorry about that."

"It doesn't matter, Mom. Nothing matters except getting Chelsea back."

"I know," Patsy said. "Remember when you asked me, what's on the other side of now?"

"Yeah," he said.

"I just . . . I just wonder if anything means anything. Does the past really disappear into the void? Or do you keep reliving your nightmares, keep recreating them?"

"Mom, the past is in the void. What's happening now is now."

They stopped for gas. The fluorescent lights glared as they both got out and stretched.

"I'll drive," Patsy said, taking the keys from him.

"Isn't it dangerous to drive in weather like this?" Kyle asked. "You know how you hate to drive in snow storms."

"This isn't like snow or ice. I grew up with hurricanes, baby. And this one is still a long ways away. We'll be down there before it hits full force."

"Full force?" Kyle asked.

As they drove back onto the interstate, Kyle was thoughtful.

"I remember how, when I was about ten and Chelsea was five, you took Chelsea's Barbie doll and placed the doll's hands on the steering wheel so that Barbie could drive. Barbie would swivel her head both ways and then say in a nasal voice, 'Get out of my way, assholes!' Then Barbie would flip over and scream as the steering wheel turned. Chelsea would laugh so hard. Me, too. I had a feeling you weren't like any other mother," he said.

"I guess I'm not like any other mother," Patsy said as she remembered what it was like to have young children. It was the happiest time in her life. "Maybe I just appreciated it more because I knew it could be over at any minute."

"When are you going to finish your story?" he asked.

Patsy pushed the hair behind her ear. She wore a small gold hoop in her earlobe. Her profile was lit by the oncoming headlights. She was beautiful but seemed different than he had ever known her.

"My name is Vera Lee Gifford," she said to him. "At least that's the name I had for the first eighteen years of my life. I was seventeen when I went on my infamous killing spree."

Kyle sat still as stone.

"I murdered at least two people, Kyle, maybe three. I can't say it was an accident or that I didn't mean to do it. I can't offer any excuse at all. Yes, I did it because a man wanted me to, and I thought I had something to prove to him. I did it because I was lost and frightened and because I had this buried pain inside me. I did it because I wanted to kill my father and I was afraid of him. I did it because I was so stoned on PCP I had no connection to reality. I did it because they had sexually abused my little sister. I know now that I could have done a thousand other things. It's just that at the time I felt as if I was being pulled by strings—strings that someone else controlled. God, you don't know how hard it is to tell you this."

Kyle felt as if someone had plunged a needleful of novocaine into his chest, and it was slowly spreading.

"How could you ever have done that? You read about these things in the paper. But they're never people you know. They're never someone's mother. My mother. My mother is smart and funny and volunteers to run bake sales at the school. She was the field trip mom, the room mother, the one who'd go out in the middle of the night to find an open store for some part I needed. She's the one who took me camping one weekend—just the two of us. Remember that?"

She did. She remembered climbing the rocks by the waterfall at South Mountain, turning to him and beckoning him on.

"You used to sing that Led Zeppelin song to help us get to sleep at night," Kyle said, "about how you'd love me even if the sun refused to shine . . ."

She said, "I shouldn't have told you this."

"It's going to take me a little while to absorb this new information about you. I'm having trouble understanding . . ."

"I don't understand it either. Just that I was a very angry, scared and crazy girl. I was crying out for love in the worst way. The worst way I possibly could."

"But, Mom, you're not like that now. How can someone change like that?"

"The world is full of bad people, Kyle. But it's also full of good people, and the good people will save you if you let them. That's what your grandma and granddad did. They're not your blood relatives. You know that. But what we never tell anyone is that I was already eighteen when they adopted me."

"Why was your dad so crazy?"

"He wasn't always crazy. My mama was only about sixteen when she met him and supposedly he stole her from some other man. They got married when she was seventeen. The first few years of their marriage weren't bad, but Mama had a wild streak. One time an old boyfriend came back and she took off for a couple of days. Daddy paced the floor, drinking and carrying on. Fancy Lee and I hid under the bed or anywhere else we could find when he was like that."

"Your sister's name was Fancy Lee and you were Vera Lee?"

"Yeah, and Momma's name was Mari Lee. Randall thought it was so funny—our names. Merrily, Verily and Fancily, that's how he'd say it. Randall wasn't such a bad man. Not at first. He came from West Virginia. His dad was an itinerant preacher and his mom committed suicide, so he was at loose ends when he was about your age. He managed to do fine until he met Mama. He loved her so much and she kept running off with this guy and that guy.

"So one night, Randall said they had to go to do some work on the boat. He made her go along. They went out on his boat—his boat named *Daddy's Baby*. They were gone all night. I finally woke up Fancy Lee and we went down to the marina. When the boat pulled up, I was so relieved. Fancy Lee was asleep. I pretended to be sleeping, too. Daddy got off the boat and picked up Fancy Lee and took her inside. I got up and went on the boat, looking for Momma. It wasn't a real big boat—a twenty-eight-footer. But it did have a little cabin down some steps. I looked over every inch of that boat, but Momma wasn't on it."

"God, Mom. I can't believe this."

"That's because it's so different than anything you ever experienced. I wanted your life to be normal. And now this has happened. I've failed you."

"How did you wind up with Grandma and Granddad?"

"I escaped from a prison in Florida. And I went to them because I knew the girl who had killed their daughter in a car accident. And they took me in. They loved me."

"Did you love them? Did you love Dad?"

"I didn't know how to love anyone. I used them at first. I used your father. Then I got pregnant, quite by accident I assure you. And the moment that nurse placed that little baby in my arms, my heart cracked open like a safe that someone had finally figured out the code to."

"Are you going to kill these people who have Chelsea?"

"I hope not, but I'll do whatever I have to do to get my little girl back," she said. "I don't have a gun or a knife or anything. All I've got is my son, my really smart son, and he's going to help me solve this problem."

Chapter 41

Once upon a time, there were two princesses. They lived in a magic tower of light by the sea. The princesses wore pretty dresses of silver and gold. They sang and played games every day. During the day, birds flew around them calling their names, and dolphins leapt from the sea when they were near. At night the ocean waves whispered words of love to the two girls.

The elder princess was as beautiful as the stars in the sky. She took good care of the younger princess. She brought her mangoes and pomegranates and good things to eat. Whenever the younger princess skinned her knee, the elder princess kissed it and magically it was healed. They laughed together and were quite content never to leave their magic tower.

But there was a monster who lived down below the surface of the sea. Whenever the moon was dark, this monster would raise its green head and breathe flames at their tower.

"I will eat you both," the monster bellowed. "The elder girl will be my dinner and the younger one my dessert."

Whenever the monster said these words, the two princesses would cower in their bed and hold each other in fear.

"Please stay with me. Don't ever leave me," the younger princess begged the older one. And the older one promised she would not leave.

But the older princess lied. One day the sea monster rose from the sea and the dark waters churned as he came stomping toward the tower. The older princess climbed to the window and as the sea monster shot flames from its claws at the princesses she laughed and turned into a giant bird. With a soft flap of her wings, she flew up into the sky. The younger princess had no idea how her sister had turned into a bird. She closed her eyes and begged the gods to turn her into a bird, too. But to no avail. She was stuck in the tower.

Every night the sea monster bellowed and sent flames all around the tower. The young princess was all alone. She was scared. One day the sea monster came all the way up to her window. He was hungry and he was going to eat the princess. That was when she saw her sister's sword leaning against the wall. With one swoop she picked up the sword and cut off the sea monster's head. It rolled into the water with a mighty splash and caused a tidal wave all over the world.

"That's not how the story goes."

Yes, it is. The older princess finally came back. She came back to get her little egg that the younger princess had found lying by the road. But the younger princess was not happy and she shot down the bird which had once been a princess. And she lived happily ever after.

"I don't think I like that story."

"That's okay. It's time for you to sleep anyway."

Fancy glanced back at the little girl in the back seat. She was kind of a pretty thing. Fancy had hoped the little girl might look like her, but she didn't. Where the hell had she gotten that red hair from?

It had been easy enough to get her to drink the chocolate milk there in the ice-skating rink parking lot, easy enough to convince her that the doctors wouldn't allow her to go in to see her momma. You could tell a kid just about any damn thing and they were dumb enough to believe it. She just hoped the drugs wouldn't kill the child. Not that it would be a bad thing if the girl died. Better to die innocent, uncorrupted, pure. And it would give Vera Lee something to think about, wouldn't it.

There had been all those fruitless searches—going to bars and strip clubs, searching the nasty parts of town where girls sold their bodies. Of course Vera Lee was a little old to be out on the meat market like that. But Fancy Lee couldn't imagine where else someone like Vera Lee could come up with hundred dollar bills to give away every few months. She laughed at the irony of it. There she was looking in all the down-and-out places and Vera Lee had set herself up as a suburban mom! Now that was a group of people that Fancy Lee truly couldn't abide. They lived in their nice little houses and sent their little children off to school in big yellow buses. Their husbands played golf and the wives watched the food channel for new recipes. They drove their tanks down the road with their cell phones glued to their ears and their big hair sitting on their heads like helmets. And their cars bore the signs of their private schools, their private clubs, their badges of this or that. Vera Lee would have been better off as a whore.

She glanced again at the child asleep in the back seat. She was just about the same age as Fancy had been when Vera Lee left. And just a couple of years older when the man in the white Cadillac came for her. Now it was time to bring Vera Lee back home, so she could atone for what she did.

Chapter 42

"Mom, the hurricane is screwing up the sat signal. The last place I have them is getting off I-95 near some place called Jupiter," Kyle asked. "Do you know where they'd go?"

Patsy thought. She stared down at Rodney's cell phone. He had tried to call her on it several times. Now, it was time to call him back. She dialed the last incoming call.

"Yeah?" Rodney said. "Patsy?"

"Are you here?" she asked. "In Florida?"

"I'm in Jupiter. I just met your dad, Patsy. He doesn't have Chelsea. Patsy, I think it's your sister, Fancy, who has her. And she's probably the one who murdered Trent."

Patsy felt as if she'd been punched in the solar plexus.

"You're lying," she said.

"No, I'm not. You got to trust me on this one. Let me meet up with you, Patsy. We'll find her together."

Patsy pushed "end". If it really was Fancy who had Chelsea, she knew exactly where she'd go. A pair of headlights panned across her eyes, and it seemed like a sign.

"To the lighthouse. That's where she is."

"The lighthouse?"

"Fancy Lee and I used to go there and pretend we were kidnapped princesses."

The rain fell steadily. They were twelve miles from the exit.

Patsy hadn't been here since Trent Lewis had taken her away almost thirty years ago. Fast food places and mini-malls had sprung up like mushrooms, but she knew how to get to the lighthouse. All she had to do was find the intercoastal waterway and she would see its light flash. She even remembered how long the flash lasted: 1.6 seconds.

The streets were deserted. All the stores and restaurants boarded up. Palm fronds and pine branches littered the roadway. A traffic signal had been yanked off the pole and was flapping dangerously in the wind as if it were a flag of surrender.

"This place is under some kind of mandatory evacuation, Mom," Kyle said. "No one is here."

"A lot of the locals won't leave. I've been through a few hurricanes. They're scary, but most of them aren't that deadly if you stay inside." A causeway loomed ahead of them. Then the sweep of white light in the sky.

"We're here," Patsy said. "Turn to the left here, see the sign?" No ships would be out in the water now. She wondered if it were still possible to get inside the lighthouse.

They pulled into the lighthouse parking lot. The old wooden house with the big porch was still there on the inlet. The waves of the inlet were riotous and huge. Patsy tried opening her door, but the wind was like a wall against it.

"Let me out your side," she said. "Then, Kyle, you wait for Rodney."

"Don't go in there without me."

"Whoever has Chelsea is very dangerous. I want you to call Rodney and tell him where we are. But they can't come in until Chelsea comes out. Then whatever happens doesn't matter."

"Mom, it does matter," Kyle said in a panicked voice.

"Baby, I love you so much," Patsy said, holding his face in her hands. "It would kill me if anything happened to you. Please do what I tell you."

Kyle let her out of the car and got back in to wait.

There had been no fence when she was a kid, but now standing between her and her child was a nine-foot chain-link barrier. She kicked off her shoes, grasped the cold metal in her hands and hoisted herself up, one, two, three. The barbs at the top gouged into her thighs as pulled herself over. She ignored the blood that leaked through her slacks. The howling wind battered her as she dropped to the ground on the other side. Then she slipped on the wet grass. Rivers of rain ran everywhere.

She looked up. There it was—a dark tower of brick rising into the night. When she was a child, it had been painted bright red, but it was impossible to tell the color now. The wind moaned and shredded a toppled cabbage palm. She got up and ran through the inches-deep water rushing down the sidewalk. Just up the hill were the steep stone steps leading up to the lighthouse and the old oil house beside it. Above her the bright beam of light blinked on and off, faithfully through the storm. Branches from the giant banyan tree flew past her. That was the tree where she and Fancy had whiled away summer afternoons, playing in its long roots and imagining it was the dungeon of the sea monster.

Patsy struggled up the steps, the wind like a pair of hands shoving her low to the ground. At the top of the steps, she ran to the lighthouse and tugged on the big wooden door. It didn't budge.

Chelsea, baby, she whispered, hang on. Then she remembered the window. She and Fancy had maneuvered their way through that window often. She felt her way around the base of the tower. The window, buried in a foot-deep recess, was already cracked open. She heaved it open enough to crawl through and then she was in. Every inch of her was soaked, but the wind no longer had its fist wrapped around her. She caught her breath.

The room at the bottom of the tower had the same smell of damp stone and fresh paint that she remembered, but now a ghastly howling was all around her, echoing up the tower. She looked up into a spiraling dark well. Was Chelsea up at the top? What if she'd been wrong? What if there was no one here at all?

Patsy clung to the railing as she began the long climb up the ninety-nine steps to the lamphouse. It was completely black inside the tower and the hurricane outside cried like an angry child. The door to the lamphouse was closed and it was black as the inside of a gun barrel. The rage that had fueled her so far had begun to dissipate; it was replaced by raw fear. Her stomach clenched and unclenched violently as she silently prayed, God, please let Chelsea live. Please don't take her. Was this the payback she deserved? She had taken life, and so life would be taken from her—but not her own. That would be too easy. As she climbed the steps, she remembered the first time Chelsea stood up on ice skates. Patsy had sat in the bleachers and watched the small girl struggling to stay upright. By the end of the day, Chelsea was twirling in circles. As Patsy went round and round the spiraling steps, her daughter twirled in her mind.

At last she reached the door of the lamphouse. It was exactly as she remembered it, a big oval slab of wood. She pushed up and saw the light faithfully scouring the sky—hurricane or no hurricane. The glass rattled and up here the wind virtually screamed. Then she saw her. Fancy Lee. It took a few seconds for the image of the eleven-year-old girl she had left behind to become a middle-aged woman with dark hair and a wide heavy face, but Patsy knew it was her little sister crouched under the trajectory of the light. Patsy climbed into the lamphouse, leaving the door hatch open.

"Where is she?" Patsy screamed. "Where's my daughter, Fancy Lee?" The great light blinked on and off.

Fancy Lee didn't answer. She just flicked her eyes up to the metal platform above her head. Patsy saw a man holding her daughter's body.

Suddenly the wind died down, and the room was quiet except for Patsy's breath.

The man spoke, "We're in the eye now, Vera Lee. But you always were in the eye of the storm, weren't you?"

"Lance?" Patsy said. "I thought . . ."

"Officially, yes, I'm dead. It makes it much easier to do business this way. I've been living in Haiti, courtesy of some old friends of mine."

Patsy stood still and tried to discern his face in the dark. He was older now, but it was his voice, that same calm, smooth voice that sent her back twenty-five years to when she was a scared girl running from the law. He sat just outside of the path of the blinding light.

"I want my daughter, Lance. Give her to me," Patsy said.

"You're still beautiful," he said. "Like your mother was."

"Chelsea," Patsy called. "Chelsea, are you all right?"

The child groaned and moved on the floor, but did not open her eyes.

"She's okay," Fancy said.

"Shut up," Lance said.

Fancy ignored him. "I just gave her something to knock her out."

"I said, shut up," Lance repeated in a steely voice.

The lamphouse was cramped and Patsy only stood a few feet from her sister. She noticed that both of Fancy's hands were duct-taped to the iron staircase that led to the platform. As the light passed over their heads, she could see a bloody gash on Fancy's skull. Behind Fancy was the bolted door that led to the balcony outside where, as children, the two of them had sat hour after hour, looking at the rivers running north and west and then the big blue monster that slept to the east.

"We don't have a lot of time, dear Vera Lee," Lance said. "I need you to do one more killing for me. Then you and I can leave. There's a gun on the edge of this platform. Please take it. We need to get rid of your sister."

Patsy felt as if the air had been sucked from her lungs. He couldn't be asking her to do this again? Fancy Lee began to cry.

"No, you bastard. Wasn't it enough that I killed your wife for you?"

"You didn't kill Lois, Vera Lee. I did. But you did kill Chuck and Lorenzo, and I'll always appreciate that."

"I wouldn't have killed them if you hadn't shown me those pictures, you son of a bitch," Patsy said.

"The pictures?" Fancy Lee asked. "You saw the pictures?"

"Yes, I saw them."

"He told me that if I let those men do that to me then he wouldn't hurt you. He said you would come back to me and you never did, Vera Lee. You never came back," Fancy Lee accused. "Do you think I give a damn if you shoot me. You killed me the day you left me."

Patsy bent down and looked into her sister's eyes.

"I'm sorry. I called Daddy and told him to watch out for you, not to let them get you again. But I couldn't take you with me, Fancy Lee. Too many people wanted . . ."

"Shut up, both of you," Lance interrupted. He pulled Chelsea's head up and placed a straight razor against the girl's throat. "Take the gun and shoot her, Vera Lee, or your daughter will die. That's your choice. Now, who will live? You decide." His voice was level and resonant in the small room. It was the reasoned voice of a lawyer, but spouting the commands of a madman.

Patsy saw the gun he indicated. It was black and small.

"A Walther?" she asked, hoping to distract him.

"A P88. Very few of those little treasures. But I'm going to give you the honor of shooting it."

Patsy lifted the gun and held it.

"Go on," he said. "The eye won't stay over us forever and we have to go."

"Why did you do this? Why come find me after all these years?"

"I had to, Vera Lee. I would have been happy to leave you alone, but your enterprising former boyfriend and your sister were sure they had found a clue to your whereabouts. Trent had been doing odd jobs for me in the states for years. So he came to me and offered to find you. I knew if he could find you, then the police weren't far behind. The FBI knew I wasn't dead and they'd love to find you and then come after me. Just to spite my friends at the CIA, of course. And you, clever little thing that you are, don't you remember the note you left me when you broke into my house? You said you had found Lois's evidence and you threatened me with it. You thought that would protect you, but it didn't, did it?"

Patsy thought of the jacket. What had she done with it? Everything had been so confusing, she'd forgotten that it was in her car. It was still there.

"I do have the evidence, you piece of shit. Lois turned it into microfiche and sewed it into a jacket. I still have it after all these years, and if you don't let Chelsea go right now, I'll make sure the police find it."

"No, you won't. Because after you kill your sister, you and I will go away together. We'll move to Paraguay," Lance said. "I've missed you, Vera Lee. You're all I have."

Patsy squeezed her fingers around the gun's grip.

"What happens to Chelsea?"

"The police come, they find your dead sister, they find your live daughter, and they find that you're gone—vanished once again. Vera Lee, don't be afraid now. We'll have fun together. We'll go gambling. I'll give you everything you want."

Patsy tried to make sense of his tone. He seemed so earnest, so insistent. She remembered the power he had once had over her, the way his arms felt around her. She had loved him so intensely and yet he never touched her sexually.

"Why, Lance? Why do you want me? I have my own life," Patsy said, tears streaming down her face.

"Honey, you can't stay in that life anymore. The police will know who you really are. Which is something even you don't know. Who you really are."

"Who am I, Lance?" Patsy asked.

"You're my daughter."

Just then Fancy Lee screamed out, "You pig! You used me to get to her."

"Just kill her," Lance said in a weary voice. "Get it over with. She had no compunctions about killing Thelma Jackson or hitting Trent Lewis in the head with a hammer when she thought he was going to leave her. She killed your friend Mandy, too. Now, it's your turn."

"This is the last one, Lance," Patsy said. Then she kneeled down beside Fancy.

"Once again, you betray me for him," Fancy said bitterly. Patsy placed the gun against Fancy's smooth white forehead and held her breath. In the seconds between light flashes, she fired the gun. Fancy Lee grunted and slumped over, slowly shutting her eyes. Lance stood up on the platform, and Patsy wheeled around and pointed the gun at him.

"There was only one bullet in it," he said. "I knew you wouldn't miss so close. Besides, I know that you still love me." He climbed down the ladder steps and took the gun from Patsy's hand. He gently kissed her on the forehead.

Patsy stared at him. Yes, he was older. His hair was a little grayer, skin a little more weathered, but still the same smooth brow, the weak chin, the inscrutable eyes. He smiled. "You know I wouldn't have hurt your daughter. My own flesh and blood."

She heard Chelsea stir. All right, she thought, just get him out. Lance then pulled another gun from behind his waist and pointed it at her head. "Don't do anything crazy, precious."

The room became cold; she shivered. Then the light stopped its rhythmic pulse, and the door to the little balcony surrounding the lamphouse flew open. What was happening? Patsy thought of the ghost stories her mother had told her about the tower. *It always gets cold when a ghost is present.*

Someone screamed. Fancy's legs shot up and thrust against Lance's body. He grunted and then fell into the hole down the wrought-iron steps. He banged and thudded down the steps, falling down the spiral, falling until finally he stopped and didn't move. Patsy stared at the open door, shaking. Something seemed to hover in the air. The light suddenly flicked back on.

"Fancy Lee, are you okay?" Patsy asked, kneeling beside her. The bullet had grazed the top of her head but had done no serious damage. She had averted the gun in the dark and prayed that Fancy wouldn't move into the path of the bullet.

"Did you see her?" Fancy Lee asked. "Momma was here. Momma opened the door."

Patsy looked around the small room. Black windows surrounded her. She saw no one else. She climbed the short iron ladder to the platform where Chelsea still lay. She touched her warm little body and felt the girl's chest rise and fall gently. Lance's razor lay beside her.

"Vera Lee," Fancy called to her. "Your friend isn't dead."

"Mandy's still alive? Where is she?" Patsy asked. She grabbed the razor and dropped back to the floor. Then she slashed the tape binding Fancy's hands.

"She's in the bait box on the boat," Fancy said. Fancy's fist opened to reveal a key. Patsy took it from her hand.

"Where's the boat, Fancy Lee?" Patsy asked.

"In the marina across the street," she said.

Patsy stood up and crawled up the ladder to the platform where Chelsea lay, still wearing her velvet skating outfit. She placed her face next to Chelsea's warm cheek. "Mom?" Chelsea whispered.

"Thank you, God," she said and tears fell down her face. She hugged Chelsea close to her. "I've got to get you out of here."

Fancy gasped and Patsy turned to see Lance coming through the hole in the floor. Blood dripped along his face. Fancy stood and ran through the open door to the balcony. Patsy watched horrified as Lance followed her sister outside. She had to get Chelsea out somehow. She gathered the child in one arm and with the other she clung to the ladder. Just as she reached the bottom of the ladder, she heard a scream. Lance stood on the little lookout alone. He turned and pointed his gun through the open door directly at Patsy's head.

A shot rang out, and Lance's head jerked forward, pieces of his skull flying. He dropped to the metal balcony floor, dead.

Chapter 43

Rodney handed the rifle to Lanelle and raced toward the tower. One of the coastguard families who lived on the lighthouse land had let them in the main gate. The eye was passing quickly and soon the rain and wind would race across the spit of land between the mainland and the ocean.

He'd heard enough on the headset to know that Patsy and Chelsea were inside. The man from the coastguard had gone ahead to unlock the door. Rodney stopped and looked at Fancy's crumpled body on the ground. He bent over—the fall had broken her into pieces. She was lifeless. Rodney ran inside.

"Patsy!" he called.

"Up here," she yelled down. "Chelsea's drugged. Get an ambulance."

"We've got one coming," he said, mounting the steps two at a time. Patsy came down from the lamphouse and met him on the steps. Her lip quivered as she grabbed him. Her dark eyes searched his.

"I'm afraid to try to bring her down alone. I don't want to fall and hurt her," Patsy said. Then she handed him something, a key. "Mandy is in the boat in the marina across the causeway. It's called *Daddy's Baby*. She's in the bait box. Hurry, Rodney. Please hurry."

Rodney took the key.

"I'm gonna send my partner up here to help you."

Patsy nodded.

"Rodney?" Lanelle called from downstairs, shining her flashlight up the middle of the spiral.

"Come on up, Lanelle. Help Mrs. Palmer get her daughter down, okay," he said. He looked at Patsy and touched her ashen face. "You'll be all right. Lanelle will take care of you."

Then he turned and hurried down the steps. He met Lanelle halfway down the steps. A tall blond teenage boy was right behind her.

"Is my mother okay?" he asked Rodney.

"Yes, she and your sister will be fine."

The causeway had been locked down—standard procedure during any hurricane. The winds had started up again and the rain screamed. Rodney put Twyla in Lanelle's patrol car and drove the Volvo out of the parking lot. The wind pushed it sideways, but he maneuvered into the wind as if he were on a sailboat, tacking to get to the road. Crossing the causeway in a hurricane was terrifying, but there was no other way to get to the marina and the waves began to pitch the boats below as if they were toys.

By the time he got to the other side and out of the car, the wind and rain howled like a pack of wolves. Boats reared up out of the water, lunging at the dock. Where was *Daddy's Baby*? Then he saw a wooden fishing boat down at the far end of the dock. It was older than any of the others, stockier. A wave pushed up the stern of the boat and then the bow slammed down under the edge of the dock. Rodney caught his breath. Water sloshed over his feet and rain stung his face. He lurched along the dock, holding onto pilings as the wind tugged at his clothes and water drenched them.

Finally he was there, the boat a forlorn wreck. Somehow he had to get on it. He jumped from the wet dock into the water and landed on the bow. Clinging to the windshield of the boat, he felt the water roiling around him. He pulled himself up over the top of the cabin and slid down to the slanted floor of the boat. He jabbed his ribs and bruised his hands, but ignored the pain as he found the bait box. Then he fumbled for the key in his pocket and tried to jam it into the lock. It fell.

He scrambled on his knees and found it. Once again he reached for the lock. A wave splashed over the end of the boat. The dock groaned and splintered as *Daddy's Baby* twisted underneath. The lock turned. Rodney whispered a prayer to whatever gods might be on duty as he pulled the lock from the latch and threw open the top of the bait box.

Bound and gagged, Mandy looked up at him with wide, terrified eyes. He eased the tape from her mouth.

"Are you okay?" he yelled.

She nodded. He realized he couldn't carry her off the boat in this weather. He had to find something to cut her free. It was a fishing boat; there had to be a knife on it somewhere. He pulled her out of the box and hurried to the pilothouse. The boat pitched and Mandy slid along the deck. Rodney finally found a knife in a drawer that flew open as the boat tilted sideways.

"Come on," Rodney yelled, cutting her free. "We've got to get off this boat."

Mandy shakily reached for his arm. The boat tossed underneath them and water splashed in arrhythmic beats against anything that stood in its way. Rodney leapt over to the dock, held the stern of the boat fast and helped her clamber out of it.

As they fell to the dock, the rain swirling around them, Rodney felt the solidness of Mandy's body against him. Her hair and face were dirty. But she was all in one piece. As they dashed off the dock, Rodney looked back. A hungry wave hammered *Daddy's Baby*. It broke apart and all that could be seen was a piece of hull that flew up into the air.

Patsy was waiting in the hospital lobby with the woman detective when Rodney brought Mandy inside.

"How's your daughter, Mrs. Palmer?" Rodney asked.

"The doctors say she'll be fine," Patsy said and turned to Mandy.

"Are you okay?" Patsy asked her.

Mandy nodded.

"Of course, you aren't," Patsy said. "This was my fault. I hope you'll forgive me."

Mandy shook her head. "Not your fault, girlfriend. Let it go. I'll be okay. I'm just so glad you got me out of there. I want to go home."

A young woman with frizzy hair came up to them. She was carrying a brown jacket.

"I knew you'd be cold, so I looked in your car. This was all I could find," she said, handing Patsy the jacket.

Patsy held the jacket for a moment before giving it to Rodney.

"See that stuff between the patches?" Patsy asked.

"It feels like plastic," he said.

"It's microfiche. Lois recorded all of Lance's records. She was going to turn him in, Rodney. That's why he killed her."

"Wait a minute," the woman detective said. "Just who are you? How did you get this evidence?"

Patsy's eyes met Rodney's. Then she turned to the woman detective.

"Don't, Patsy," Mandy said.

"I have to. It's time." She took a deep breath, then confessed. "Detective, my name is Vera Lee Gifford. I've been wanted by the State of Florida since I escaped from prison in 1978. Here I am." Patsy smiled grimly and said, "It's done, Rodney. I'm going home."

Rodney nodded.

"I just want to say goodbye to my children before you take me in," she said. "Can you let me do that?"

"I don't know," the woman detective said. She looked at Patsy. "Did you kill Thelma Jackson or Trent Lewis?"

Patsy shook her head.

"That woman who kidnapped me did it," Mandy said,

tearfully. Lanelle's eyes traveled back and forth between the two women and then she looked at Rodney.

"Okay, let's let her see the kids. Then we're taking her in."

Rodney placed an arm around Patsy's waist as he led her to her children.

Chapter 44

Rodney drove through the orange groves to the maximum security women's prison west of Fort Lauderdale, noticing the squat trees heavy with fruit. His mind drifted back to Amy's wedding. So many people had come to watch his girl make her vows to be with one man and only one man for the rest of her life. It was an old-fashioned idea, an illusion that love lasts forever. For some people it probably did, but not for many. Still if anyone could make it work, he gave his daughter good odds.

It was interesting to Rodney that when he finally saw Cheryl, he hardly recognized her. Her short hair framed a lightly freckled face, a cute turned-up nose and thin lips. She wore two sets of earrings in her delicate ears. She had hugged him, and he felt absolutely nothing. No anger, no sorrow, no longing. For fifteen years he'd held a torch for her—a torch of rage. Somehow in the past few weeks, the flame had been extinguished.

It probably didn't hurt that he had woken up that morning next to Katherine Chevalier, who was standing by his side in a beautiful lavender dress while he and Cheryl got reacquainted. The good doctor had healed his dog and healed his heart—not to mention his sex life.

He wished Willie could have been at the wedding, but somehow he felt like Willie would always be with him now. The dead didn't exactly leave you. They became more present. He knew Willie would approve of the direction his life had taken. He would still be involved in finding the bad guys—and girls, but now he could do it his way.

Rodney sat at a round table in the visiting park of the women's prison. He stretched his legs out and shifted uncomfortably in the orange plastic chair. An inmate in a gold dress walked past him, holding onto a little boy. She was smiling a big gold-toothed smile. He watched her walk around with the boy, bouncing him on her hip. If she'd known how much she was going to miss him, would she have done things differently, Rodney wondered. Then his eyes were caught by an attractive woman with short blond hair. She smiled at him and he stood to greet her.

"How are you holding up?" he asked, as she gave him a quick hug. She sat down before answering.

"Okay. I thought it would be so hard but it feels good to not have to hide or worry that someday someone might find out the truth. It's been a little lonely, but I'm managing," she said.

"I notice you're a blond again," he said. "And there are those blue eyes."

"Yeah, I'd forgotten what I looked like," she said and smiled wryly.

"So I don't know what to call you. Vera Lee or Patsy?"

"Believe it or not, that fancy lawyer you got me—what's her name? Amy? Anyway, she helped me get my name changed legally. I'm now Patsy Gifford Palmer," Patsy answered. "So what brought you all the way down here from Gainesville?"

"I had some old business to attend to, and I thought I'd touch base with you and fill you in on some info we found out," he said. "Everything in Lois's microfiche holds up as far as we can tell. There's one thing you ought to know. According to a letter Lois wrote, Lance murdered your mother."

"You mean it wasn't my dad who did it?"

"Technically, it was your dad. Lance was telling the truth. He was your father."

Patsy swallowed hard, as if trying to digest what she heard. “Why would he kill my mother? And how?” she asked.

“Your mother wanted him to marry her apparently and she wanted to get you and Fancy from Randall. She was willing to do anything to force him to do that. Lois wrote that your mother came to her and demanded she leave Lance. I take it your mom was pretty feisty.”

“She was probably drunk.”

“Anyway, Lance told Lois not to worry about it. He took your mother on a little boat trip, and when he came back, he was alone.”

“I knew she drowned,” she said, looking at the floor. “I don’t know how I knew, but I did.”

“Look, Vera Lee, there’s a lot of evidence against Lance Underwood. The microfiche in the coat showed that he was in all kinds of dirty doings. You’ll get a new trial for those original charges. Amy will go to the state’s attorney and make a deal. You might be out of here in as little as three to five years.”

“Really?”

“Yeah. You do want to go to your daughter’s high-school graduation, don’t you?”

“Do you think that’s possible?” she asked.

“Amy does. Her argument is that you were a juvenile, under the influence of drugs and that you were forced to kill those men for fear of what might happen to your little sister. We even have the photos that Lance took of her with Chuck and Lorenzo. Child pornographers don’t get a lot of sympathy with juries. But a mother of two kids with a husband who loves her can look pretty good.”

Patsy shook her head.

“I don’t think Tom will vouch for me, Rodney. He hasn’t written to me or visited me once. He feels that I betrayed him. And I did. I pretended to be someone I wasn’t.”

“Yes, you did. But you became the person you were

pretending to be. That's got to count for something. You became Patsy Palmer."

Patsy bowed her head. "I don't know. I'm afraid he'll never forgive me."

"Give him time," Rodney said. He knew how hard it was to forgive a woman who had crushed your heart. But if Tom held onto a grudge, it wouldn't do him any good.

"What about Thelma? Were you able to prove that Trent or Fancy murdered her?" Patsy said.

"Well, we don't know which one of them actually wielded the hammer," Rodney answered, sparing her his suspicion that Trent wouldn't have had the guts. "But obviously Trent was the one who framed the preacher-man. We found Trent's prints on the car. The idiot wiped his prints off the hammer but didn't bother to clean off the car. So Reverend Moore is free, but I think he's doing a lot of praying these days. Apparently his wife has forgiven him."

"Forgiveness is hard," Patsy said. "I'm still trying to forgive Lance for what he did to my sister and my mother. You know something weird? Fancy Lee thought she saw my mother there in the lighthouse with us. But I didn't. I saw Lois."

"I guess you see whatever ghosts you carry around in your own head," Rodney said.

"Yeah," Patsy answered. They were quiet, and Rodney studied her. He'd felt almost unbearably drawn to her back there in that mansion in Charlotte, but he knew it had nothing really to do with her and more about what he had projected onto her in his loneliness and confusion. Now he realized she was just a middle-aged woman who'd made mistakes in her youth, deadly mistakes that she'd tried to make up for by living a good life. She was someone's wife and someone's mother. Vera Lee no longer existed. Rodney patted Patsy's hand. Then he said, "Listen, Patsy. I have to head on out. I've got to meet someone. I just wanted to see you and let you know what we found out."

"Oh, you know people down here?" she asked.

"Well, there's someone I got to see. A man who lives in Davie, last I heard."

He stood up, and Patsy stood up as well. He shook her hand and walked out of the large room to the gates. A bored guard looked at him from behind a glassed-in room and pushed a button. The first gate opened, and as Rodney stood between the two fences, he saw a man coming up the path with a blond teenage boy and a pretty red-haired little girl. Rodney smiled to himself. Tom Palmer had come around.

This part of Florida was like a different planet from Gainesville. The trees were fat and too green. There was no Spanish moss dangling from the branches. The traffic was deadly. But he liked the way the air felt soft and velvety. He took the exit off the interstate and soon turned down a sparsely populated road. It was hard to imagine any place in South Florida that was sparsely populated, but here it was. A ramshackle house, painted green, stood behind some Australian pines.

Rodney walked up to the front door of a screened-in porch. He looked through the screen door and saw the back of a man leaning over a table.

"Knock, knock," Rodney said.

"Come in," the man said without looking up.

Rodney opened the screen door and stepped onto the porch. Now, he could see what the man was doing. A stuffed bird was perched on a branch, and the man appeared to be painting a water color of the bird. A radio played oldies in the background.

"What kind of bird is that?" Rodney asked. "I don't think I've ever seen anything like it."

"No, most likely you haven't," the man answered. "It's an ivory-billed woodpecker. Back in the old days, them so-called naturalists used to shoot 'em and stuff 'em. No telling how old this one is. You can't find these around anymore. People say they're extinct, but I think they're still around, just layin' low, Smokey Joe, layin' low."

The man turned and faced Rodney. He was African-American, in his late forties with deep-set brown eyes and thick shoulders.

"Can I help you?" he asked.

"Are you Gavin Worthy?" Rodney asked.

"Yes, sir, I am," the man answered.

"I'm Rodney Ellis," Rodney said. "Wonder if I could talk to you for a minute?"

Gavin Worthy studied him for a good long moment and then turned back to his painting.

"Have a seat if you like. I'll be done with this in a little bit," he said.

Rodney sat down in a plastic chair near the stuffed bird.

"I'm not in a hurry," he said.

"Good," Gavin Worthy responded. "'Cause if you want to find the rarest birds, you got to be as patient as Moses."

Rodney settled back in the chair. The cold black eye of the large, long-billed bird watched him, and together they waited for Gavin Worthy to finish the painting.

Acknowledgments

I am so grateful to my agent Marc Gerald for encouragement and guidance in the writing of this book, as well as to Pete Ayrton and Amy Scholder at Serpent's Tail for their steadfast support. I am also thankful beyond words to early readers of the book: Patti Wood, Michael McClelland and Vicki Moreland. Thanks to Douglas Fletcher for valuable research information and Doug Bartholomew for his advice. Thanks to Virginia and Peter Popovich and the Ballantyne Resort for lessons in real estate. Thanks also go to Tony and Turk, my South Florida buddies, and Pam and MJ, my North Florida chums, just because. Much credit goes to my husband for keeping my computer running and my daughter for her ability to make me laugh whenever I need it.